Time Voyagers:
The Adventure Begins

By RJ Dean Jr

Table of Contents

This book is a work of fiction by RJ Dean Jr. Incidents within the adventure stories are based in true events or history but the parts of George and his friends in these events is totally fictional. Consent was given by real life people for their names to be used in the stories as certain characters. These characters are not necessarily true representations of the living persons. Other characters are named after much respected persons who influenced the author's life. Some characters have deliberately been based on living persons but would not be recognized as such by most readers. Any other instances of resemblance to persons living or dead, places or events, is purely coincidental. Any unauthorized reproduction of this book whatsoever without written consent, except for short excerpts for reviews or educational purposes, is strictly prohibited.

Bible quotations are from the King James Bible except where noted otherwise.

Requests for information or permission to make copies of any part of this book should be sent directly to the author at: thetimevoyagers@aol.com

Forward

Set in northern West Virginia, the characters speak some Appalachian dialect. George, from a broken home, is taken under the wing of a kind science teacher. While getting ready for a school science fair his project goes haywire and propels him in time. Join him in the adventures as fourteen year old George witnesses sometimes little known but exciting history and gets entangled in other famous historical events.

Time Voyagers: The Adventure Begins © 2014

First Edition

ISBN 10:1494947773
ISBN 13:9781494947774

About the Author

Photograph by Aretha Kees © 2013

RJ Dean Jr was born in a small town in West Virginia, was a Cub Scout, Webelos and a Boy Scout. He worked on a volunteer fire department where he became nationally certified under NFPA 1001. At the same time RJ worked in WV Forestry at the Bee Mountain Fire Tower. He currently lives with his wife on a thirty two acre tree farm in Jackson county where he keeps honeybees. After they were married, his wife got into working with Ed Clevenger on location for 'Into the Wilderness: The Jesse Hughes Story.' As a genealogist, RJ discovered the same people portrayed in his family tree and got involved himself as an extra, and camera man. After the filming was all done, RJ had stories in his head busting to be told. So here is the first one, 'Time Voyagers: The Adventure Begins.'

Special Thanks To

My mother who never let me quit anything I started out to do when I was young.

Mr Watt, my science teacher in junior high school, who motivated us to think beyond our confined class.

Mr Watts, the scoutmaster of Troop 25 at the First Baptist Church of Saint Albans, WV. He taught us skills that I use on the farm and in daily life.

My wife for listening about the story, helping it along with lots of research and editing.

www.crosswalk.com for their free sermon, part of which is preached by Pastor Bess in Chapter 9, on Easter Sunday morning.

Jody of the National Park Service, New River Gorge Visitors Center for information about Kaymoor.

Fort Randolph, Point Pleasant, WV for the information about the siege of Fort Randolph that made part of this book possible.

Ed Smolder, WVU Agriculture Extension Service of Jackson County WV, (retired).

Charles Monola of the Federal Aviation Administration, Charleston, WV Office for information about aircraft regulations.

Aretha Kees for her photograph of the author.

Albert Azevedo of Electronic Specialty Company, Dunbar, WV for information about electronics.

David Turnipseed, of WV Forestry, for true information about apple trees.

Jerry Beckett, my consultant on parts of the Bible.

Pastor Benjamin Bess, (retired) my consultant on parts of the Bible.

To my niece, Amy H. Ritchie, who inspired me to get with it on this book, by writing her first book (at the age of twelve), available on Amazon., Title, T.H.E.G.R.O.U.P.

And anyone else I might have missed, thank you.

Chapter 1
The New Beginning

The story begins on March 26th 1963 at a school on the edge of the tired looking town of Chapman Grove, WV.[1] The outside is red brick marked with gang graffiti. On the front wall it says, 'Chapman Grove High School'. At least, it did. Many of the letters were gone due to vandalism. Each classroom window slid open, when they worked. Some panes were cracked. None would be replaced until the glass broke out completely. The building was all on one level, ground floor only. The school looks like it's been there for a hundred years. But in fact it's not been there very long. In its day, the school was built to be the most modern school of its time. But that's not the way it turned out to be.
Some of the classes have bright, gifted students. They'll most likely get college and university scholarships or land that job and become an executive or something. Then there's the everyday students that come, do their classes, then leave. Those will end up struggling to either pay their own way to higher education or end up in dead end jobs that nobody else wants. Which takes us to the bottom of the rung; the slow, unwanted or trouble makers. They're just there because they have nowhere else to go. Mostly, these students will end up in the worst of the worst jobs, welfare programs or prisons. Some might make a life for themselves but they'll be miserable most of their lives.
Which brings us to George, a very smart, gifted lad about the age of fourteen. Kind of thin built and five foot five tall with short black wavy hair and green eyes, George comes from a broken home. It's not certain where his mother is at this point in time but she's definitely out of the picture. However, there is a photograph of her on the mantel right next to the picture of the current president, President Kennedy[13]. George's father is not involved much in his life either. His father sees him as a no account brat, always causing trouble whether it be in school or out on the street. George's father works as a laborer down at the lumber mill

alongside the Ohio river, slaving away at pushing carts heavy laden with scrap lumber on its way to be burnt.

On this day, we enter the classroom of Mr Watts, a kind older man, large build, not much hair and the little he has is cut very short. His main interests are teaching kids and going to church every time the doors are open. Approaching the classroom, laughter is heard. Entering, the teacher is with his students, some twenty in all, talking about the upcoming science fair. Just then the principal, Mr Biggarstaff, a big fat bald mean hateful looking man, comes bashing in with a young boy named George. He shoves George into an empty seat at a nearby desk causing him to nearly crash into Stephen, a fine young boy from England.

"There boy, sit and try to stay out of trouble! Here Watts, this boy's your problem now." Mr Biggarstaff slams a file folder down on Mr Watts' desk, turns and stomps out of the room giving a glaring look at young George who cowers in his seat.

Mr Watts replies, "Yes, Mr Biggarstaff sir. We'll take care of him." The door slams shut and Mr Watts exhales and puts his hand to his chest as a sign of relief that he's gone. About this time the bell rings for the students to go to their next class. All the kids go charging out the door in a very undignified manner.

"Well now, George," Mr Watts says, "what was that all about?"

George shrugs his shoulders and just says, "Nothing."

"Well, sure doesn't look like nothing to me."

George shrinks into his seat even more until Mr Watts says, "Well, all that's behind you and in the past. Let's start fresh tomorrow and have a better day of it. Now, you go on to your next class before you're late."

George sits up in amazement. Nobody ever spoke to him like this before. He jumps up out of his seat and charges for the door, "Yes, Mr Watts. Thank you, sir!"

Mr Watts just goes to his desk and looks through the file Mr Biggarstaff had left. He looks up then back to the file in astonishment as he can't believe what he reads.

Wednesday, March 27th 1963

The next day was much better than it's ever been for George. The small act of kindness from his science teacher, Mr Watts, started to turn George's life around for the better. The students were piling into the classroom. They were talking about stuff that was on TV last night, homework and how hard it was, and did you get the answer on question fourteen? Then Mr Watts comes in and tells them all to take their seats as he proceeds to mark in the roll book everyone that's present.

"Class!" Mr Watts speaks. "Class, we need to get ready for the science fair coming up. Most of you know the school doesn't think this class will amount to much but I know better. Every one of you can excel at you dreams and goals if you set your mind to it. Now, if any of you want to work the rest of this class time to plan your project, go ahead. Otherwise read chapter 16 of your textbook." Most of them look over their plans for the science fair.

"George, how about you come up to my desk and let's talk about the science fair and how it works."

George eagerly approaches the teacher's desk.

"George, we know you haven't been in my class very long, but I know you can achieve anything you set your mind to. Have you got anything you would like to enter into the science fair? There's not much time to work on anything."

"No, not really. I do have this magnetic motor that can run all by itself without any power added to it. I built it all by myself when I had nothing else to do."

"That sounds intriguing, George. But you are required to write out the plans on how it works. So get started on that, if you want to enter the fair. Your father will have to sign your permission slip to enter since it's not on school time."

"I don't think he will, Mr Watts. He works hard in the mill all day then falls asleep drinking beer and watching TV. Dad says it takes away the pain in his aching back."

"Well, you take it anyway. If you can't get him to sign the permission slip, I might have a talk with him."

George looks somewhat pleased, agrees and heads back to his desk.

This is how George wrote the paper on the magnetic motor:

How the Magnetic Motor Works

As you know, in magnetism like poles repel and unlike poles attract. If this can be set up on a governed rotating system with a constant repelling-attracting the motor would run until it wore out. Also with the constant repelling and attracting the only thing one would have to do is to maintain a constant speed with a governor or it would spin so fast it could burn up.

Imagine hooking the magnetic motor to a generator. America could generate all its energy needs or make cars run or planes fly forever or even go to the moon.

Then the bell rings to go to the next class. George says, "Oh man!" The next class was math. George was pretty good in math, but he thought the teacher wasn't all that great. She'd sit at her desk doing her knitting and just mutter at them to do which chapter and page, unless one of her 'special' students needed assistance.

"George!" Mr Watts called out. "Time for your next class. Don't want to be late."

"Yes, I do!" said George. "Mrs MacQueen doesn't have time for her students. I wish she go to Ohio and we get a new teacher."

"Well then George, I'll have a talk with her. She'll listen to me." The two of them walk along to the classroom where the math teacher is waiting for all her students to arrive and be seated. George takes his seat and opens his math book. Mr Watts speaks with her at her desk. She seems intrigued and agrees with him. Mr Watts leaves the room as the second bell rings. The rest of the class seems to go normally but the teacher hands George homework to do as he's leaving to go home. Homework, he thinks, I never been given this before.

George heads out the door to walk home. Home was just a few blocks down the road and across the railroad tracks, one of the houses built for the workers of the lumber mill in the past. As he walks along the street, girls from his classes start mocking and making fun of him, chanting, "♫Georgie porgie puddin' and pie ♫kissed the girls and made them cry!"

At this moment some bullies start to chase him.

"♪When the boys came out to play ♫Georgie porgie ran away!" the girls continue chanting at him.

But Susan and another girl scream at them, **"You all can be so mean!"**

George beats them all to his house and runs inside, missing most of the steps up to the door. The kids shout they'll get him next time.

"GEORGE!" His father is home. "What are you doing, coming in the house like that? Don't you know you bust something it comes out of MY paycheck! Now, get in the kitchen. I have to work the night shift also."

George's dad is an average size man, about five foot ten, one hundred and forty pounds and with black hair and a bald spot near the back of his head. His body looked tired and really worn out, typical of a hard laborer. His face was sun scorched from working out in the hot sweltering sun year after year. The look of this withered man showed he smoked all his life and drank too much. George is nothing but the family slave to his dad. He goes in the kitchen and starts preparing supper; beans, potatoes, cornbread. That's about all George could fix. Sometimes it would be spaghetti, macaroni and cheese or anything that just needed you to open the box. It was all they could afford.

After supper George thinks this would be the best time to ask about permission to enter the science fair.

"Dad?"

"What is it, boy?"

"Mr Watts, my science teacher, said I had to give you this. It's permission to enter the science fair. He said to enter I need your signature."

"I'll think about it," his dad grumbled, dropping the paper to the floor and picking up the bottle of liquor to take a quick drink. Now, George knew the translation of this meant 'no'. So he just slunk away, rejected.

A few hours later George hears the TV shut off and then the front door opens and closes. He is all alone. Looking out the dusty window he sees his dad walking down the filthy potholed street towards the mill. Then he's gone, leaving George to fend for himself. George does his homework then reviews his science project that now just seems like a pipe dream.

Thursday, March 28th 1963

Next thing George knows, his alarm clock is going off to get up for school. He fell asleep at his desk as he'd done many times in the past. George drags himself to the kitchen to pack a lunch for the day, without changing clothes, wearing what he had on the day before, all wrinkled.

Out the door he goes. His father would be home soon and he didn't want to see him. George was still upset about the permission to enter the science fair. The walk to school was met with no incidents of girls chanting or bullies chasing him.

The first class of the day was history. They had been studying the War of 1812 and what the cause of it was. What a drag, thought George. Next class was English. You would think by now I know English. I been speaking it since I could walk. When would anybody need to conjugate a verb or know nouns?

Then came study hall. Here, George would work on ideas he had or he'd just read. He loved reading. In the book he could be anything, imagine being anywhere. Then the bell rang. That's the fastest forty five minutes of the day, when George is reading. Shop class was next. George could build anything. He was great with his hands. Shop was noisy, but halfway through it wasn't nearly noisy enough to drown out the fire engines going by. The whole class came to a stop to watch them head down the street. You could see the smoke billowing up and the wind fanning the flames and smoke, down in the shantytown.

George and some of the others walked to the fire quickly, to not miss a thing. Then, as George came closer, he realized the fire was at his house. Knowing his dad would have been home, he tried to race into the house to save him. A firefighter and the county sheriff grabbed him. George put up a fight, trying to get to his father. The firefighter said, "If anyone's in there, they're gone by now."

George just stood back and watched, crying, as the fire department tried to keep the fire from spreading. The wind wasn't helping at all.

Mr Watts came up to George and they held on to each other. The sheriff came, and said, "Dad, you know this boy?"

"Yes, he's one of my students. I'm going to take him home for now."

"Okay, Dad. You were always there for me, now for him."

The school had closed early after everyone ran out to watch the excitement. There wasn't much of the school day left anyway.

Mr Watts leads George to his house. It was a big two story wooden house with a large covered front porch. On the porch, hung from the wooden tongue and groove ceiling, were wooden swings at each end. Both swings had been painted white and suspended with slightly rusty chains. Set out on the porch were old green and white metal chairs and tables, like those you might find in a yard. All of them were in need of a paint job. The floor of the porch was also tongue and groove. The same tongue and groove floor construction continued inside the house. Large casement windows looked out from the house onto the porch. Faded green matching curtains were in each window. Entrance ways at both the front door into the living room and the back door into the kitchen had walls painted a bright cheerful blue.

The kitchen was a yellowish tan color. This color continued through the living room and the rest of the first floor. The HUGE kitchen was decked out with all things a kitchen might need including two stoves with ovens, one electric and one gas. Even the refrigerator was huge. If you were snowed in for a month, and the fridge was full, you wouldn't go hungry. In the center of the room was a table large enough for an army. Just off the kitchen, down a short hall, was a spare bedroom furnished with bunk beds, a blackboard on one wall and a desk and chair. From the short hall a set of stairs led down into a root cellar that was once used for a secret underground railroad before the Civil War.[15]

The living room too was huge; if you wanted to, you could hold a convention in there. At one end was the OLD fireplace, original from the time the house was built. And away on the other end, in a corner, was a gas fireplace. On the opposite end of the house, still on the first floor, was a modest sized bedroom. Next to it was Mr Watts' room. Not much is known about his room. Only he is allowed in there.

When Mr Watts arrives home with George he tries to make him comfortable. He gives him the spare bedroom down the short hall from the kitchen and fits him up with a few changes of clothes. Leaving him to settle in a while, he fixes them a nice meal of chicken, mashed potatoes and green beans. When George comes back to the kitchen Mr Watts tells him, "George, tomorrow you and I need to go to the courthouse to see the judge."

"Why, Mr Watts? I didn't do anything wrong. Are you mad at me for something? I can make it right."

"No George, nothing you've done. But now you're without a home and family so we need to see what the judge says about this. For now just enjoy your food, then why don't you get some rest. It's been a trying day. You need anything, just knock on my bedroom door."

"Yes, sir." George goes off to bed; can't say it's a restful night for George. What's going to happen to me, he keeps thinking.

Friday, March 29th 1963
The next morning he wakes to the smell of eggs, bacon and toast filling the whole house. George follows the smell to find the kitchen.

"Good morning, George. I hope you got some sleep last night. Now the sun is up and it's a great day the Lord has made. Have a seat, George." Mr Watts fills his plate. "There's jam, jelly, honey and apple butter on the table. Just help yourself. There's plenty to go around. Like some milk?"

"Yes, sir."

Mr Watts pours him the biggest glass of milk he ever saw. "George, after you get ready we're going down to the county courthouse to see Judge Hanson. She's a good person to get to know. She'll determine what's the best course of action."

"Okay, sir. The judge is a woman?"

"Yes, she is in the family court system. All she deals with is matters of the family. So everything's going to be okay."

They walked down the street past the school and a store, within sight of George's burnt home, until they got to the main part of town where they caught a bus to the county seat of Marshall. The courthouse was built of red brick, had tall arched windows and doors. The steps, built of stone, were huge; built to last. Inside, they went down a long hallway then up more stairs and down the end of the hall was the courtroom of Judge Mary Hanson. Inside were some people; the sheriff who was at the fire, the fire chief and also a few others that he'd seen around town. They took a seat on the front row. They just sat there quietly.

Then a BIG MEAN looking man comes out in an officer's uniform and announces, "ALL RISE. The Honorable Judge Hanson in and for the county of Marshall, in the matters of family court, is now in session. You may be seated."

"Ben," the judge asks, "what's on the docket for today?"

"Your Honor, the care today is for one boy, George, who lost his house in a fire and lost his one and only known relative, his father."

"Yes, I saw the fire on the news. Very tragic. Well now, young man, I see your home is gone, father is too."

"Your Honor, may I speak for George?"

"If he has no objections, Mr Watts."

"Your Honor, George stayed with me last night with permission of the sheriff."

"Yes, I'm aware of that, Mr Watts. You're always stepping in to help."

"Anyway, for now, I would like to foster George until the court has more time to think about his future."

The judge strikes the gavel and says, "Approved! Dismissed for six months from now. Ben, what's the next case?"

Mr Watts and George leave the courtroom and head out the courthouse door. George looks a bit puzzled.

"Mr Watts? What just happened?"

"Well, George, I've fostered kids here for many years. Some were like you, orphaned due to some accident, others were abandoned. Somebody needed to do something, so we did. Many of the people

around town here were raised as foster kids by my wife and I."
"What happened to Mrs Watts?"
"She died a few years ago of lung cancer while working as a nurse at the steel plant in Wheeling. But she worked helping others till the end."
They catch the bus back to Chapman Grove.
"Sorry to hear that, sir. She sounded like she lived at the steel mill."
"No George, she didn't live there but she did lots to help others. She also loved the Lord. Every time the church doors were open she'd be there when she could. So, while we could, we took kids in to foster them. The orphanage was so overcrowded. Members of the church decided it was a calling. The orphanage dwindled to just a few kids. Today the orphanage is a foster home itself."
"WOW, lots of good people here, sir."
"George, you're a good boy and a smart one too. I saw that from the first day I met you. The judge saw it too. I grew up with her. She's my wife's sister, Mary."
At this moment they get to school just in time for lunch. Mr Watts goes to the kitchen and tells the clerk to add George's lunch to payroll deduction.
"Raising me a little brother, Dad?" asked Rick, the kitchen clerk.
"Something like that." Mr Watts replied.
Today's lunch was: spaghetti and meatballs, homemade rolls, green beans, followed by chocolate cake with icing and milk. George never ate this well. Most of the time he brought a bag lunch of a sandwich, maybe an apple if lucky. His poor diet made him a skinny kid.
After lunch George went outside to read under the old apple tree that's been standing there since the beginning of time. George loved reading under that old apple tree. Today he had a book on understanding electronics. He was like a sponge, soaking up everything he read. Then lunch was over and a physical education class was next. He had little use for this class. It was just required. Then came Mr Watts' class, the best time of the day. Mr Watts opened up your mind and got you thinking.
"Class, the science fair is fast approaching. First off, those of you

who are ready can tell us about your project, if you want to. I know some of you like secrets and I'll not press you for it."

"Mr Watts, I know what Georgie been planning. Bet it started the fire."

 Some of the students laugh.

"Okay Margaret, I'm sure it's none of our business till George tells us. And no, it didn't start the fire. Susan, how about you go first if you want."

"Yes, sir. My project takes account of the language barrier. For centuries, to communicate with others, people had to have an interpreter or learn the language themselves. What if a person could just speak into a microphone and others could hear it in their language in headphones?" Susan sets a huge contraption on the table. It has wires going every which way, tubes lighting up and makes a buzzing sound. "In this demonstration, Angela will speak French into the microphone and I, who knows no French, will tell you what she said."

"Bonjour. Comment allez vous aujourd'hui?"

"Angela said, 'Hello, how are you today?' I am doing very well, Angela. Can you hear me okay?"

"Oui, je vous entends très bien."

"Just think, this could be used at the United Nations, talking to foreign countries, almost anybody. This is my first model and it only does French. Someday it be great if it was a universal translator. Also, thank you Angela, for helping me program the French into it."

The class applauds then Mr Watts calls the next student.

 "Okay Mathew, you're up."

Mathew gets up to the front of the class and Mrs Harless, the school secretary, comes to the front also.

"As you all know and have seen, Mrs Harless has arthritis really bad. Sometimes so bad it can be very painful till she misses work. With the help of her doctor, we have been treating her hands with bee stings."

Lots of the class comment with "Ye-ugh!" and "Never get me to do that!"

"Anyway, this treatment is apitherapy," continues Mathew, "the use of bee venom to treat the body."

Mrs Harless holds up her hands and wiggles her fingers and says, "See class, not hardly hurting at all."

Mathew smiles and finishes, "This is not a cure, by far. It's only a treatment. But if it makes life better then it could be worth it. Please do not do this without a doctor's supervision. Some people can go into shock and that can be bad enough to kill you."

Mr Watts stands up as everyone applauds, and says, "Great work, Mathew. Who wants it next?" Just then the bell rings. "Okay, we'll get into it next time."

The kids all go charging out the door. Their next class period is the last one of the day so they're all eager to have their school day over.

George's last class of the day went well, without a hitch. He even showed a great mind for math, at college level. Most of it he could do in his head, which impressed Mrs MacQueen. She instructed, "George, your answers on these are one hundred percent correct, but you need to write out how you got the answer."

He thinks for a minute and says, "I just thought about it, and it just came to me."

"That's great, George. Later I'll help you figure out how you got the answer."

"I know how, ma'am. I saw the question then wrote down the answer."

"I'll show you what I mean later."

"Okay, Mrs MacQueen."

The two of them are starting to get along better.

School lets out for the day and George waits outside for Mr Watts.

"Hey, there's teacher's pet, Georgie porgie!" calls out one of the bullies standing around in the yard.

Susan stands up to them, hitting one of them with her text book. The boys just run off, laughing. Susan picks a flower, a black-eyed susan, and gives it to George and smiles.

"I don't want any trouble with them," George tells Susan as he accepts the wildflower.

"I know, George, but you got to stand up to them or you'll never

hear the end of it. I think you're awesome."
George smells the flower then presses it in his book as Susan walks away.
"George? You know she's right." Here comes Mr Watts. "If you don't stand up to those bullies, they'll hound you till the end of time. I bet if you stood up to their ring leader, Eddy Gulch, all of them will either turn tail and run or become your friend."
George considers what his teacher said but stays silent.
"George, you lost everything for your project?"
"Yes, sir."
"No, you didn't. Bet it's still in your head. Maybe even a better way to do it."
George's voice gets excited as he blurts out, "Yes, I do."
"So, George, let's see what we've got in the garage and get busy."
George starts to smile and walks taller; a girl that likes him and a teacher that has faith in him.

Saturday, March 30th 1963

George woke up early in the morning to the sounds of cars going by, people cutting the grass and so forth. After getting dressed he wandered around then found Mr Watts under the hood of a green 1952 Oldsmobile® that still looked fairly well taken care of.
"What's up, Mr Watts?"
"Oh, just fixing Mr McKee's car. He said it was running badly and making a noise, so I told him to pop on over with it and I'll have a look-see."
Then a voice came from inside the car. A man in his fifties was inside, "I found a speedometer cable loose but I don't think that would cause it to act the way it has. Oh, you must be George. I heard a lot about you. Sorry about your dad and home. I'm Mr McKee." George didn't say anything. Then Mr McKee got out of the car and proceeded to the hood. He had only one leg. George stared.
"Excuse me, George, let me get past you here."
"George," Mr Watts calls out, "it's really not polite to stare."
"I'm sorry. What happened to your leg, Mr McKee?"

"I lost it on December 7ᵗʰ 1941 when the Japanese attacked us at Pearl Harbor, Hawaii. I was on a service vessel called the Vestar, right next to the battleship Arizona. The Arizona took a bomb in the magazine and when it blew, the whole ship blew. It raised that whole ship up out of the water. When that happened, the sound of the blast blew me right off the deck of the Vestar. I crashed into the battleship West Virginia and my leg twisted till it had to come off. Yep, I spent World War II in the base hospital. I also was lucky to count my blessings. I was really off duty that day but I filled in for a shipmate who wasn't feeling well. My barracks took a bombshell and nobody survived. They really kicked our tails that day but look who won the war."

"Need some work done around the house, Mr McKee?" George asked.

"Well, George, can you run a lawnmower?"

"Yes, sir!"

George takes off like a shot, heading for Mr McKee's tool shed. This lawnmower was unlike the one his dad used to have; this one had a motor. He gets the lawnmower out, checks the oil and fills the tank with gas. Then he's off and running with the mower, working systematically, starting at the front yard and working towards the sides.

"He's full of energy, Mike."

"He sure is, Tom. I saw he's a good boy from the start, just needed to belong."

George didn't stop with cutting the grass. He got out the hand clippers and trimmed around the trees and the walkway then came back to the shade tree mechanics, looking proud of himself.

"All done, Mr McKee."

"All done, George?"

"Yes, sir." George is still standing tall, smiling.

"Did the back yard too?"

"Yep, also trimmed around all the trees and next to the walkway."

"You forgot one thing, George."

George looked puzzled. "What could it be, sir?"

"You forgot this tall lemonade."

George took the glass as a pleasing reward for a chore well done. As the glass turned up, he could feel the cold lemonade going down.

"Aw, that was good."

The next sound he heard was the car starting up and purring like a kitten.

"Hey Mike, you all come over this evening to the cookout I'm having."

"Sounds great! We'll bring drinks, ice and cups."

Mr McKee got into the car and drove it across the road to his house. Mr Watts and George went into the garage to find parts for his science project.

"Okay George, what do you think you need?"

"Well, I need five round bars of metal to magnetize, about six inches long."

"Okay George, I have one long rod that we can cut to the lengths needed."

"I need wire."

"It's over on the top shelf."

"And I need three feet of conflux."

"You need what?"

"Conflux. Plastic tubing with a high iron content mixed in an oil based fluid. I can make it."

"Long as it doesn't blow up the garage, George!" Mr Watts and George laugh.

George heats up some Vaseline® and mixes in lots of iron dust. Then, while still a hot liquid but on the verge of becoming a paste, George squeezes it into the plastic tubing. When cooled, the stuff stays in the tubing.

"Okay George, I cut the rods to the length you said."

George measures each rod and says, "Perfect! I need to mount them equally spaced on a bracket."

"Would this scrap lumber work, George?"

"I think it would. I need to drill five holes in two round sections to hold the rods in place."

"The drill press and bits are all in the corner."

He drills the holes at equal distances around the wooden bracket for the rods to fit into. In the center of that is a tiny hole for the axle to pivot on. Then from the axle it mounts on its base to hold it all together. The rods had been magnetized already. So, next the conflux gets installed. One length comes close to, but not touching, one end of the rod. Then the other end comes to the opposite end of the rods to line up with the next rod. He keeps doing this until all rods always line up with the conflux, so the poles will always be NS, SN, in an alternating fashion.

"George, we been working all day."

"Yes, sir. It really feels good, Mr Watts."

"George, let's go inside and get cleaned up for the cookout."

"A cookout, sir?"

"Yes, Tom McKee invited us both to a cookout in their backyard."

"WOW, just like a picnic, Mr Watts!"

"Okay George, you clean up first and I'll run down to the store for cookout stuff. What's your favorite drink?"

"Well, I like many kinds of pop."

"Alright, I'll select a variety of drinks."

"Ah, Mr Watts, I'm kind of partial to orange."

"Hmm, I'll bring some orange also, but first let me quickly wash up a bit and change my shirt."

Then Mr Watts goes to the garage where he collects a kid's Radio Flier® wagon with railed wooden sides, and takes off down the street for the store, wagon banging on the bumpy sidewalk. George darts into the house to his room. He strips off all the grungy clothes, runs into the bathroom and takes a nice hot bath. He's never had it so good. But George begins to wonder why. Why has all this acts of random kindness happened to me? Why, after all is said and done, why are people helping me?

After twenty minutes he gets out of the tub, dries off and puts on fresh clean clothes then puts the bathroom in order and goes to his room. George looks at the few treasures salvaged from the fire: a pocket knife that he traded his spare baseball cards for; a G.I. Joe® toy that he found in the trash and cleaned up; a yo-yo he carved from scrap lumber; a small faded photograph of his mom with dark brown hair and a nice flower behind her right ear, all now smelling of smoke.

"George?" Mr Watts had come in. George was so engrossed with his treasures that he didn't hear him. "Are your things okay from the fire?"

"Somewhat, sir." He sniffs one of his things. "Mostly they smell of smoke."

"Is this a picture of your mom? Very pretty. She looks like someone I knew," Mr Watts says thoughtfully. "The rest of your things that could be salvaged are in the garage for now."

George doesn't say anything.

"Well George, time we go over to the McKee house and help set up for the cookout. Bet you're hungry."

The two of them head out the door and Mr Watts grabs the handle of the wagon. It was piled so high with drinks of all kinds and with ice and cups, it's surprising it all stayed on. But it did. They arrived and went right into the backyard, dumped some ice in a cooler then a mixture of drinks then more ice on top of that. About then Tom McKee comes out, carrying a big bowl of food. George runs up to him and grabs the bowl, "I got it, Mr McKee."

George puts the bowl on the now empty wagon. Then he catches up with Mr Watts who's gone to the garage to get saw horses before fetching planks to make tables for all the food that will be coming. Next, the grill was dragged to the concrete patio. A big load of charcoal was dumped in and spread evenly. Lighter fluid then saturated the charcoal and, when Mr McKee lit a match to it, a big ball of smoke and flames sent up a smoke signal.

First came Mr Watts' sister, Mrs MacQueen, carrying what seemed like a barrel of potato salad. She also brought in tow her next door neighbors, Mrs Fitch and the Bowmans; some sweet old people that grew up here with the rest of them. Then in came a bunch of folks carrying tons of food. George wondered, where did all these people come from? Looks like most the town is here. Then more came. Mr McKee seemed so pleased to see everyone. When you thought everyone was there, here came more till there were over a hundred or so.

Mr McKee spoke loudly, "I'm so pleased that you all came. It's so joyful that we could be together again. Pastor Bess, please could you give the blessing on the gathering and thanks for the food here today?"

Pastor Bess stands. Everyone becomes silent. "Lord Jesus, thank you for this beautiful day, all the abundance of the land for nourishing the body. Thank you for seeing everybody here safely, watch over them returning. Let us be thankful for this gathering. Amen."

A group of people broke out playing music on guitar, fiddle and banjo. It sounded great while they mingled, talking about everything and anything. Mr and Mrs McKee were at the grill, making sure enough food was cooking. Some of the young ones were dancing in front of the band, having a grand time. Mr Watts and Mrs MacQueen were talking and laughing. George was standing near the grill, just in case something was needing done. He enjoyed being helpful and tasting the grill-cooked foods.

On the grill were the usual hot dogs and hamburgers to eat with chilli sauce. Roasting ears of corn wrapped in foil, with the smell of real butter, filled the air also. Some were feasting on hot dogs. Others were munching on corn. A few loved the hamburgers with onions cooked on top. The makeshift table was loaded. One end of the table had potato salad, macaroni salad, deviled eggs, baked beans; and these were not small containers either. The smallest must have been at least a couple of gallons. In the middle of the table was the overflow from the grill. A crew at the grill kept it full and people kept eating.

Homemade breads were loaded on one end while the other end of the table held desserts: chocolate cake, apple pie, cherry pie, sweet potato pie, large tubs of ice cream; any flavor you could want. Strawberry seemed the most popular. Of course there was chocolate and vanilla. All this went on for hours. Even the streetlights started to come on.

"Well well, isn't it Georgie porgie. Still hanging around old man Watts, are you?"

George just kept his back turned, trying to ignore Eddy Gulch. He didn't want to ruin the feast.

"Hey Georgie, why don't you go home, back to Kaymoor.[6] Your kind don't belong here."

Some of the others started looking at what was happening. Susan was watching also, with some of her friends.

"Georgie, why don't you run home to your mommie. Oh I forgot, you were hatched, not born."

A few of Eddy's buddies were chuckling.

"Your old man burned down one of my mom's rental houses. Now she's out of the house and income."

George felt ready to burst. But he didn't react.

"Your drunk father was no 'count."

George didn't know what happened next. Eddy was on the ground with such a bloody nose you couldn't see it anymore. George thought, did I do that? It felt good.

Lots of the crowd started applauding. Eddy had been asking for this for a long time. Mrs Gulch came over to help pick Eddy up. He got to his feet then started running away.

"**SHERIFF**, **you saw what happened? Arrest that juvenile delinquent!**"

"I didn't see a thing, Mrs Gulch. Besides, I'm off duty."

"**JUDGE Hanson!**" she yelled. "**You saw!**"

"Not a thing. Besides, my jurisdiction is in the courtroom chambers."

"**You all will pay for this. All of you!**" She stomped off.

Little Susan comes and hugs George, "You don't realize what you've done. Those bullies has tormented us for years and everyone was afraid to do anything 'cause she owned so many of our homes."

Susan's dad came over to get her and gave George a pat on the back. The party started breaking up. People started gathering up their bowls and things. People smiled at George when passing.

Eddy's buddies showed their true colors now, "Sorry to been so mean to you, George. You're one cool dude. If we didn't hang out with Eddy, his mom threatened to throw us out in the street."

Everything was cleaned up and stuff put away.

"George, you ready to come home? It must be near midnight."
"Home, sir?" George is still a little dazed.
"My home is your home, long as we can. Let's go home, we've got church in the morning. You ever been in church?"
"No. What do we do there?"
"We learn about God's word, the Bible, and sing praise to Him."
"Will he be there too?"
"Yes, George, He's everywhere."
"Hmm, sounds amazing."
"He certainly is, George."

Sunday, March 31ˢᵗ 1963
The next morning, Mr Watts and George start walking to church. As they were walking, a bell started ringing.
"What's that bell ringing for, sir?"
"It's the church bell, letting people know the church doors are open to welcome them in."
"Everybody?"
"Yes, everybody."
"Even Eddy and his mom?"
"Them too. But I've never seen them there."
They approach the church, a nice looking place with flowers growing all around. A tall steeple projected upward, reaching for the sky. A round window with a nice stained glass design was centered in its middle. Steps led up to the church and through the bottom part of the steeple. The doors were solid wood with brass handles that gleamed from the sun shining on them. They go inside and Mr Watts introduces George to Andy Brown, the Sunday school teacher for George's age group.
"Hello, George. You can call me Andy. Welcome to church. Is this your first time here?"
"First time I ever been in a church, Andy."
"Well, you just follow me and we'll be fine."
George follows Andy down a hall which leads to the classrooms. Their classroom was packed with many kids, some from his school.
"Class, this is George. I want you to help him as this is his first

time here."
A few kids wave, some say 'hi' and that's about it.
"If you have your Bibles, hold them up so I can get a count."
They all hold up their Bibles, except George. He sees Susan away in the back of the room. She's a titchy little thing, about five foot tall, nicely slim, with wavy black hair that comes down to her shoulders. Her eyes are baby blue. He can spot her a mile off.
"George, you need a Bible?" asks Andy.
George doesn't answer but Andy hands him a black book with gold lettering saying Holy Bible. George feels the cover. He thinks it feels good.
"Here, we use the King James Bible. Today's lesson is in the book of Matthew, chapter 14 and we'll start at verse 14. *'And Jesus went forth, and saw a great multitude, and was moved with compassion toward them, and he healed their sick. And when it was evening, his disciples came to him, saying, This is a desert place, and the time is now past; send the multitude away, that they may go into the villages, and buy themselves victuals. But Jesus said unto them, They need not depart; give ye them to eat. And they say unto him, We have here but five loaves, and two fishes. He said, Bring them hither to me. And he commanded the multitude to sit down on the grass, and took the five loaves, and the two fishes, and looking up to heaven, he blessed, and brake, and gave the loaves to his disciples, and the disciples to the multitude. And they did all eat, and were filled: and they took up of the fragments that remained twelve baskets full. And they that had eaten were about five thousand men, beside women and children.'* So class, what did we see or learn from this?"
One girl said Jesus didn't need the market to feed so many. Susan said, "I forget where it is but this same story appears and it's a shepherd boy's meal."
"That's right, Susan, it was. A shepherd was the one to look after the sheep. Similarly, Jesus tends us like sheep. He takes care of us and will feed us."
George was listening but was still puzzled. How can a person feed five thousand men then women and children and end up with more

than he started with? If I keep quiet and listen maybe the answer will come. But the math don't add up.

"So class, why did Jesus feed them all?"

Another girl speaks out and says, "Because God loves us, He wouldn't let us suffer and be hungry."

"John 3:16 says God loves us," adds Jennifer. "'*For God so loved the world that He gave his only begotten Son that whoever believes in Him shall not perish but have everlasting life.*'"

Everlasting life, George thought. Does this mean living forever? How can a person live forever? You have to die sometime.

"George! You still with us? You seem to be in outer space."

Some of the others chuckled.

"I was thinking how can one live..." the bell rang for the main service, interrupting him in mid-sentence, ".... forever?"

"One can't live forever in the body, but in the spirit with Jesus Christ as our savior."

"How could a person feed over five thousand people with only five loaves and two fish?"

"That's an excellent question, George. Best thing I can say on that, is that God's son, Jesus, performed a miracle."

"But the math don't add up, Andy."

"You're right George, that's what makes it a miracle."

"So why did he do it?"

"Because He loves us. Okay, let's go to the eleven o'clock service, see what Pastor Bess says."

"Okay."

George went into the main part of the church. Some of the kids from class called out for George to join them. Mr Watts pointed his thumb to go join the young folk in the back. The music from the piano started playing and it seemed like everybody knew the song, except George. He felt left out. A young boy smiled and handed him a hymnal opened to page seventy two, To God Be the Glory. George smiled back. George didn't really know any gospel songs but he did the best he could.

At the end of the song Pastor Bess stood up and said, "I heard, on Paul Harvey News yesterday, this story that he tells every year. It was originally told by a Boston preacher, Dr S.D. Gordon.[8]

'Dr Gordon placed a beat up, bent, rusted old bird cage beside his pulpit. An unkempt, unwashed, little lad about 10 years old was coming up the alley swinging this old caved in bird cage with several tiny birds shivering on the floor of it. The compassionate Dr Gordon asked the boy where he got the birds. He said he trapped them. Dr Gordon asked what he was going to do with them. The boy said he was going to play with them and have fun with them. The preacher said, "Sooner or later you'll get tired of them. Then what are you going to do with them?"

The lad said, "I have some cats at home. They like birds. I'll feed them to my cats."

Dr Gordon said, "Son, how much do you want for the birds?"

The boy, surprised, hesitated and said, "Mister, you don't want these birds. They're just plain old field birds. They can't even sing. They're ugly."

The preacher said, "Just tell me. How much do you want?"

The grubby little lad thought about it. He squinted up one eye. He calculated and hesitated and said, "Two dollars?" To his surprise Dr Gordon reached into his pocket and handed the boy two, one dollar bills. The preacher took the cage. The boy, in a wink, hurried up the alley.

In a sheltered crevice between buildings, Dr Gordon opened the door of the cage and tapping on the rusty exterior, he encouraged the little birds, one at a time, to find their way out through the narrow door and fly away.

Thus, having accounted for the empty cage beside his pulpit, the preacher went on to tell what seemed at first like a separate story, about how once upon a time, Jesus and the Devil had engaged in a negotiation.

Satan had boasted how he'd baited a trap in Eden's garden and caught himself a world full of people.

"What are you going to do with all those people in your cage?" Jesus wanted to know.

The Devil said, "I'm going to play with 'em, tease 'em. Make them marry and divorce and fight and kill one another. I'm going to teach them to throw bombs on one another. I'm going to have fun with them!"

Jesus said, "You can't have fun with them forever. When you get tired of playing, what are you going to do with them?"

Satan said, "Damn them! They're no good anyway! Damn them! Kill them!"

Jesus said, "How much do you want for them?"

Satan said, "You can't be serious! If I sell them to you, they'll just spit on you. They'll hate you. They'll hit you and beat you. They'll hammer nails into you! They're no good."

Jesus said, "How much?"

Satan said, "All of your tears and all of your blood. That's the price."

Jesus took the cage and paid the price and opened the door. All you have to do is accept the gift of eternal life.'"

Pastor Bess ends the story, turns and signals to the choir. The choir stood up and sang a song about coming to Jesus. George heard the words of the song and was pondering the message. Something was tugging at his heart and he didn't know what it was.

Then the service was over and everyone started going out the front door, some getting into cars and others walking, like George and Mr Watts. The walk was very quiet.

"George, you okay? Not said much."

"I'm okay, just thinking."

"You can always talk to me if you want."

"I need a Bible to read. You have any at home?"

"George, I got a box full of Bibles."

They got home and Mr Watts reached into a box and pulled out a brand new Bible. "George, this is yours. Put your name in it and keep it. Might start in the book of John."

"Is that another book?"

"No, no. It's in the New Testament, written by one of Jesus' disciples, John!"

Mr Watts turns to the book of John, and George takes it in his hand, walks out the door and sits under an apple tree in the front yard. George sits there all afternoon, reading. Next thing you know he fell asleep.

George finds himself in a cage. Satan was jabbing him with a rod. Satan looked like Eddy. Then he shook the cage. Then Satan grew. He was ten times bigger, now, than George. Satan shook the cage more, then ripped the cage open and reached in and...

"GEORGE, wake up!"

George woke up in a cold sweat. Mr Watts was holding his shoulder.

"You having a bad dream? Time to get ready for the evening service. You want a bite to eat before we go?"

George just nods his head. They go inside for a quick bite then out the door to church. Church wasn't as crowded this time but George still had lots on his mind.

Walking home, Mr Watts said, "George, when you have something on your mind you can always ask me."

George says nothing. They get home and George goes to his room to bed.

Monday, April 1st 1963

Next morning, George wakes to the smell of sausage and biscuits.

"George, we have your father's funeral today. Your father's insurance has taken care of everything."

They ate breakfast quietly then headed out the door to the church. Chapman Grove was a small town and had no funeral homes. The funeral went off without a hitch. It was quiet and dignified. The casket was a closed one for reason of the burnt body. After the service ended the casket was loaded onto a horse drawn wagon and driven up to the city cemetery.

The graveside service was modest. Pastor Bess reads from the Bible, and as it begins to rain with a little bit of rolling thunder, umbrellas begin to open. George just stood there, feeling numb. This was the only family he knew. Then the graveside funeral broke up. People passed by George, giving a caring touch. George seemed to notice Susan's hug most. The last two remaining were Mr Watts and George. They turned and slowly walked away.

"Wotcha want to do today, George?"

"Got school, don't I?"

"No school for you and I today, canceled for the funeral. We go back tomorrow."

"I'd rather go back today to get my mind on other things and forget this day."

"I understand. Let's go for a walk."

"In the rain?"

"It won't hurt us George, besides we have umbrellas."

They walked down to the Dairy Queen®.

"I'll have a double strawberry cone," Mr Watts said to the person at the window. "You having anything, George?"

"Hmm, I'll have the same. Strawberry's my favorite followed by chocolate then vanilla."

"You got your priorities in order, don't you George?"

They both chuckle a little.

"Here ya are, Grandpa." The young girl handed out two ice cream cones.

They walked on, trying to enjoy the day more. The bank was open so Mr Watts took him in, to the account manager. The bank was inside a building not originally meant to be a bank. It was an old red brick building with two entrance doors side by side in the center front, with the second entrance going into the other half of the building where another business had been but was now gone. That half used to be a toy store, then a clothing store, then a hobby shop. No business lasted long. The bank interior was passable but it was a secondhand building. The vault was nothing more than a huge safe. It was big and would take an army to move. A few desks and chairs placed in a row, and some filing cabinets comprised all the furnishing for the bank staff.

"George, this is Mrs Harper. She watches over your bank account."

"How do I have a bank account, Mr Watts?"

"Ask her."

"Well George, your father had life insurance. You know what that is? No? Well, if something happened to your dad a lump sum of money comes to you. But seeing as you're underage, I've been appointed by Judge Hanson to see it's used wisely. Also, the child foster parent program from the state deposits money needed for your welfare."

"How much do I have?"

"Well George, Mr Watts supervises it along with Judge Hanson and I monitor it. But as of today, you have one hundred fifty thousand, three hundred and sixty dollars total." She hands him a bank deposit book. George's mouth drops open and he gets big eyed, looking at it.

"Two percent of that is in a checking account to help buy you food, clothes, things for school and for things like going out, like the movies. Three people watch over your money to protect you. Mr Watts has done this time and time again. He never fails to take care of anyone."

The two of them thank Mrs Harper and proceed out the door.

"Wow, $150,360! Wonder if that's enough for college?"

"I would say so, George. Got a college in mind?"

"No sir, I just like learning stuff and I have some great ideas."

"I bet you do, George. Let's head for home."

"Home sounds nice."

The two of them walked home and got some supper. Mr Watts and George clean up the kitchen.

"George, thanks for helping."

"You called it my home too, so I want to take care of it also."

"George, see that cake pan lid; how about hand that to me. I'll give it a good washing."

George takes the lid off the pan only to find a cake with Happy Birthday on it.

"George, things have been so hectic the last few days but I wanted to let you know I hadn't forgotten your birthday."

They sit down to some homemade cake with Neapolitan® ice cream. Then Mr Watts hands him a card. The card was his first ever birthday card. Taped to the inside was a key.

"What's this for?" George asked.

"That's the front door key so you can always come home."

George hugs Mr Watts. After all that, George goes to his room, maybe to read or do school work. A little later music starts coming out of the room, a little bit loud. Mr Watts goes to investigate. He cracks the door open and peeks in. There's George dancing to the music and every few seconds he would mark a number on a blackboard. What kind of equation is that, he wondered. Then George is startled as he sees Mr Watts.

"Is the music too loud, sir?"

"Not much, but will you turn it down just a bit?"

George turns the radio down and goes back to enjoying himself. Mr Watts chuckles and closes the door. A few hours later the music ends.

Chapter 2
Fort Randolph[3]

Tuesday, April 2nd 1963
The next morning George is up before the sun. He is really loving school now. He gets dressed fast and starts darting for the door. "Hold on George, school won't start for another ninety minutes and it's a five minute walk from here. Come have a hot breakfast." George sits down to eat as Mr Watts says, "Don't forget your science project for school and any other homework you had. I never saw a kid so excited about going to school in all my born days." Mr. Watts feels like a parent again.
After breakfast the two of them go out the door and walk to school. Classes go normally, meeting friends in the hallway, lunch room and classrooms. Then came science,.his number one favorite class. "Everyone take your seats and we can begin. Margaret, you too. It's been a long weekend so I hope you all enjoyed it."
A boy raises his hand frantically. "Mr Watts, can I show my project first?"
"If nobody minds, Timmy. Come on up since you seem to be set up and ready."
Timmy comes forward. "My project is to make propellers quieter in the water for use on navy ships and submarines. Here you see a regular propeller driven by a small motor. I hold a microphone to the side of the tank and the sound meter shows a recording of eighty six decibels. Now here is the same type propeller except I modified it with a shroud, and ran by the same type of motor. Now hold the microphone on the side of the tank and we see the sound level has been reduced by about seventy five percent. Our submarines could be totally silent one day."
"Well done, Timmy!" exclaims Mr Watts as the class explodes in clapping and cheering. Timmy makes his way back to his seat, blushing and grinning. Mr Watts turns to George and asks, "Okay George, you ready?"
George gets up and announces, "Thanks to Mr Watts for helping me rebuild my project since the first one was ruined in the fire.

Here we have the use of magnets on a rotating axle. As it turns, the magnetic waves travel through this specially made conduit tubing. As you know, in magnetism like poles repel and unlike poles attract. If one can set this up on a governed rotating system with a constant repelling-attracting, the motor would run until it wore out." He gives it a spin and it keeps going and going and going. Then a governor comes up to keep it from going even faster. Margaret jumps out of her seat and says, "I see what's doing it! It's this thing that popped up." She grabs it off of the project. George screams to give it back. The project screams even louder than George. Then something like a vortex opens around the project and sucks the machine and George in. All the other students run like mad, knocking over Mr Watts in fear they will be next. Then, he's gone! George was nowhere to be seen, nor the machine. Mr Watts gets back to his feet. It's true, George and the machine are gone. Mr Watts looks around and sees part of the desk is also missing. All that's left is the governor that Margaret had taken and dropped.

Thursday, October 9th 1777[7]
George and his project land on the edge of a clearing but fall, rolling down an embankment. In the distance are two rivers, one flowing into a larger one. At the intersection of the two rivers was a structure made of tall logs. From a distance you could see that, inside, there were some buildings and people.
George hides his project then proceeds to walk towards the strange looking place. Coming up from inside was a flag pole with what seemed like the American flag, but it didn't look right. People were at the top of some kind of log wall and seemed to have guns. Was this some strange kind of prison, he wondered.
A voice comes from inside. "Sergeant of the guard, somebody is approaching."
George looks over his shoulder. Do they mean me? George slows his pace. As he gets closer a gate opens and three men come out and take him in.
"Boy, what were you doing way out there? Don't you know Indians

are all over this countryside and could attack any moment?"
"No sir, I didn't know. Where am I anyhow?"
"You're at Fort Randolph, the most farthest outpost in northwestern Virginia."[4]
George keeps his mouth shut until he figures out what's going on. That night he sat around a campfire and some of the men fed him what they had; some kind of brown meat cooked on the fire, biscuits, beans and potatoes. He ate good that night.
Later that night an officer, at least that's what he looked like, came up to him and spoke, "Hello lad, I'm Captain Arbuckle. Who might you be?"
"I'm George, sir."
"George, is it?"
George just nods his head.
"Well, how did a strangely dressed lad like you get way out here in northwestern Virginia?"[4]
"I got separated from my friends and now I'm lost," George responded truthfully enough.
"Where's home, then?"
"It's in Chapman Grove, on the Ohio River."
"Well George, I'm not sure where that is but I'm sure we can find it and get you home to your family and friends. But for now I have a meeting with the officers. You get some rest."
"Thank you Captain, your men has been very kind to me." George lay down near the campfire, looking up at the stars. Not realizing the danger he's in, he falls asleep.

Friday, October 10th 1777
George woke up early the next morning. Men were coming in at the gate, while others were going out. Some ladies with baskets were speaking to a guard at the main gate then they too proceeded out. Some other men moved to a platform so they could look over the fort wall. Others were having some kind of hot drinks near the fire as it was a cold morning. Dew covered the grassier areas of the grounds.
"Captain Arburkle! Indians approaching. Looks like Chief

Cornstalk bearing a white flag. Get some men to the bastions and blockhouses just in case they're not alone."

An Indian came into the fort. A real live Indian! George had never seen one before. Leastwise none he recalls. This was an Indian chief? The Chief and the Captain shake hands. Some of the other men step back with their rifles in a ready position.

"Captain Arbuckle, it is good to see you again," Chief Cornstalk said. "Captain, we must talk. I have kept my warriors at peace since the signing of the treaty with your former governor, Lord Dunmore."

George decides to back up a little bit as the others had been doing. You can't never tell what might happen next.

The Chief continues, "But I can no longer restrain my warriors. They will fight again. I regret this information, but I must flow like a river and join them."

Flow like a river, George thought. What does he mean by that? So George goes into a nearby cabin for safety. Inside was somewhat warmer than outside. George went up to the roaring fireplace. It felt nice. George turned around to warm his back and could see out the window. People, including all the ladies that had gone out, were hurrying back in. Then the gates closed and more men went to the fort walls.

Captain Arbuckle and Chief Cornstalk talked a little longer then the Captain motioned for the Chief to go inside the cabin. Oh man! George couldn't believe it. He came into the cabin for safety and what does the Captain do? He sends an Indian in here.

The Captain gives something to a couple of men on horses and they go charging out of the gate. Chief Cornstalk enters the cabin and some of the men start grumbling about it.

Then another Indian comes into the fort. Is this Indian central? The Chief goes back out to meet them. They talk the longest time. What could they be saying? But I'm not going out there to find out, George thinks. Then he hears, **"Lies! We came alone."** That was the last George heard of their talk outside. He also saw an Indian woman. She was very pretty.

"Who is that woman?"

"That's Cornstalk's family," a man told him, adding, "Any more come in here they'll just know how to hit us."
The other men were getting more restless. Then the Chief started heading back toward the cabin. Some of the men started slowly loading their rifles.
"Boy, you better step back."
A minute later Chief Cornstalk came in, poured himself a drink and broke off a large piece of bread. He seemed a peaceful person, just different. The tension in the cabin was growing. More of the men had loaded up their rifles, and knives were being sharpened. Suddenly a shot went off in the cabin and Chief Cornstalk started stumbling. More shots were fired and he then fell to the floor, dead. Some of the men pulled knives as big as butcher knives. They jumped on the body of Cornstalk. George couldn't see what was happening. Next thing he knew they had the Chief's bloody hair in their hands. The men who did the horrible murder ran out the door, yelling that was one less Indian to deal with. The bloody body of a great person, who only wanted peace, lay dead on the floor.
Some other Indians that hadn't been noticed, crept out the back door of the cabin. George followed them. The Indians unlocked and went out through an unguarded gate in the fort. George continued to follow them, securing the gate behind him. Keeping his distance, George came up to where he had hidden his project. All this time, George had been pondering what had happened and how to reverse it. George pulled out all the weeds that had got rooted in the magnets and axle. Taking one last look around, George thought nobody was going to ever believe this place. George started the motor for the return trip. As George vanished, an Indian came by, perhaps investigating the noises made by George's machine.

Wednesday, October 10th 1963

George lands back at Chapman Grove, but in the middle of a highway. A car swerves to miss him, and he jumps at the last second to avoid being creamed. The man in the car screams, **"Get out of the road, you stupid brat. I'll report you to the sheriff!"**

Then he sped off. That looked like the principal, Mr Biggarstaff. George sees he landed on the far south end of town. He's even past the lumber mill where his dad had worked. So guess got a long walk ahead.

George passes homes and stores. Some of the stores have posters displayed. He looks closely at all the posters. Then his mouth drops open as he sees a poster with his picture on it. It said 'Missing' then his name. 'Last seen in school on April 2nd 1963. Age fourteen, height 5' 5". Weight about 115 lbs. If seen contact Mr Mike Watts at 158 Marshall Street, Chapman Grove or the Marshall County Sheriff Department.' George yanked a poster off the window and tried running home. But the machine was kind of bulky and got heavier as he ran. Then he could see, in the distance, home. Home is the greatest place to be. Oh, this thing is heavy. Next I'll build a smaller project or put it on wheels. As he got closer he saw someone on the front porch. He steps up his pace. It could only be Mr Watts.

 "Mr Watts!" he calls out. Mr Watts stands up, and papers from school fall all over the place. He runs down the steps to meet him. George drops his motor on some hedges then meets Mr Watts on the sidewalk. They hug each other, seeming like they'd never let go, both of them crying.

"George, I love you boy! Where have you been?"

"I love you too, sir. It's hard for me to believe where I've been."

"Let's go inside. I need to tell everyone you're home and safe." George goes to his room. Nothing's been touched. It's just like he left it. He sits on the edge of the bed then lies back. Oh, a nice soft bed feels good. George falls asleep.

Thursday, October 11th 1963

The next morning George wakes up in a fright. Looking around, he realizes he's home. Maybe it was all a dream. He gets up and walks out to the living room. There, sitting with Mr Watts, are Sheriff Shamblin, Judge Hanson and Mr McKee, who is a court clerk.

"Good morning, George," said Mr Watts. "Hope you slept well. Get yourself a snack or drink in the kitchen. We all need to talk about your whereabouts."

"Okay, sir." George goes to the kitchen and gets a small drink of orange juice. He then comes back into the room.

"George, have a seat. You realize what today is?"

"Yes, Your Honor, it's April the 3rd."

"No, George," stated the judge. "Today is October 11th. You've been missing since April. George, when was the last time you remember being in Mr Watts' science classroom?"

"We were showing our projects for the school science fair. Timmy raised his hand wanting to go first. He showed his project; a demonstration of a more silent propeller for the Navy. Then Mr Watts called me up next. I told about my project, a magnetic motor that could run without outside help once it started. Margaret broke it by yanking off a part, causing it to run out of control. Things got a little fuzzy then. I'm sure this is when I was no longer in the classroom."

"Where do you think you were, George?" inquired the judge.

"I'm not sure of the exact location but the place was called Fort Randolph."

Mr McKee raised head in amazement.

"You have a question, Mr McKee?" asked the judge.

"Yes, Your Honor. George, you say you was at Fort Randolph?"

"Yes sir, at least that's what I was told."

"Who told you that you was at Fort Randolph?"

 "An officer called Captain Arbuckle."

"Can you describe this fort?"

"It was tall, walls made of logs, like a square box. Some buildings were inside with men carrying guns. It was on the banks of two rivers and land cleared around it, sir."

"That's all I have, Your Honor."

"Okay George, continue. You said you were at Fort Randolph."

"Yes ma'am. I was outside the fort a little distance away. I walked towards the fort and some men came out and got me. They asked who I was and I just told them 'George'. That seemed to satisfy them. They fed me and then I fell asleep around the campfire while they told stories. I remember about one man they called Jesse

Hughes."

"Then, when you woke up what happened?"

"The men around me seemed tense."

"How so, George?"

"I don't know, it was just a feeling. Later an Indian was let into the fort. I think they called him Cornstalk. Anyway, he talked with the Captain awhile. I snuck into the nearby cabin for safety."

"Good thinking, George," commended the judge.

"I got a drink from the water barrel but it was vile tasting and I spit it out in the fire. I was looking out the window and saw Chief Cornstalk coming toward the cabin. He then came in. Some of the men were grumbling and loading strange looking guns, none of which I've seen before. Then he went back out when another Indian came into the fort. They talked awhile then the Chief came back in. I'm not sure what happened next or what started it. I couldn't see everything."

"Go on George, just describe what you saw."

"A gunshot went off; it really smoked up the place. Then I saw the Chief stumble. A few more shots sounded and he fell to the floor! Then the men jumped him and cut his hair off skin and all! They ran out the door screaming, being pleased with themselves. Chief Cornstalk only wanted peace." George's voice was trembling and he started crying uncontrollably.

Judge Hanson said, "Let's take a break here. Mr Watts, you take George and get him something to eat."

"Yes, ma'am. You all like anything?"

"Coffee would be good,]" the judge requested, and the others agreed.

In the kitchen, Mr Watts tries to comfort George. "You're doing fine. Just tell what you know. This is not a trial, it's more like an investigation to see what happened."

George sits down with an apple and takes a crunchy bite. "I think I'll be okay in a few minutes, sir. It's just the stress of the last few days for me."

George finishes his apple then helps Mr Watts with carrying the coffee for the others. He goes back to the kitchen and brings himself a small glass of milk.

"George, are you going to be alright now?" Judge Hanson asked.

"Yes, Your Honor. Sorry about my outburst."

"It's understandable, young man. Let's continue, George. After the men ran out the door, what happened next?"

"A couple of Indians was still in the cabin but was unnoticed by all the others. They snuck out the back door of the cabin and then an unguarded back gate. I thought this might be my only chance to get out of the fort without being seen. I kept my distance and tried staying hidden. Went up to my magnetic motor, cleaned out the weeds tangled in it and ran it in reverse. I guessed this would get me back. I just wasn't sure about the amount of running time needed to get back. Guess I overshot my target time, huh. I landed in the middle of Route 2 about the same time a car was coming. I think it was Mr Biggarstaff on the south end of town. He swerved and I jumped fast. I started walking back home and as I passed some stores I saw the posters of myself. Then I got home and found Mr Watts on the porch watching for me while grading papers. And that's it."

"George, what about this motor? We can't get it to do anything." George gets up, walks over to the machine and gives it a try. It just slows back down and stops cold. "Well," George said, "it use to work."

"Alright George, I think we're finished here."

"But it did something! It took off with me!"

"It's alright, George. Everything is, how you kids say, cool." George goes to his room, maybe to rest or read.

"Well gentlemen, what do you think? Mr Watts?"

"Many of the students that day saw something happen. Many of them ran in fear. He disappeared right in front of us. Also, I've never told this to George but Jesse Hughes is in my family tree. I feel George is telling the truth."

"Mr McKee," asked the judge, "beyond your capacity as court clerk, you seemed interested."

"Yes, Your Honor. After Captain Arbuckle transferred from Fort Randolph, my fourth great-grandfather took command. Also,

George described the fort pretty good."

"Sheriff, do you have anything to add?"

"Yes, I do, Your Honor. All the kids in Mr Watts' classroom were pretty much unaffected, no harm done. However, here are photos of the table the device sat on. As you can see, the metal and wood pieces are cut clean in a roundish shape, like a ball was once in its place."

Judge Hanson listened and was tinkering with the motor. It seemed dead. "Mr McKee, as the court clerk please put this hearing in George's file, and sealed, for George is still underage. It seems something mysterious happened but with the lack of hard evidence I see no reason to pursue this. Mr Watts, would you bring that young man back in."

Mr Watts gets up and leaves the room. Seconds later the two of them come back. Mr Watts sits while George remains standing, looking at everyone.

The judge speaks, "I have been listening to your story, George. I find it incredibly hard to believe, myself. But with what you said today and Mr McKee confirming about Fort Randolph and all the statements made by your foster parent and classmates, I have no recourse but to dismiss this investigation. On the other hand, George, the next time you leave this time for times unknown..." Judge Hanson seems puzzled by her own words, "...you need to take Mr Watts or one of us with you."

George leaps for the judge giving her a nice tight hug saying, "Thank you, ma'am, thank you very much."

"George, you are in contempt!" Then the judge hugs him back, saying, "You're a good boy, George."

Chapter 3
The First Thanksgiving

Tuesday, November 26ᵗʰ 1963

The days turned into weeks. Then came Thanksgiving season. George never had a Thanksgiving day. Most of the time he never knew what it was all about, except the time his dad sat at home watching a ball game. Mr Watts was downstairs in the basement, singing cheerfully. The basement was once a root cellar which had been under the house before the house was constructed. It had almost as much floor space as the first floor. George went creeping down the steps from the back hall into the basement. Mr Watts' singing was heard louder now.

> "♪God is good all the time
> Even with rain and shine
> uh huh He's good to me♪"

"Mr Watts?" George called out.

"Oh, hello George, what are you doing down here?"

"Seeing what's making you sing so cheerfully, sir."

"Well George, God has been good to me with an abundance from the apple trees and garden."

"Yes, I love being under that tree to read, Mr Watts. You really put up lots of stuff in jars. Got enough here, sir?"

"Oh yes, George, and sometimes I'll give some to church dinners or make something up when invited to a party, and some I just give away."

"Who planted the apple trees? It seems like they been here a long time. They so big."

"George, they were here when I bought the place some fifty years ago. The past owner said all the apple trees were here before his grand-daddy was born."[2]

"So they been here for centuries?"

"Kind of looks that way, George. But the reason I'm down here was to get ready for one of my favorite times of the year, Thanksgiving."

"Then comes Christmas, sir."

"You're darn tootin'!" Mr Watts said, while chuckling. "I also like lots of the kids that were raised here, coming back to visit. It will be mighty crowded, George. You ready for it?"

"So these would be my foster brothers and sisters?"

"You can kind of look at it that way, George. We're also all God's children. George, will you carry this box up to the kitchen. I need to get in the deep freezer for a turkey." Mr Watts opens a huge freezer which seems packed ready for an army.

George was up and back in a flash. By this time Mr Watts had selected a turkey that looked like it weighed a hundred pounds. He struggled to get a grip on the icy frozen bird with not much luck.

"I can get it sir, let me tackle that turkey."

"Okay George, just put it in the sink. Don't try to eat it on the way, it's frozen too hard." They laughed.

That afternoon Mr Watts and George were busy in the kitchen when a couple of young women came in the back door.

"Dad! You in here?"

"Judy? Barbara?"

Judy and Barbara Watts were the only children born to Mike and Eileen Watts.

"Daddy, it's so good to be home again. We can't be home for Christmas so we came now."

"Oh girls, you make an old man happy. How did you get shore leave from the Navy, Judy, did you jump ship?"

"No Dad, don't be silly. So, is this George we heard so much about?"

"Yes, it is."

"Hello George, I'm Judy and this is my sister Barbara."

"Nice to meet you, Judy and Barbara."

"Dad," Barbara comments, " you never said my new brother was this handsome. George, Dad has been a foster father for decades. So Dad, how can we help? I've done a lot of KP in the Air Force. This won't hurt me a bit."

The four of them sat down at the table, making pies and peeling potatoes, preparing yams and sweet potatoes, all the time swapping stories and catching up on things.

"So George, did you really travel back to Fort Randolph? I think that's so cool! I had a time of it, but found a little bit of information. Fort Randolph seemed to be a stronghold for a while but was later abandoned," Judy said.

"They ought to rebuild it for a tourist attraction," George suggested.

"It would never happen, George. People got too much other stuff," said Barbara.

"Gosh, you all look how late it is. You girls want to bunk upstairs in room one?"

"Okay Dad, that sounds good. We just have the one bag each and we know where everything is at."

"Okay, good night girls."

George washes his hands and says, "I'm turning in also, sir."

"Me too, George. See you in the morning."

Wednesday, November 27th 1963

The next morning he rose to a sunny day. George was up and in the garage tinkering on a project.

"George, you in here?" Mr Watts called out.

"Yes sir, in the back at the workbench."

"What you doing up this time of morning?"

"Well, since I missed the science fair I thought I'd make my motor useful. You have no objections do you?"

"No, George, not as long as tests are supervised. You planning another trip?"

"Was thinking about it. But this time like to anchor it down till I don't travel way down the river."

"That's a good idea, George. Any ideas how to do that?"

"Not really, sir. How about you?"

"How about stake it down to the ground? Maybe this motor's got lots of get up and go."

"Yes, sir. That could be it. I've overhauled the wooden part with metal. And where the axle mounts to the frame, I put in roller bearings that I found."

"You cleaned and repacked them with grease?"

" Yep!"

"Well done, George."

"I'm going to fix the governor with a speed control. This might control the time travel speed. If I can find another governor."

"OH! That reminds me." Mr Watts goes back into the house then a few minutes later reappears with the original part.

"You found it! Whereabouts was it?"

"On the floor of the classroom after you departed."

"Thank you, sir." George takes the part and it fits back in perfectly. But he then takes it back out and files a groove before putting it back on again, and inserts a washer and cotter pin. "THERE! That will hold it in there."

The two of them looked it over and made more improvements, one being it could fit into a small case for carrying. Those two were happier than kids at Christmas time.

About noon, a car pulled up in the driveway to the garage. They got up and looked out the dusty window and saw five people get out. But with the dust on the window it was hard to tell who it was. So both of them go to get a good look at who it is.

Mr Watts shouts, **BOYS!** It's so good to see you. Where have you all been?"

"Well you know, Dad, we just so busy working all the time," Robert said. "The newspaper presses would quit running if David took a day off. College keeps me busy with exams. You know James is always after anyone trying to cheat the government of taxes and Andy is busy working his farm, trying to feed the world single handed."

They all laugh. "So Dad, is this George, the future Stephen Hawking?"[14]

"Yes, it is. We were just tinkering in the garage when you all pulled up. Let's go in and raid the icebox."

"Yea!" says George. So they all pile into the kitchen where they find the girls making hamburgers and cold tea.

"Oh, you girls are so incredible, fixing all the food."

"Well," Barbara said, "we remember how Mom had to run the kitchen like a big name restaurant."

For hours they sat at the kitchen table chatting, catching up on the family news. George learned so much, but most of all he now has a family that loves him so dearly.

Later they sat on lawn chairs out in the front yard under the grand old apple tree, waving at passing neighbors and talking more than ever.

"Robert, what is the future of electronics? I might want to study it also."

"George, technology is going to depend on electronics in the near future. The federal government is going to need it for the space race to the moon. We want to beat the Russians there, don't we?"

"Yes, we do! SO, how do we do it, Robert?"

"You stay in school George, study hard in all subjects. Find a good college or university. You're the future of this country."

 That night George had a dream he was an astronaut on his way to the moon. They were going through all the pre-launch checklists.

"Launch control, this is Captain George. Doing test of all electronics."

"All seems a go of this first flight to the moon. You're looking good here, Captain George." Static crackles in. "All circuits are green."

"Roger, control. But you're breaking up." A few moments pass by. Nothing new to report. Then the silence is broken with blood curdling screams, **"Control, we're on fire, we're on fire."**[7]

Thursday, November 28th 1963

George jumps up in the bed in a cold sweat, breathing heavily. In the room were Mr Watts and two others, all looking at him.

"George, you having a bad dream?"

"No sir, it was a nightmare."

"Okay everybody, false alarm, you can put the fire extinguishers back. George, you need to change your clothes and change your bed sheets. They're all wet from sweating."

George did all that he was told then joined the others. Some more family arrived during that morning. Macy's Thanksgiving Day Parade was on and they were enjoying it immensely. The floats were decked out in spectacular designs. The old TV was black and white, and if it were color they would have jumped out at you. Then came more floats and marching bands, big balloons in all kinds of shapes like superman, clowns and animals. This took up most of the day. More family had been arriving during the day. Some traveled a couple of hundred miles with their families. Others were just in the next town nearby. All of them brought more food or something to brighten the day there. Mr Watts and the oldest girls, Judy and Barbara, were in the kitchen taking care of the dinner plans. They simply loved the kitchen.

A football game started and George didn't really care about it. So he just got up and wandered around to the kitchen. Even though it was a gigantic kitchen, too much was happening in there and George just felt in the way. So he said he was going out to the garage to tinker on the motor.

"Okay George, just don't leave the present!" Mr Watts said. George replied good naturedly, "I'm not intending on it with all this food around."

So George just meandered out towards the garage, setting back up a few things that seemed to have been knocked over. He went on into the garage, back to his project. It all seemed fine but he thought of a speed brake to slow it down automatically. This would take hold if the governor failed. It could also work like a hand brake should you want to stop it. He made a framework over it, to the base, to protect it from being damaged. All this took the better part of the whole afternoon. Then Robert came out to tell him supper was ready.

"George, you still in here?"

"Hi Robert, yes I'm still in here."

"So George, this is the magnetic motor that took you back in time, is it?"

"Yep! I still want it to do what I intended, an unlimited supply of energy."

"You're really ahead of the times, George; thought of doing away with these tubes and doing it like an electromagnetic motor? But let's go in and see who can eat the most turkey."

"I'm right with you, Robert."

The two of them went in and the table seemed as big as a football field. Counting George, there were fourteen there this day. And this wasn't all the foster kids. Many couldn't come. Some sent letters saying so, others realized at the last minute it was impossible to make it, so they telephoned. Anyway, all that could come were there at the table. So much food was on the table you couldn't see its surface.

Mr Watts stood. "It's so good that those of you that could make it, did. This has been a hectic year. But I've had a new blessing by taking care of George. He's given new life to this old man. Let's say grace." They all bowed their heads. Mr Watts gave the blessing, "Lord, thank you for all that you do for us in ways that we see and can't see or understand. Thank you for bringing everybody here safely and watch over them going home. Please bless this food that you've given us an abundance of, in the name of your son Jesus Christ. Amen." And everyone else said **AMEN!**

Then Mr Watts, while still standing, started carving that huge bird. He put slices on a plate and it started being passed around. He started loading up a second plate and sent it in the other direction. Then the first plate came back empty.

"Didn't I just load up this plate?" Mr Watts said.

Then they all laughed. He just started to load more on.

"Here Dad, let me serve the rest up. You get your plate filled or you'll never get any!" said one of his daughters-in-law.

All of them continued chatting and eating. It wasn't a race to see who could eat the most, but everybody ate their fill. Nobody had room for any of the pies right now. Their table was loaded to breaking under the following:

30 lb turkey

20 lb ham

a ton of mashed potatoes with gravy

a large pan of candied sweet potatoes

a medium size pan of broccoli & cheese casserole

corn, green beans, peas

cranberries

homemade dinner rolls
bread pudding
apple, pumpkin, sweet potato and cherry pies
apple cider and fruit juices

Slowly, one at a time, they started getting up, taking their plates and scraping stuff off either into the compost bucket, garbage disposal or trash can, then rinsed off the plates, utensils and cups and placed them in the dishwasher before heading out to the front family room to collapse. This continued for about another hour till most of the kitchen was cleared out. Mr Watts, Helen (one of his adopted daughters) and George were all that remained.

"So Dad, you want to adopt George?"

"If he wants me. I'll have him in half a heart beat."

"You're not getting any younger, Dad. A young teenager can be a handful."

"I know, Helen, but if George will have me, I want a fine young man like him."

"George," Helen said, "what do you think?"

George just sat there looking shocked that somebody would want him so much that they would want to adopt him. "Could I keep my own name?"

"Yes, that could be worked out. So George, would you like me to start the paperwork? I work at the State Capitol in the Department of Child Welfare. It takes months to get it all approved."

"Yes ma'am, I would like that. What if I change my mind?"

"If you change your mind before a judge signs the final order, you can stop them. But I don't think you will."

"I don't think I will either, Helen. Will you be my official sister then?"

Helen smiled and said, "Yes, and you will be my brother."

"I like that, Helen."

All of them get up and go out with the rest of the gang. A football game was playing but for the most part nobody was watching. They just kept up the visiting with each other and reminiscing about growing up. George started getting tired and said he was

56

going to bed. It's been one fine day.

Friday, October 29th 1963

The next morning everybody started slowly getting up and making their way down to the kitchen. Judy and Barbara are at it again.

"You girls sure do love the kitchen, don't ya?" said Mr Watts.

"We don't get to cook very much, Dad. Mom showed us it could be fun."

"Where's the rest of the family, Barbara?"

"You know them, Dad, out on the front porch next to the apple tree. That old tree that's been standing there forever. I remember the rope swing hooked to its branches. Andrea is out there singing a little bit. I'm so glad she took time out of her gospel singing tour to come home. I love her voice. It echoes over the town."

So Mr Watts went out to the front porch with a plate of food and found everybody else out there talking and laughing, just having a grand old time.

"Dad, good to see you up already, we want to speak to you about something."

"Okay, fire away, Ruth," Mr Watts said.

"Dad, you're not getting any younger."

"Yes, I am," he said in a joking way.

"Now Dad, listen up! We're all for you adopting George. But what if something happens to you? We want to carry on your ministry to help foster children in need. And that will include our new brother, George, who will always have a home and family."

Mr Watts, Ruth, George and the rest of them on the porch hug one another as a happy family. This brings tears to George's eyes.

Some of them left that day, having other commitments or getting called back to work for emergencies. More than a dozen came this Thanksgiving holiday and left with a new gift of a little brother. Before they left, they had one family tradition they had to tend to.

"Okay Dad, you got the fish bowl with everybody's name in it?"

"Yes I do, Raymond. George, what we do the day after Thanksgiving, is draw a name out of the fish bowl to get a gift for that person at Christmas. Those who did not come this year but still

want to participate, well their names are on the board. So for now, from the oldest to youngest."
Then each one comes to the fish bowl, swirls their hand in and pulls out a name. Some say, oh goodie goodie, I know just what they want. Some say, I'll have to think what to get them. Each one of them came and pulled a name out. Then it was George's turn. He did the same and pulled out a name.
"You got one, George?" asked Andrea.
"Yep!"
"But you're not going to tell us, are you?"
"Nope," George said with a smile, and Andrea smiled back.
Then they pulled the names for the ones that wanted to buy gifts but couldn't be there. Those were all placed on the blackboard, matched up to others to exchange gifts. And it was all said and done. "Remember, guidelines are try to stay around twenty dollars. You can trade names if you want to. If you want to get a special gift for someone, try not to go overboard. You need to get the gift sent to them to arrive before Christmas," Mr Watts reminded everyone. Some started to get up, ready to leave. It's so sad that all too often they might not be able to get back for a long time. But some can drive in from nearby. Others were just so busy with work and family. They do, however, stay in touch. Mr Watts was comforted by this last thought.

Chapter 4
Three Shots[7]

Saturday, November 30th 1963

Mr Watts and George were alone now that the last car, full of family, left that morning. Some traveled by car, others took the train, and some went to the airport for long flights.

"Well George, what did you think of the family?"

"I like them, sir. I didn't know I had so many."

"You've got thirty one brothers and sisters. We need to hang your picture on the wall with the rest of them."

"Really, sir?"

"Yep, really, George. Let's go in and grab a snack. Want to watch Saturday morning cartoons or something else? Maybe even go to the library?"

"I wasn't ever much on cartoons and I don't think much is ever on TV anyway."

The two of them go in and raid the refrigerator like two kids. Having George around has brought new life to Mr Watts. Then they do go into the living room and warm up the TV set. They flipped through all four channels with nothing intelligent to watch.

"How about a walk in town?" George suggested.

"Great idea, it's a sunny day. We should be out in it."

The two of them talked while walking down the street and waving at people they knew.

"Mr Watts?"

"Yeah, George."

"If you could continue to travel in time, you would have to be careful, wouldn't you?"

"I would suppose so. If one went back in time and changed one little tiny thing how would it affect the present? Let's say you stepped on a butterfly fifty million years in the past, how might it affect today? Or you went back and met your younger self, what would happen?"

"I think, sir, you would have to be careful not to step on bugs and try not to interfere with the time line. For example, if a person went

back in history and shot their own grandmother, how could they be born to go back and do that evil deed?"
"That's a good point, George."
The two of them come upon the place that has the best ice cream cones around.
"It's a little warm today, George. Shall we?" said Mr Watts as he pointed at the Dairy Queen®.
"I'll have a triple."
"Okay, two triple ice cream cones, please."
"Yes Grandpa, coming right up," said the girl inside.
"Mr Watts, does everybody in the world know you?"
"It seems like that, George. But she's the daughter of one my foster kids."
The weekend goes by and it's back to school. Days went into weeks at school and at home. George was a straight 'A' student, had become a good friend to all classmates he knew, and worked around town cutting lawns and doing other odd jobs.

Wednesday, December 11th 1963
Then one evening George came up with a brilliant idea.
"Mr Watts?"
"Yes, George?"
"Wasn't the assassination of President Kennedy tragic?"[13]
"Yes, it was."
"If a person could have stopped it, wouldn't it be their patriotic duty to try?"
"I think so, George." Then Mr Watts realizes where George is going with this, literally.
"I have a machine that could go back to before he even leaves Washington and tell him he's in danger."
"First off, George, you can't just walk into the White House and talk to the president. To think so is crazy."
"But don't you think he should be warned?"
"Yes I do, George, but it could never happen."
"But it should be tried, shouldn't it, sir?"
Mr Watts was getting nowhere with this line of discussion.

"George, we got to think about this."

"You not having second thoughts, are you sir?"

"No, but we've got to have a plan. Quick, let's go down to the newspaper office. I have an idea."

The two of them reached the newspaper offices and were directed to where they'd find the editor of the local paper, a childhood friend of Mr Watts' daddy. In strict secrecy, they got about half a dozen leaflets printed up real fast.

"Now remember, Clark, not a word to anybody about this. If we're successful then the president will still be alive."

"You got my word on that, Mike. Good luck and God bless your voyage."

hey hurry home and set up the motor.

"George, you can get us there at the right time and place, can you?"

"I think so, sir."

"What do you mean, you think so?"

But it was too late. George had disarmed the speed regulating governor, aimed the machine in what he thought was the general direction and had given the motor a spin.

"Hang on Mr Watts, it can be a bumpy landing."

Mr Watts grabs hold of the frame just as it lifts off and they disappear.

Wednesday, November 20th 1963

No sooner do they take off than George slams on the brakes and they come crashing into the side of a building. Mr Watts says, "I'm too old for time travel."

"You okay, sir?"

"Is my head still on? Am I bleeding anywhere?"

"Yes to the first and no to the second."

"Then I think I'll live. Ouch! What building did we hit, George?"

"Well, it's tall and white."

"That might be the Washington Monument. That's pretty close for a guessing aim, George. Next time try to miss tall monuments and you might consider some kind of seat and belts for this thing."

"I'll try to remember that, sir."

The two of them packed up the time machine and proceeded out in the direction of the White House. When they got there, they were met at the gate by a man with the Secret Service.

"Can we help you, folks?"

"Yes sir, you can. I'm Mr Watts, this is George. We would like to meet the president. But more than likely, that's impossible," Mr Watts replied.

"You're correct, sir. What do you want with President Kennedy?" That question answered an unspoken one of their own; he's still alive. Mr Watts catches sight of a newspaper dated November 20th 1963.

"Well, we come from the great state of Texas and feel obligated to bring this to the president." Mr Watts hands him one copy of the paper that he'd had printed. "You see sir, we feel the president is in grave danger."

According to his name tag, the secret service agent was Mr Lawson. He looks at the paper they handed to him. On it is a photograph of President Kennedy and a caption reads, Wanted For Treason Against the United States.

"You see, Agent Lawson, we love our country and we'll defend it the best we can, sir. We found dozens of these all over the place."

"We see this kind of trash all the time, Mr Watts."

"Please Mr Lawson, don't let him go," George said, tears starting to come down.

"Look son, we can't stop the president from going out. He'd become a prisoner in the White House. But I can assign my best team to look into these papers, and post more men around the president. But you really have nothing to worry about. President Kennedy is the best loved ever." Mr Lawson closes the gate door. Mr Watts and George turn and walk away slowly.

"Mr Watts, I could sneak in and give the president one of those!"

"George, the secret service would be on you like a pack of dogs on a three legged cat."

"They not going to do anything, are they?" says George hopelessly.

"They will George, but I don't think it will be enough. Let's get to Dallas, Texas."

"What we going to do there, sir?"
"I'll let you know when we get there."
The two of them book a flight, arriving on November 22nd.

Friday, November 22nd 1963
"We've not much time, George. We have to see Governor Connelly."
"What can he do, Mr Watts?"
"I'm not sure, but we got to see him. He was in the president's car also, at the time Oswald shot the president."
The two of them take a cab to the state Capitol and race in to his office. Both of them say, "We must see the Governor, it's an emergency!"
"Just one moment. I'll see if an aide can come out and speak with you."
Thirty minutes pass while they wait.
"I'm the governor's aide, can I help you?"
"George, let me do the talking," mutters Mr Watts under his breath.
"Yes, sir," George whispers back.
"I'm Mr Watts and this is George. We found lots of these papers in the city and need to have the governor warn the president. We feel he's in grave danger."
Another man came up and looked at the paper.
"We love America, sir, and don't want anything to happen. So could you please tell Governor Connelly to tell the secret service."
The other man spoke, "I'm with the secret service. You two were in DC just days ago?"
"Yes, we were, sir."
"And you were told we get these all the time. Now go on out to where the president will be passing and wave like good citizens."
George and Mr Watts leave, sad hearted.
"Mr Watts, I have one last idea! If we can't stop the president...."
"You're right, George, stop Oswald! This could be dangerous. We can get hurt or shot."
"Yes, but if we don't do anything President Kennedy will be shot at 12:30pm. The country needs him. I'd take a bullet for him, wouldn't

you?"
"Yes, I would, George. Let's go."
They get a cab and hightail it for Dealy Plaza. Traffic was starting to become congested in anticipation of President Kennedy's arrival.
"Okay George, can you find Oswald?"
"That building there?"
"You got it, young man."
George races off to try to stop Lee Harvey Oswald. In the meantime, Mr Watts sees a police motorcycle decked out with jacket and helmet. He crept up to it. A few other officers were nearby but not watching. Mr Watts used to ride motorcycles a long time ago. He pushes the big machine away into hiding.
Meanwhile, George had entered the building of the Texas Schoolbook Depository. He hears some noises up a staircase. So our young hero crept up the stairs and entered the mostly book filled room where Lee Harvey Oswald had a rifle, dry fire practicing out the window. George continued to slowly creep up on Oswald. He picked up a board he saw lying there, crept up closer, thinking he could hit him hard enough to knock him out. He really doesn't want to kill him. Best, he thinks, to just hit him real hard. George raised the board, took careful aim, but bumped a building framework, alarming Oswald. Oswald took the rifle and rifle butted George in the head, knocking him out as George tried to strike.
Back on the plaza, Mr Watts couldn't wait any longer for any kind of sign that George had been successful. He put on the police jacket and helmet, and reached down for the key. Oops, no key.
"Oh great, I've stolen a police motorcycle with no key." Mr Watts proceeds to see if he can hot wire it. On the first attempt, sparks fly out and Mr Watts burns his fingers. "What has George gotten me into. That boy is a bad influence on me."
The motorcycle fires up and he keeps the engine idling. Then comes the motorcade. Mr Watts pulls out to precede them, going slowly so they can catch up.
Time, 12:28.
Then the president's limo comes alongside.
Time, 12:29.

Mr Watts calls, "**Mr President, sir! You think this open limo is safe?**"

The president just smiles, waves and nods his head.

Time, 12:30!

If Mr Watts is going to save him, he has to stop the limo. He races in front of the limo and tries slowing down in front of it. No good. So he tries to block Oswald's view. But the bullets would just go right over his head. The angle was just too high. Next thing he knows, shots have been fired. Three in all. Mr Watts swerves out of the way of the motorcade which now seems to be blasting off at a high rate of speed. He stops the motorcycle and starts to cry, knowing he's failed. He turns around and parks the motorcycle near where he stole it.

Mr Watts runs off towards the book depository where George had gone. The place was swarming with police.

"**Officer!** My boy is missing. I think he went in that building to watch the president's motorcade."

"Let's go in and see." Both of them went in and up the stairs and found George with a bloody forehead. "Mister, we need to get him to a doctor."

"I'll take him," Mr Watts quickly exclaims. "You got your hands full with that gunman."

As they get outside, George starts to come to. "Did we do it? Is the president safe?"

"No George," Mr Watts says, crying.

"We can go back and try it again."

"Let's go home, George. I don't think it's going to work. You could have been killed."

George reset the machine and it was ready. "Are you sure you don't want to try again, sir?"

"No, George, let's go home."

George was crying as he gave the roller a spin to return home. This time they hit Thursday, the day after they left.

Thursday, December 12th 1963
As before, they landed at Chapman Grove, almost at home. This time it's 6:50am on the far side of the school.
"George, you need to look after that wound on your head. How about go see the school nurse."
"Yes, sir."
"After that, get on to your class and not a word about how you got hurt. Make something up. I'll put your machine in my locker for safe keeping."
"I agree, sir."
The two of them go inside. George's day at school was really uneventful. Some asked how he hurt his head, but he stuck to a story that he hit it while going down into the basement. They never mentioned the trip to try and save a president that day.

Chapter 5
John Chapman

Sunday, December 15th 1963

Sunday morning came and George woke to the sound of church bells ringing. Hurrying to get dressed, he was thinking about the recent events but was trying to forget about them. Coming into the kitchen, George finds Mr Watts having a cup of coffee.

"Good morning, George."

George just smiles back and says, "You ready for church?"

"I think so, George."

They finish getting ready and out the door they go.

"Mr Watts, was it right what I tried to do? I thought about killing a man. The Bible says killing is wrong. But if I didn't try to stop him, he was going to murder someone."

"George, many people have wrestled with those same questions. In World War I, a man filed for objecting to go to war for religious reasons."

"So he didn't go, sir?"

"Yes, he did have to go. But the Captain of his unit gave him a book about America. He got to go on leave back home and read it."

"Did he go back to the army, is it?"

"Yep, the army. And he got promoted till he was a sergeant. One time when his unit was pinned down under enemy fire, he saved the lives of many of his men by shooting them."

"I don't get it, sir. He shot the enemy?"

" Yep! You see, George, he shot the Germans to save his men. But more people might have died if he hadn't shot the enemy."

"Who was he?"

"His name was Alvin York, a countryman from Kentucky. Earned the Congressional Medal of Honor."

"WOW! He was a hero."

"He didn't look at it that way, George. He said he had something to do and did it."

The two of them make it to church in time to meet the pastor and get in for Sunday School class. George still had thoughts in his mind about 'Thou shalt not kill.' Sunday school had barely started up and right away George raises his hand.

"George, the class hasn't even started yet," said Andy, the teacher.

"I know, but I have a question."

"Go ahead, then."

"The ten commandments says, 'Thou shalt not kill.' Is there exceptions to the rule? If there is, where is it?"

Andy was stunned by the question. But it was a good one. "George, let me ask you this. Do you think about trying to go and kill someone because you're angry with them?"

"No, Andy, if anything I usually just let it go."

"So you'd not be hating them, wanting to murder anyone, would you, George?"

"No way! So, is the commandment about murder cause you hate someone?"

"Something very like that, George. It's not talking about protecting yourself and others. Would you think of killing one to save another?"

"Yes sir, maybe."

"Maybe pray about it George, we need to have class before the 11am service begins. Let's not be late for Pastor Bess."

"Yes, sir."

When class is finished, George, Andy and the others head on out to the main sanctuary where he meets the rest of his friends.

That afternoon after church and lunch Mr Watts says, "Hey George, it's almost Christmas time and we haven't even got the Christmas tree up."

"A CHRISTMAS TREE! WOW! I never had a Christmas tree before."

"Then let's get the saw and ax and go find a Christmas tree."

The two of them get the tools needed for tree cutting. Up through the back hills of Chapman Grove they go. There were lots of good pine trees but they had not found that perfect one; the one just tall enough and wide enough to fit in the living room.

"Mr Watts, sure is a lot of BIG trees here that are dormant now."

"Yep, lots of them are apple trees. Someone planted them, maybe at

the same time as the one in the yard and around town. But this area's all grown up and neglected. The section we're on now is my land, about thirty acres, more or less. It use to be grown up clear down to within a few feet of the house. When I bought this place, when I was younger, the wife and I started clearing the land. We had dreams of running a big farm. But then, seeing children in need of a home and we had all this space, we started fostering children."
"Mr Watts, we ever learn who planted all these apple trees? It looks like it was a part of a larger orchard. Maybe a forestry man can help us determine how old the trees are and then go back to their planting. What harm could there be in that?"
"I'm afraid to answer that, George. But no harm in researching the trees. Go ahead and phone the local forestry people in the morning."
"Sure will!"
"Well, George, I'll bet that tree over there is the one for us."
"Yeah, that's a great tree."
George takes the saw and cuts down his first Christmas tree. Mr Watts trims up some of the branches, then they proceed to drag it back to the house. At the porch they shake off the dirt, rip out the vines, then set it up in the corner of the living room.
"Now what?" said George.
"I'll bring the decorations up from downstairs."
"I'll help."
The two of them go down into the basement and bring up two boxes marked 'Christmas tree.'
"What's those other Christmas boxes downstairs for?"
"Those are for the outside of the house."
"WOW! Bet it will be seen for miles."
"Maybe, George. But let's do them tomorrow. The tree will take us clear up to church time."
With half an hour to spare after finishing the tree, the two of them put on their sweaters and go out to the porch and relax for the rest of the quiet afternoon, swinging on the front porch. Then off to church for an enjoyable service. Pastor Bess always brings a good message and it always makes you think.

Monday, December 16th 1963

The next morning, before school started, George was on the phone to the nearest local office of the department of forestry. But of course, that early in the morning, no one was in. But he did leave a message on the answering machine. George made his way to the kitchen to surprise Mr Watts with a simple hot breakfast. But just as he gets in there, Mr Watts comes in.

"Good morning, sir. I was going to make breakfast for us."

"Well, George, that will be very nice. You need some help?"

"No, but tell me where something is if I can't find it. Got you a cup of coffee ready."

"Oh good, I can't get my motor running till I've had a cup of Joe."

"I called forestry and they weren't in the office this early. So I left a message about what we're interested in and how to contact us."

"George, you seem like you have a level head on your shoulders."

"Thank you, sir. It might make a good school research paper in English or history."

"Hmm, good thinking, young man."

"Refill on your coffee?"

"No, I'm fine."

Then George put a plate of bacon, eggs, sausage and toast in front of Mr Watts.

"Mmm, that looks good."

George put a plate of the same on the table for himself.

"Lord," Mr Watts prayed, "thank you for this food that George prepared for us. Amen."

"Amen," echoed George.

"Ready for classes today?"

"Yep, I got a math and a history test today, then things should be cool till after the Christmas holidays. I'd like to test out to a higher grade level than sophomore. I think it be a great challenge to try."

"You'd be a year ahead of your classmates, George."

"Hadn't thought of that. I wouldn't get to see them as much. Think I'll stay in the tenth grade for now."

The two of them got up and started heading out the door. Then the phone started ringing. Mr Watts answered. "Hello? Oh, okay, just a

minute. George, it's for you."
George took the receiver. "Hello? Yeah. Huh-uh. Right. Yes, sir. Okay. About noon during my lunch time at school? Great. Look forward to seeing you."
"Forestry man, George?"
"Yep, he'll be over today and I'll meet him at noon during lunch. He'll be round here this evening after school is let out for the day."
"Sounds good, George."
"Yep, he'll meet with people that has big apple trees in their yard, measure and tap those trees and see if he can come up with an age." "Maybe you're right and it was part of a larger orchard at one time. It will be interesting to find out, George. But let's get to school before we're late."
"Right, sir."
They both hurry out the door. They get there just as the bell rings.
"**WATTS,** your watch is running late!" Mr Biggarstaff scorns at them.
"Yes, sir, we're both here." 'That man! That man!' Mr Watts thought.
Both of them race off to where they need to be.
About noon, George went outside as it was lunch time. He spotted a dark green forestry truck and saw Mr Biggarstaff and a forestry person by one of the big apple trees.
"Boy, what are you doing snooping around here? Isn't it bad enough to have forestry meddling around on my school property?"
"Yes sir, no sir," George stutters.
Mr Biggarstaff stomped back into the school, scowling.
"What was that all about?"
"I'm not sure, sir. My name is George. I'm the one that phoned this morning."
"Pleased to meet you, George. I'm Mr Clement with the state forestry service."
"Well, I'm pleased to meet you, Mr Clement."
"George, what prompted you into calling forestry?"
"Well, Mr Clement, I love sitting under this tree and the one just like it at home."

"You mean there's more of these apple trees, like this one?"
"Yes, sir. I can show you many of them. My foster dad, Mr Watts, might even know of more of these apple trees."
"Does he? Well, we're all going to have to get together and talk about this. Can I meet him after you get out of school?"
"Yes, sir. Mr Watts is a teacher here too. Sounds good, Mr Clement. We live in that house up there."
"In the meantime, I'll get out of the school area since it seems to upset Mr Biggarstaff."
George laughs and says, "Yep, it does."
George heads back inside to grab something to eat before racing off to afternoon classes. Mr Clement drives off to patrol the town for more apple trees of the right size, like the ones he's been looking at. Much later that evening, the forester meets them at their house.
"Hello," Mr Watts calls out. "You must be Mr Clement. George spoke to me about you."
"Yes I am, Mr Watts. I'm glad George called. I been driving around town measuring apple trees and taking samples. The results were fascinating. The oldest trees are about 125 to 130 years old. And that's really old for apple trees. I'd love to know who planted them, cause they did a good job. It was well organized. I made a map of your town, and the trees seem to be in a grid form. Like an orchard. Bet there was many of those apple trees here too. But none seem to be on the other side of the railroad tracks. Just think about it; the name of the town has the word grove in it. Yes, sir, this was the mind of an orchard planter at work."

Thursday, December 19th 1963
On Thursday morning, Mr Watts, George and Mr McKee were all having breakfast together in the Watts kitchen when a knock came on the back door. George jumps up to go answer it. In the background they could hear George inviting somebody in. Then Mr Clement from forestry walked into the kitchen.
"Hello, Mr Clement. This here is my neighbor, Mr McKee."
"Yes, I met him while making my rounds of your fine town."
"So, Mr Clement, what have you found out so far?" George asked,

with a grin. "Bet those trees are a thousand years old."

Mr Clement replied with a chuckle, "Not that old, George, but they do seem to be planted about the same time. Around 1792 is the best guess. And they resemble the way John Chapman planted apple trees."

"Who?" George asked.

"Johnny Appleseed," explained Mr Clement, "went across this part of the countryside planting apple orchards. Most people become a legend after they die. He became one while he was still planting apple trees. But there's no real way to prove he did plant these trees."

Mr Watts looks at George, smiling. George looks back, smiling.

"George, you thinking what I'm thinking?"

"I think so, sir."

"George, you're definitely getting to be a bad influence on me." They both laugh.

"What are you two laughing about?" Mr Clement wants to know.

"Mr Clement, what would it mean if it could be proved John Chapman DID plant those trees?"

"Well, Mr Watts, this town could enjoy an economical boom. Everyone that has any trees planted by him could have extra money coming in. Just imagine, Johnny Appleseed apples. So what do you have in mind to prove it?"

Mr Watts, Mr McKee and George smile. George simply tells him, "We got a tool that will help prove who planted every apple tree and how many. Be here Friday after school lets out and we'll take you on an incredible journey. You'll not be disappointed."

Friday, December 20th 1963

Friday afternoon came and Mr Clement was at Mr Watts' house, ready for the trip.

"So, Mr Watts, whereabouts are we going? I got the service truck all gassed up and ready to roll."

"I think we're there, Mr Clement." George sounds quite mysterious.

"What do you mean, George?"

"The mode of travel is right here."

Mr Clement looks at a strange looking device, sitting there twirling and making just as strange a sound. "What's that?"

"It's our transportation," George informs Mr Clement.

"Really? So how does it work?"

"About what was the approximate year these trees were planted?" asks Mr Watts.

"Ah, that be about 1792."

"Here, Mr Clement, put these clothes on over top of those. Where we're going you'll be a little out of place."

George sets up a big yellow post to use as a marker for the return trip. George and Mr Watts grab a hold of the frame, and Mr Clement takes the hint and does the same.

"Mr Clement, keep your eye on our apple tree."

George releases the brake for full power. Mr Clement watches as the huge apple tree starts shrinking. The sky was making a blinking, like a light turning on and off super fast. At the same time, the huge apple tree became just a sapling. George slows the motor down then they come to a halt.

Sometime around 1792 (they think)

The apple tree was gone. The house was gone too. Across the main highway, which now seemed like a cow path, was a large cornfield. On a knoll above that cornfield was a huge house. It looked like a grand place. Down in the field there appeared to be people working. All of them seemed to be black people. Another man down in the field seemed to be the boss. About then he started beating a man who was hoeing the cornfield.

George said sharply, "Look what they're doing to that person! WE GOT TO STOP HIM!"

Mr Watts grabs George as he tries to barrel down the hillside and stop the abuse being inflicted. "George, where do you think you're going? We're not in the twentieth century anymore."

"But that person needs our help."

"George, that person is a slave. People owned others back then. Some were indentured servants, paying off their passage to America. These are negro slaves. They were captured most of the time in Africa and sold. Their owners can legally do what they want."

"But it's not right to treat others like that, Mr Watts."

"And we have no right to stop them either, in this time period, George. Let's continue with why we came here."

George had brought a camera with him this time, and took pictures. The three of them started heading south. The land looked so different without a town. On their side of the road it was mostly clear, no buildings except way off in the distance. Alongside of the road, around what would be the middle of town in their time, was a lone man working at putting up a fence. It looked to be about the length of four city blocks of the town. They continued to head towards him. As they got closer they heard singing from the man, who seemed poorly dressed.

"♪God is good all the time♪

♪Even with rain and shine♪

♪And I thank him for He's so fine.♪

♪uh huh He's so good to me♪

♪Oh the seeds I plant He grows♪

♪here beneath the big blue sky♪

♪I wake up happy as I can be♪

♪because♪

♪God is good all the time♪

♪uh huh He's good to me♪"[16]

The three of them came upon the man who appeared to be about twenty five to thirty years of age.

"Hello, folks and young lad. What can I do for you?"

"We heard someone was planting apple orchards in the area and wanted to check it out," Mr Clement said.

"We love apples," George added.

"Well folks, you're right. I'm the one planting this whole side of the road with apple seeds and seedlings. This section will be seedlings. The fence will hold off that farm's livestock from tearing it up." He points up to the farm on the knoll above the cornfield, then continues, "The way they treat the slaves is horrible. Absolutely horrible. And when they die, the poor souls, they're just thrown in a

75

grave and forgotten. Old man Gulch is giving me a hard time too. Wants to take the apple trees and burn them all. He'll not do that for he knows the law will be after him. But better keep my eye on his whole family. That older Gulch boy, Edward, is not very bright but wicked."

"We've had dealings with them before," Mr. Watts comments aloud, not thinking.

"Sorry about your trouble. But where's my manners? I'm John Chapman."

"Mr Chapman? You're the man we've been looking for," Mr Clement says happily.

Mr Watts whispers to Mr Clement, "Careful what you say about where we're from, the future. Keep that hush hush."

"Right," Mr Clement whispers back, then turning his attention to the orchard planter, says, "Mr Chapman! Whereabouts are you from?"

"I was born in 1774 in the little town of Leominister, Massachusetts."

"So you're a long way from home, aren't you?"

"You could say that, but anywhere I can lay my head is home. The Lord is good to me wherever I am."

"Any family with you?"

"I had a half brother with me but he went to help Pop on the farm." All this information seemed correct from the history that Mr Clement knew.

"So folks, where do y'all hail from?" Mr Chapman asked.

"We're from up the road a piece and on the hill. We're still somewhat new to the area. We come from a place called Chapman Grove. Ever heard of it?"

"No," Mr Chapman replied. "But I like the name of the place."

"So we might like to plant some trees too. How do you do it?" asked George.

"It's simple. I put up a fence to keep livestock out. For the little seed, I plant one here then pace off ten large steps then plant another one. All the trees when full grown will be some thirty feet apart. Then the little honeybees pollinate the flowers, and that fall you have an abundance of apples."

"Can we help you, Mr Chapman?" George requested.

"Why, sure, young lad. I'm done with the seeds. But I have a wagon load, full of seedlings."

"WOW, that's lots of trees," Mr Watts exclaimed in surprise.

"Then let's get started, folks. You see how I started. If any questions just ask."

John Chapman, George, Mr Watts and Mr Clement started right away. Two would dig the small holes. George brought the trees from the wagon and held each one straight in the hole as Mr Watts filled in around the roots. Time and time again the process went. The hours went by until it was late that afternoon.

Then George said, "Mr Chapman, these seem to be the last of the trees. I know a few places that they might love to grow, sir."

"Very well George, lead the way."

They all went up the hillside at the north end of the clearing.

"Why up here, George?" Mr Chapman asked.

"I think I would like this spot to read underneath an apple tree and look over this valley with the trees growing." George's eyes held a faraway look.

"Sounds like a good place then," agreed John Chapman.

"Mr Chapman, I'll dig the hole," said George, "if you'll plant the tree."

"Very well, young lad, you got it. My, this is a great site up here for a home," John Chapman commented.

"George, whereabouts for these other trees?" asked Mr Clement.

George led them to a few more places and they planted them the same way.

"All done! Every tree is in the ground. Men, I'm so glad you showed up. I made new friends. This week's worth of work took one day. Join me at my camp for supper," John Chapman invited.

"Thank you, Mr Chapman, we'd be honored. We have some food with us to share." Mr Watts hands out apple pie and apple cider.

"That looks good, sir," John Chapman says thankfully.

"Let's build a fire to ward off the chill in the air," Mr Clement suggested.

"Don't make it too big," John Chapman warned, "insects might come. Get killed in the flames."

Everybody sat down by the campfire.

Then John Chapman started telling them a story that he recalled from the Holy Bible, "It was a long time since the days when God walked with Adam and Eve in the garden of Eden and things had changed. Everyone forgot about God. They didn't pray to him anymore. They didn't care about pleasing him. All they cared about was themselves. God's beautiful world became a mean awful scary place to live. That's what happens when people forget about God. But God saw one good man. His name was Noah. Noah still cared about God. He listened to God and he always tried to do what God said. And God was pleased with Noah. God said to Noah, *'Noah, I have decided to put an end to this mess people have made of my world, and start all over.'* So God said to Noah, *'I want you to build an ark.'"*

"What's an ark?" George interrupted.

"It's a kind of ship to keep special things safe in," John Chapman informed him, and went right on with the story. "Then God said, *'But your ark is going to be a very BIG boat!'* God told Noah exactly how to make it. It was going to be very long and higher than any building with one door and a window beneath the roof."

"This was going to be a big job for a five hundred year old man," Mr Watts remarked.

"Yes. That's how old Noah was when God gave him his little project to do," continued John Chapman. "Now, Noah might have thought, 'This job is too big and I am too old!' But he did have God, and with God on your side anything is possible. So Noah went right to work. He did everything just as God had told him to. His neighbors must have thought he was crazy. While they were spending all their time doing wicked things just to please themselves, Noah was hard at work pleasing God. Noah kept on working day after day, year after year. And day after day, year after year, people laughed at him. And then one day Noah put down his hammer. The ark was finished. There it was, this giant boat, resting on dry land and no water in sight! What was God thinking? He was thinking he had another job for Noah! A really BIG job. God said to Noah, *'Now I want you to take two of every kind of animal, a male and a female, and bring them into the ark. They will come to you. And bring enough food for them all too.'"*

"Just think what a noise that must have been. It must have smelled pretty bad too. What a noise! And what a mess!" George interrupted again. "And how do you keep the tigers from eating the little lambs?"

John Chapman continued, "Still, with God's help, Noah did it all just as God told him to. Until finally there was just one more to get up onto the ark. Noah was pushing on the wrinkly behind of a big grumpy elephant. And so, with one big last push, he got that reluctant elephant up into the ark. Whew! A hundred years is a long time to work on one job! Noah sat down by the door of the ark and wiped the sweat from his forehead. At last he was finished with all that God had asked him to do. Noah was six hundred years old when he did all that God asked him to. Seven days went by, one for each day it took to make the world God was about to wash clean. So Noah and his wife, and his three sons Shem, Ham and Japheth and their wives all got into the ark. Then the Lord himself reached down from heaven and shut the door. Water poured from the sky and gushed up from the ground. It rained hard, and I mean really hard. Lightning flashed. Thunder crashed. The winds blew huge waves across the water. The water lifted the giant boat from the ground. It rained for forty days and forty nights. It rained so hard that Noah's ark floated above even the highest mountains. There was no dry ground left at all. And everything that breathed on the earth died. What terrible things happen when people sin. Noah and his family waited in the ark. Up and down, and up and down, they tossed on the waves."

George felt a little seasick but was fascinated by the story.

"Everywhere they looked, they saw nothing but water. For one hundred and fifty days the ark tossed on those waves."

"That's a long time to be on the ark, Mr Chapman," George commented.

"What do you suppose they did all day, George?" asked Mr

Chapman.

"Maybe that's when they played checkers, and pin the tail on the donkey was invented. I'll bet the donkey wasn't too happy about that, George," Mr Clement said before George could answer. George's eyes had lit up and he reeled off quite a speech, "But there was probably enough work to do every day, just trying to keep all those animals fed and the ark cleaned up. And maybe at the end of a long day, they sat around the kitchen fire and told stories, and tried to remember what it was like to take a walk through the trees on a warm summer evening. But with the racket of all those animals, and the creaking of the heavy wooden beams of the ark, how did they get to sleep at night? And how did they keep from rolling out of their beds?" George's vivid imagination was making it all very real to him.

John Chapman smiled at George's enthusiasm and went on with the story, "But God hadn't forgotten about them. One day God caused a wind to blow. The rain stopped and the water began to go down. It was another a hundred and fifty days before the ark came to rest on the very top of a mountain range called Ararat. Noah and his family and all those animals had all been together in that ark for almost a year! After forty more days, Noah opened the window of the ark and sent a raven out. He wanted to see whether it could find some dry ground. But none was found yet. So Noah tried again. This time he sent out a dove. The dove flew around and around. But it couldn't find any dry ground and it had to come back. Noah waited seven more days, and then he let the dove fly out again. That evening the dove came back with a fresh olive leaf in its beak. That was a sign for Noah. Now he knew the water had gone down because the dove had found an olive bush growing on dry land. Noah waited another seven days and then he sent the dove out again. This time it didn't come back. It had found a new place to live.

Finally God told Noah it was alright to leave the ark. God opened the door and all those animals rushed out! They found new homes in the world God had washed clean. God had saved them!

God provided the ark and it had brought them all safely through the water. It carried them to a new life. Noah was six hundred an one years old when he left the ark. And was he ever glad to be walking on dry ground again!

Then Noah does a strange thing. At least it would seem very strange to us today. The ark was safely on dry ground again. A few minutes before, it was filled with animals. Now the door was wide open and the giant boat sat on a mountain top, all empty and quiet."

"So what was Noah doing, Mr Chapman?" asked George.

"He was so thankful to be alive, he was going to build an altar to God. Then he took the best of some special animals he had kept aside, killed them and burned them on the altar. This was a sacrifice Noah offered to God to thank him for saving his life. It might seem like a strange thing to do. It couldn't have been an easy thing to do either. But that's what people did in those long ago days. That way they would know that dealing with God is a very serious thing. God was pleased with Noah's sacrifice. But most of all God was pleased that Noah was truly thankful.

And so God made this promise to Noah, *'Never again will I destroy the world with a flood. I make this covenant with you and with all creatures.'*

God knew that there is something inside each of us that tries to keep us from doing what is right. That is what causes all the trouble in the world. God also knew that one day He would send His Son to save us from that. God saved Noah and his family to show us that He has the power to save us all and one day bring us to a new life with Him in heaven.

So God blessed Noah and his family. He told them to have many children and fill the earth with people again. He gave them the animals as well as the plants for food. And he appointed people to take care of everything on earth. Think of it this way; you might have a pet dog or a cat. There aren't any dogs who have pet people! And then God said to Noah, *'Look up in the sky.'* Noah looked up. The storm clouds were drifting away, the bright sun was shining against Noah's back. And against the dark gray sky God made a brilliant rainbow appear.

God said to Noah, *'You see, I have set my bow in the cloud. This*

will be the sign of the covenant I have made with you and all creatures, never again to destroy the earth by a flood. It will always remind us of the promise between you and me.'
So, the next time you see a rainbow think of Noah and the flood. Remember that God loves you and that no matter how bad the storm, there will always come a bright new day. That is God's promise and God always keeps His promises."
The three men looked upon George, sound asleep by the campfire. While John Chapman was telling the Bible story of the great flood, old man Gulch was having his son Edward foil John Chapman's plans to get the apple orchard growing. They had been watching the planting from a distance.
"Edward! Get over here, boy. That Chapman had help today. All those seeds and trees are already in the ground, thanks to those no good outsiders. So we going to help a little bit too."
"We going to plant more trees, Pa?"
"NO BOY! They seem to be settling in for the night. Now quietly take the wagon from behind the barn and spread its contents all over those trees. I don't want none of them to be alive."
"What's in the wagon, Pa?"
"It's old watery rotten black walnut husk. Now you keep to the road till you get to that apple cuckoo's trees. Spill that on the corn and we're done for. It will kill the crop. Now get busy!"
Edward Gulch went to the barn and hitched up the wagon after dark. Nobody could see what he was doing on this moonless night. Without light, Edward took longer to even see the wagon. He walked the team so it would make less noise. He walked down past the cornfield all the way back up to the north side of the orchard. As he gets clear up to the north end, Edward takes a shovelful and throws it on each tree. He gets to where the seeds had been planted and does the same. As he gets near the south end, Edward sees he's running out of stuff to throw on. He backs the team up and gets a little bit from what he'd already shoveled out, to add to the remaining apple trees.
As Edward Gulch was finishing up the dastardly deed, rain started falling. Edward jumped on the buckboard and hightailed it for

home. As he got back to the Gulch farm he was met by the old man.

"Pa, I put the whole load on every tree. And with that downpour of a rain it soaked in real good."

"Good work, boy."

Meanwhile back with the Chapman planting crew, when the rain started in a heavy downpour, waking George, they took shelter under the canopy of the buckboard.

"You folks got time to view some other groves over the river?" asked John Chapman.

Mr Watts turned to the others and asked, "What do you think, Mr Clement?"

"I think time's on our side. Sounds good to me. I'd love to see more of Mr Chapman's groves."

"Let's start in the morning," Mr Chapman says as he begins to settle down for the night in the bed of the buckboard. The others follow suit.

The next morning, still sometime around 1792

That morning they set off in the wagon, over the mountain into the next state by way of the ferry, to see the groves. It was good that the rains had about ended.

A few days later they arrived in Ohio in sight of a well established apple grove; about five hundred of the prettiest trees one every saw. "Folks, we're here. What you think?"

"Mr Chapman, you got a fine apple grove. Let's get out and inspect them," says Mr Clements, excited to look at more.

Walking between the apple trees, it was obvious many of them were loaded, about ready for picking.

"Mr Anderson will be picking and selling the apples from this grove as part of share cropping," John Chapman told them.

Back on the Gulch farm, old man Gulch has discovered his boy had taken the wrong wagon. Instead of taking black walnut husk to kill the apple seedlings, Edward had put manure on them, giving them an extra high boost in growing.

So what about the husk? With the rain pouring down all that night, right through the wagon load, and the runoff down the hillside, the whole northern field was ruined. Old man Gulch was chasing Edward, kicking him in the rear.

"Boy, how can you be so stupid! That field is useless. Look there, everything is dying because of you."

Now, back in Ohio, they admired how well everything was doing.

"Folks, this apple grove is just ten years old. Now look at it, an abundance ready for picking. If Mr Anderson has a few more seasons like this he'll own this land."

They spent three days checking out the apple grove.

"Folks, let's start heading back. I need to get more seed and seedlings for planting. It's very good what God has done."

The wagon went rolling down the bumpy road, up the river to the ferry, crossed over to Wheeling, VA[4] then back down south to the new apple grove. As they approached the seedlings, they were astonished to see the little apple seedlings coming alive and growing faster than you would expect.

Mr Chapman's mouth had dropped open. "Well!" he said, astonished, "I never saw anything like it! These trees shouldn't be growing like this! They seem to like this soil. And the seeds over there are already spouting. Look at those little varmints. They're poking their little heads up to say hello. Praise the Lord."

"Mr Chapman, it's been so enjoyable to be with you for over a week but we might need to be on our way," Mr Watts said.

About that time they saw old Gulch yelling at Edward, and chasing him.

"Wonder what that was all about, Mr Watts?" George asked, watching Edward run for his life.

"I'm not really sure, George. Let's go home."

"Yes, let's."

The three of them shake hands with Mr Chapman and start heading back to the north end of what will become Chapman Grove.

"Mr Watts, sir, what you going to do when we get back to the twentieth century?"

"George, I'm going to take a nice hot bath and sleep in my own bed for a year."

George chuckles. "And you, Mr Clement?"

"I got a tricky report to write till people won't think I've lost my marbles."

"Can you hold off your report till I get these pictures developed?"

"Pictures? I plum forgot you were taking pictures."

"Yes sir, Mr Clement, I have pictures of the town, Mr Chapman and everything till I ran out of film."

"Oh, George, you're a life saver."

"Well, here we are. Our ride is still here, hidden away waiting on us."

They look around one last time.

"It's kind of pretty here, Mr Watts," George exclaims.

"Yes, it is, but it's time we left. The year 1963 is waiting for our return. How are we going to hit the right day, George? Any ideas?"

George smiles and says, "Yep."

All of them grab hold of the machine's frame, and George releases the brake, then gives the motor a spin in reverse. George slows the motor after a few minutes. Then a bright yellow post appears and George slams on the brakes. Right back where they started from. On the porch was Susan. She comes running down the steps.

"GEORGE! I been waiting all day for you." She wraps her arms around George.

Mr Watts tells Mr Clement, come on in for a cup of coffee and let's leave these kids alone.

"By the way, Susan, what day is it?" asks George.

"It's Saturday, George, December 21st 1963. Why you ask?"

"Until you experience it, you'd never believe it."

"I love you, George."

"I love you too, Susan."

Notes to the reader: the residents of Chapman Grove did get a nice little extra income if some of Johnny Appleseed's apple trees were on their property. Also, the story of Noah's ark told by John Chapman from memory, and written here by RJ Dean Jr, comes from the King James Bible. Some versions of the Bible are copyrighted. However, the Kindle® version of the KJB used for this part of the story, contained no copyright symbol.

Chapter 6
1963 Christmas Blizzard

Sunday, December 22nd 1963

Sunday morning came and winter had started to show he hadn't forgotten the little town of Chapman Grove. Half a foot of snow fell during the night. The Christmas lights on the tree, and outside on the house, had come on this morning on the timer. It lit up the whole living room and the outside. It was still dark this time of year. But many people were getting up to attend Sunday school and morning worship service. Many walked to church every Sunday. But this Sunday more were driving. As Mr Watts and George started out the door, their lights on the outside of the house had clicked off. They continued walking and the snow was really coming down now. It didn't act like snowflakes; it was more like snowballs.

When the two of them got inside the church door, they and others looked like walking snowmen.

"Woo-ee, it's really coming down out there," Pastor Bess said. "You folks go to the kitchen in the back and get a warm drink. There's coffee, tea and hot chocolate."

They went into the kitchen, following some others. It was a great atmosphere to come into. Somebody was making hot biscuits with honey, jams, jellies and apple butter. The room was filled with the aroma of wonderful baking. The bell rang to get to Sunday school class and everybody took their goodies with them.

Some were getting ready for the Christmas play that would take place at the 11am service, and a cantata to follow. George wasn't in any of the actual performances, but he was one of the stagehands that help build all the props to put on a great show.

Everyone started coming into the main worship area in a hurry, to get a good seat for the program. It began with Andy's young teen class who came out first and read from the Bible, Luke 2, NIV.

"'In those days Caesar Augustus issued a decree that a census should be taken of the entire Roman world. (This was the first census that took place while Quirinius was governor of Syria.) And

everyone went to their own town to register.
So Joseph also went up from the town of Nazareth in Galilee to Judea, to Bethlehem the town of David, because he belonged to the house and line of David. He went there to register with Mary, who was pledged to be married to him and was expecting a child. While they were there, the time came for the baby to be born, and she gave birth to her firstborn, a son. She wrapped him in cloths and placed him in a manger, because there was no room for them in the inn.'"

Mary, played by Susan, sits on a rocking chair with a baby. Baby crying. Mary sings to the baby.

"♪Baby Jesus, Baby Jesus,♪
♪please don't cry, please don't cry.♪
♪Don't you know we love you, Don't you know we love you,♪
♪Yes we do, yes we do.♪"

A Shepherd comes in and offers a lamb to the baby. Mary continues singing.

"♪Baby Jesus, Baby Jesus, ♪
♪Look who's here, look who's here.♪
♪A shepherd come to praise you, a shepherd come to praise you,♪
♪With his lamb, with his lamb.♪"

Kings comes in with presents and offer them to the baby. Mary sings on.

"♪Baby Jesus, Baby Jesus♪
♪Look who's here, look who's here♪
♪A King with lots of presents, a King with lots of presents♪
♪Just for you, just for you.♪"

Angels come in. Mary sings on.

"♪Baby Jesus, Baby Jesus,♪
♪Listen now, listen now,♪
♪Angel voices singing, angel voices singing,♪
♪We love you, yes we do.♪"

The church loved this program as it was very well done by the young people. The stagehands got busy taking the props apart. The well designed props were removed in minutes. Then the church choir came out. All wore matching colors; not robes, but they did look professional. They took their places and waited. Andy came back out and read this story:

[8]"Father Joseph Mohr sat at the old organ. His fingers stretched over the keys, forming the notes of a chord. He took a deep breath and pressed down. Silence. He lifted his fingers and tried again. Silence echoed through the church.

Father Joseph shook his head. The pipes were rusted, the bellows puffed with mildew. The organ had been wheezing and growing quieter for months and Father Joseph had been hoping it would hold together until the organ builder arrived to repair it in the spring. But now, on December 23, 1818, the organ had finally given out. Saint Nicholas Church would have no music for Christmas.

Father Joseph sighed. Maybe a brisk walk would make him feel better. He pulled on his overcoat and stepped out into the night. His white breath puffed out before him. Moonlight sparkled off the snow-crusted trees and houses in the village of Oberndorf. Father Joseph crunched through the snowy streets to the edge of the little Austrian town and climbed the path leading up the mountain.

From high above Oberndorf, Father Joseph watched the Salzach River ripple past Saint Nicholas Church. In the spring, when melting snow flowed down the mountains and the river swelled in its banks, water lapped at the foundation of the church. It was moisture from the flooding river that had caused the organ to mildew and rust.

Father Joseph looked out over the mountains. Stars shone above in the still and silent night.

Silent night? Father Joseph stopped. Of course! 'Silent Night!' He had written a poem a few years before, when he had first become a priest, and he had given it that very title, 'Silent Night.' Father Joseph scrambled down the mountain. Suddenly he knew how to bring music to the church.

The next morning, Father Joseph set out on another walk. This time he carried his poem. And this time he knew exactly where he was going... to see his friend Franz Gruber, the organist for Saint Nicholas, who lived in the next village. Franz Gruber was surprised to see the priest so far from home on Christmas Eve, and even more surprised when Father Joseph handed him the poem.

That night Father Joseph and Franz Gruber stood at the altar of Saint Nicholas Church. Father Joseph held his guitar. He could see members of the congregation giving each other puzzled looks. They had never heard a guitar played in church before, and certainly not during midnight mass on Christmas Eve, the holiest night of the year. Father Joseph picked out a few notes on the guitar, and he and Franz Gruber began to sing. Their two voices rang out, joined by the church choir on the chorus. Franz Gruber's melody matched the simplicity and honesty of Father Joseph's words.

When the last notes faded into the night, the congregation remained still for a moment, then began to clap their hands. Applause filled the church. The villagers of Oberndorf loved the song! Father Joseph's plan to bring music to Saint Nicholas Church had worked. A few months later, the organ builder arrived in Oberndorf and found the words and music to 'Silent Night' lying on the organ. The song enchanted him, and when he left, he took a copy of it with him.

The organ builder gave the song to two families of traveling singers who lived near his home. The traveling singers performed 'Silent Night' in concerts all over Europe, and soon the song spread throughout the world." As Andy finished the story the choir begins to sing:

"♪Silent Night, Holy night♪
♪All is calm, all is bright♪
♪Round yon virgin mother and child♪
♪Holy infant so tender and mild♪
♪Sleep in heavenly peace, Sleep in heavenly peace.♪"

The choir was excellent. Silent Night was followed by; The First Noel, O Come All Ye Faithful, I Heard the Bells on Christmas Day, We Three Kings of Orient Are, It Came Upon the Midnight Clear, Hark! The Herald Angels Sing, While Shepherds Watched Their Flocks, and O Little Town of Bethlehem.

Afterward, the choir came down to join the rest of the congregation and Pastor Bess came up to the podium.

"Just a few announcements. Tuesday night at midnight the church bell will ring in Christmas at the same time as the other churches. Since Christmas falls on Wednesday there will be no service that day. A bridal shower, presented by ladies of the church, will be held in the annex building Friday, January 3rd at 6pm. In case of bad weather the following Friday will be the alternate day. This will be for the wedding of Kay Williams to Mark Jones. Now for the news on the weather. Since we came in, there's been another foot of snow during the past hour. Mr Watts said anyone that feels they can't make it home safely can stay with them till the road is cleared. For those who must get home, for example to turn off the pot roast, Sheriff Shamblin said he can give a limited number of people rides to their homes." Pastor Bess gave the closing prayer.

Folks started heading out to see what the weather had become. By this time the snow was twenty inches deep. A few were able to make their way home as it was just a few blocks away. Some went with the sheriff to get a safe ride home, abandoning their vehicles to the church parking lot. Then six people came up to Mr Watts.

"Can we stay at your place till the road's been cleared?"

"Only if you bring an appetite with you." Mr Watts was always a kind man, feeding people who were coming for any stay.

This time it was the Hill family (Mr and Mrs Hill along with Susan), Stephen and his dad, and Andy Brown. All of them trudged the best they could up the road, leading to Mr Watts' house. They finally made it to the house and into a nice warm place. George just had to know how many more inches had accumulated. He took the yardstick out in the snow and stuck it in a few places. Twenty two inches. It was really coming down. Looked like it would never stop.

"Folks, I welcome you to take off your wet shoes and boots. Just sit them by the fire and let them dry out. You need any dry clothes, I've got it here, just let me know. If the snow keeps this up we might be here a while. We have plenty of room here for everybody," Mr Watts assured his guests.

Then the lights went out.

"No problem, folks. If the lights aren't back soon I have lamps for when it gets dark."

Then the lights flickered but stayed out.

"Okay, we're still all nice and safe. The gas fireplace has been warming up the room."

In fact they had to turn the fire down. Then George opened some bedroom doors upstairs to let the heat in there, should anyone stay the night.

Mr Watts checked the phone and it seemed fine for now. "Anybody want to use the phone, let family know where you are, now's a good time. Lunch is going to be chilli with crackers. Is that okay?"

No one objected. "If you need, we can always raid the icebox or the root cellar."

"Mr Watts?"

"Yeah, Susan?"

"I'm thirsty."

"Come on into the kitchen, Susan, let's see what you like," George said.

Susan went with George, smiling. The two of them went to the refrigerator. They poked their heads in to look around. Susan saw apple juice.

"I like that!"

"Okay, let's close the door quickly." George poured Susan a nice glass of apple juice and they sat down at the kitchen table. "Susan, what does your dad do for a living?"

"I'm not allowed to tell, really. Let me just say he works for the state but don't repeat it at all."

"Your all's secret is safe with me. Until you give me the word, I'll not repeat it."

Susan smiles.

Back in the living room, Mr Watts and the others were just sitting and chatting away. The battery powered radio was on to hear any news about the weather.

"Mr Hill, you have a fine smart young lady," said Mr Watts. "She should pass science class with no bother."

"That's all very well, sir, but what good will science do a girl these days? It won't get her a husband. A man doesn't want a smart woman. And what kind of job could she get anyway? All she might get is nurse, secretary, childcare or a cook. And that's about it. You don't need a diploma for any of that."

"Yes, Mr Hill, but I'm thinking in the near future opportunities are going to open up for bright gifted young men and women; and they've got to be ready or be left behind."

"I'll be satisfied if Susan finds a husband and makes me a bunch of grandchildren."

"Hey, listen to the radio!" Stephen said loudly.

"This is the national weather service forecast office in Wheeling. The national forecast office has issued a winter weather warning for all areas in the listening area, ..."

"Gee," someone commented sarcastically, "no kidding."

The radio went on, "...if you are in the listening area, stay off the roads to allow road crews to clear them more readily."

"Well, I see the trains are still getting through," Stephen observed.

"I see passengers getting off at the station way down there."

Mr Watts and others went to the window.

"Yep, quite a few getting off. Can't see who it is. Too far away," says Mr Watts, then turns back to Susan's father and takes up where they left off. "Anyway, Mr Hill, women can achieve more than just being baby makers if they want to, sir, and your daughter can be one of them. You do want her to grow up happy, doing what she wants?" "Well, maybe Mr Watts, but it's never going to happen. I'm a practical father. I got to look out for the best interests of my Susan. I just want her to finish high school."

"Guess you know best, Mr Hill."

Susan and George come back from the kitchen and look out the window.

"Susan, might as well make yourself comfortable. The weather service said stay off the roads."

"Yes, Dad. But I see some people walking this way."

"They're crazy for being out in this weather," Andy said.

"Yep, it still coming down. I saw a snowplow go by on the main road. But we better sit tight here. Electric is out all over the place.

Might be wires down," Mrs Hill adds.

The phone rings and Mr Watts gets up to answer it. "Hello? Hello, Bob. Yep, we always got room. Drop them off to us? Okay. And you come in too, to warm up, and we'll refill your thermos bottle. Bye. The sheriff is bringing up some people that were caught by surprise in this blizzard."

"Mr Watts, the walk up to the house from the road is bad. Maybe I should get out there and shovel the walk and put down some salt," suggests George.

"Good thinking, George," Mr Watts agrees.

George puts on his now dry boots, coat and hat, and races out to the tool shed for the snow shovel.

"That boy has one speed, fast. I like George," Susan says with a smile. "He helps me in study hall with my homework."

"Susan, you're not old enough to be thinking of boys."

"Yes, Daddy."

George started clearing the steps at the house, worked his way down to the road then went back up to the house, starting over, doing a much better job the second time. The snow was starting to let up but was still making roads treacherous. After his second going over, the sheriff pulled up.

"George, aren't you afraid you'll freeze to death in this?"

"No sir, this workout I'm getting is keeping me warm."

"Can you help us get these people inside? They're near froze to death when I found them."

"Yes, sir! Watch your step, it's still real slick."

The sheriff had six people in his four wheel drive patrol car which had chains on all tires. A couple of the women had babies wrapped up in blankets inside their coats. They did look frozen to death. All of them worked their way up to the porch and stepped inside. Mr Watts and the others welcomed them in. They looked stunned by the weather.

"Folks, you all come in by the fire to get warm. I've got a big pot of coffee ready for you. Hot food if you're hungry."

People helped them out of their snow-crusted coats and hung those by the fire along with their boots and shoes.

"Mr Watts, let's check these people over for frostbite. I can help, I use to be a nurse in Charleston before I got married."

Mrs Hill had each person take a seat and carefully took their cold wet gloves, shoes and socks off. Definitely cold fingers, toes and feet but nothing was found life threatening.

"Whereabouts did you dig these poor ice cubes out from?" Mr Watts addressed the sheriff.

"Dad, first off, thanks for taking them in. I found them off the side of the road down on State Route 2. Looks like they lost control and went in the ditch big time. The snowplow found them about the same time I was in the area. God was watching over them today." The sheriff went to the kitchen to refill his thermos.

About then George brought in the magnetic motor which was running, and to which he had hooked up a generator. A lantern light was connected to the generator. The motor was slowly turning, chasing away the gloom wherever it was.

"Ah, George, that's a welcome sight. Bring it in the living room and set it up high on the bookshelf," Mr Watts instructed.

With the light from the fire and the light from George's invention, the room was a lot brighter.

"George, that was a great idea. It chases away the darkness." Just then the front door opened.

"Dad!" In through the door came a bunch of Mr Watts' kids. It was Lynn, Josh, Amy, Gary, Travis, John, Jeff and their families.

"Kids, you made it in this weather. I'm so glad to see you." Hugs were spread all around.

"Travis, I could use your help. These folks were trapped by the snowstorm and were brought to us for shelter. Can you make sure they're okay? Mrs Hill has her hands full."

"Sure, Dad." Travis goes off to help Mrs Hill. "Hello, Mrs Hill, I'm Mr Watts' son, Travis. I'm a doctor. You need my help?"

"Oh gosh, yes, Dr Watts. I'm done checking these people for frostbite but it be a good idea to have a doctor look at them."

"That Travis of mine became an outstanding doctor. I'm glad he showed up, also the others. Now, let's get you all warm too." The sheriff then came from the kitchen with his little thermos bottle.

"Bob, is that your thermos? That wouldn't hold more than a cup or two. **George!**"

"Yes, sir."

"In the pantry on the top shelf is my old thermos. Would you get it and fill it for the sheriff? Right away."

"Dad, you don't need to do that," says Bob quickly.

"Yes, I do. We take care of each other in this town."

"You're a good father," says Bob appreciatively.

"You're a good sheriff, bringing these folks to us for care."

"Here you go Sheriff, fresh hot coffee." George handed him what seemed to be a half a gallon of coffee.

"My goodness, George, this will last me the rest of my shift."

"Oh, Sheriff, I packed you hot sandwiches."

"You're a good man, George."

"Sheriff, you still there?" Radio dispatch came over the hand radio.

"Yes Kyra, I'm still here."

"Power company say electric will be out till morning. A tree came down at a transformer station."

"Okay, lots of folks are holed up at the Watts house and McKee house. Looks like everybody's taken care of."

"Okay," Kyra on dispatch replied.

"Folks, you all stay put with Mr Watts, he'll take care of you till the roads are clear."

Mr Watts sees the sheriff to the door.

"Dad, I think this storm is about done for. If you could...."

"Don't even worry about them, Bob, they are my guests in this house."

The sheriff leaves and heads to the patrol car and drives away.

"Travis, how's our frozen guests?"

"They look great, Dad. Just very cold. Mrs Hill had everything under control."

"That's good. And the babies?"

"They aren't even cold. Their mothers kept them toasty warm. Mrs Hill is a great nurse. Wish I had her as one of my nurses."

"Ask her. I don't think she's employed right now."

"I will, Dad."
That evening Mr Watts and some of his family headed to the kitchen and started making supper. It looked like chaos in the kitchen but it's an event they were used to.
Mr Watts comes out to say, "Folks, we've made supper for everybody. Those who were caught by the storm, please come on in to the table first. The church members, you all come next. After everybody's tummy is full, we'll clean up and eat last."
Some of the stranded people said, "You mean you all want us to eat first, even ahead of your own?"
"The family and town does it that way. That's just how it's done here in Chapman Grove."
People get up and make their way to the kitchen table and have a nice hot meal. Then the family cleans up a bit before eating their own food. Later they join the others back in the living room.
"Dad, how are we going to sort out the sleeping arrangements?" Amy asked.
"Good question. I was thinking that the two stranded motorist families could share a room each. I don't think Andy would mind bunking with George. The grandchildren, boys can have one room and the girls another. The Hills can share a bedroom. My girls can share a room and my boys can share. Will this be okay till everything's under control?"
"We can manage for a short time," his daughters responded. Everyone else agreed, grateful for a roof over their heads in such weather conditions.
"It's been a long day. You've all got room assignments," Mr Watts said. "If anything is needed just come knock on my door. You folks with the babies, we have cribs in your rooms. By the way, we never did learn your names."
"We're the Carmichaels from Jackson County, WV, and this is our baby boy, Mitch."
"This is Joyce, my wife. Amy is my little girl and I'm Jerry Beckett. We all come from Kanawha County."
"Well folks, I'm Mr Watts and the young man that went to the back room is George."

"Thanks so much for taking us in, Mr Watts. We were so worried about where to stay on a Sunday. The car must have had some damage to it in the snow drift," said Mr Carmichael gratefully.
"Well, Mr Carmichael, you're in luck. Mr Hill works up at the gas station where they can fix you up. His wife was the nurse taking care of you. Most likely that's where your car would have been towed. And you Mr Beckett, how's your car?"
"I think we're just stuck."
"Well, your car's probably been towed to the garage too. It should be okay there. Well folks, I've had a long day so I'm turning in for the night," Mr Watts announced.
"We are, too," the family and the others agreed.
All of them started going up to the rooms they had been assigned. A few weren't sure which one was theirs but Mr Watts showed them on the chart he had made. Then they found their rooms easily. Not long afterward, all was silent that night in the Watts house in Chapman Grove.

Monday, December 23rd 1963
The sun rose up over the back hills of Chapman Grove. It was a very bright day. The blizzard had passed by without any more incidents. The sun made the snow glitter. All the women had gotten up before the men, except Mr Hill who was always an early riser. He had gotten up, had a cup of coffee and headed out the door for work at the garage. That must have been a couple of hours ago. The ladies (comprised of Mrs Beckett; Mrs Carmichael; Mrs Hill; Mr Watts' girls Lynn, Amy and four children; Travis Watts' wife Julie and John's wife Liz) were all chattering away about their lives and families. Mrs Beckett said they lived in Charleston and went to a little church up Sugar Creek Drive. It was a nice church where everybody was related somehow to someone else. Her husband worked in a warehouse for Heck's Department Store.
Lynn said, "We been trying to get Heck's to remodel the store here in Chapman Grove but not much luck."
"Our church is having a special Christmas day service since it falls on a Wednesday. It will be grand," said Mrs Carmichael.

Amy Watts said, "We always try to get to Dad's home either for Thanksgiving or Christmas. I think I only missed one year, not coming for either. It just wasn't Christmas or Thanksgiving without them."

"How long ago did your mom die?" asked Mrs Beckett.

"I think it's been almost four years now. Dad was very upset for months," Lynn told her.

Mr Watts enters the room. "What was Dad upset about?"

"We were just talking about four years ago, Dad."

"Oh okay, Lynn. Yes, I miss her very much. Mrs Carmichael, I just got off the phone with the garage and Mr Hill says the tie rod got bent real bad. He's trying to straighten it to get you on your way. If not, you're welcome to stay here till it's fixed."

Just then the lights came back on.

"Oh great, the power's back on. Hooray, for the power company," somebody exclaimed. Everyone cheered.

"Yes, it was the power transformer station knocked out; they get on to those quickly," Mr Watts said. "As I was saying, we can take care of you till your cars are roadworthy."

"Well, bless your heart." Mr Beckett came into the room.

"Good morning, Mr Beckett. I was saying I spoke to Mr Hill at the garage and Mr Carmichael's car needs a tie rod straightened. Your car was okay. Anyway, everybody can stay here till it's safe to leave."

George comes into the room. "♪Good morning, everyone.♪"

"Good morning, George. You sound lively today."

"Yep, Andy and I had a good time last night, talking."

"Is that why you look so tired?" Mr Watts commented.

"Andy got up a while ago and went to work, Mr Watts. After that he was going to attempt to get home."

"So," Mr Watts asked, "what did you all talk about all night?"

"Lots of stuff."

"Oh, okay."

More of the family and others came down to the kitchen. Some of Mr Watts' daughters had got up and started making breakfast: scrambled eggs, sausage, bacon, toast and all the trimmings. To drink, there was orange juice, apple juice and milk.

"You girls fix all this food?" Mr Becket asked.

"We always eat good here. The Lord blesses us. We just don't want anybody to be hungry."

Susan spoke up and asked, "May I have a bowl of cereal, please?"

Lynn called out a list of what was in the cupboard, "We have Capt. Crunch®, Alphabets®, Quaker Oats®, Choco Puffs®, Trix®, Fruit Loops® and Crispy Critters®."

"May I have Fruit Loops, please?"

"Susan, remember we're guest in Mr Watts' home," Mrs Hill said.

"Ah, that's fine, Mrs Hill. Little Susan is a sweetheart. I can't turn her down."

Susan blushes, "Thank you, Mr Watts."

"You're welcome, Susan."

Susan takes the bowl of cereal to the table then pours on milk. Then someone pours an apple juice and just sits it in front of her and she takes it gratefully.

Lynn continued the conversation with Dad, "How come you have so much cereal? You hardly ever eat cereal."

"You can't ever tell when a pretty young lady will want a bowl of Fruit Loops. Folks, I've got to get down to the school. Last day of school before the Christmas break. My pretty girls can take care of you."

"Bye Daddy, have a good day."

Mr Watts heads out the door and George follows in pursuit along with Susan.

The state highways crew had cleared the main road through Chapman Grove since it was a state road. The city road crews were out doing all the city's streets and back roads. School buses were running with a clanging sound of chains on the tires. The buses seemed to be more loaded this morning, the day after the blizzard of '63.

Some of Mr Watts' girls went out to do some last minute shopping up at Heck's and then to the market for a few last minute items for Christmas dinner. Others stayed to visit with the stranded motorists. The older boys started clearing snow that had blown up on the porch, then put chairs that had been blown around, back in place. Some of the Christmas lights had been rattled loose so they got the ladders out and re-secured them. Some light strings weren't working so that meant finding the burned out light.

By mid afternoon the girls had the house all decked out ready for Christmas. The boys had the snow cleared away off the porch and off the walkway over which the wind had once more blown fresh snow where George had previously cleared it. They also did the driveway to the garage and the sidewalk in front of the house. Mrs Hill left to see if she could get the car from the church parking lot to meet Susan and take her home from school.

The phone rang and Travis answered.

"It was Mr Hill, the car has been fixed and is roadworthy. The bill for towing and repair comes to $24.87, Mr Carmichael. Mr Hill straightened the tie rod and set the toe. He also inspected for any other damage and found none. But you might want to have your own mechanic check it after Christmas. But Mr Hill said this should get you on your way."

"$24.87, is that the towing or repairs?" Mr Carmichael asked.

"All of it," said Travis. "Towing, fixing and checking it over."

"Gee, that's a cheap price."

"Yes it is, Mr Carmichael, but it's not cheap work. They do good work up there at that garage. But you should have that tie rod replaced when stores open after Christmas."

"I will. You folks are good people here."

"We try to be, Mr Carmichael."

School let out and the school buses started their journey to bring all the kids home for the Christmas break. Mr Watts' sons had built a fire and got it burning in the other fireplace, the one that takes wood. A nice homey fire. As Mr Watts and George came in the front door, the blazing fire gave off a warm glow.

"Welcome home, Dad. Hard day at school?"

"Not a bit, girls. We just had an easy day in classes. All of them behaved themselves. It's like they know Santa Claus is coming."

"Oh Dad, high school kids don't believe in Santa Claus at that age."

George says, "I do!"

"Oh George, I really don't mean to burst your bubble but there's no such person as Santa Claus. No jolly man in a red suit, sliding down chimneys," said Amy.

"I agree with you Amy, on the man in a red suit. But there was a man that was called Saint Nicholas, who gave children presents. I'm not up on the full details but the symbol of Santa goes back a couple hundred years. Be nice to learn about how Santa developed to what we have today."

"NO GEORGE!" Mr Watts yells. "We need to set a quota on this time travel. I'm getting too old for time travel. That boy's a bad influence on me."

All the kids laugh with Dad and George.

"Now, let's get ready for supper."

"Dad, didn't Susan go to school with you and George?"

"Yes, but her mom stopped by the school and picked her up." Supper was going to be a simple meal this close to Christmas. Roast beef, mashed potatoes, corn, green beans and drinks for all. After supper, Mr Beckett, one of the stranded motorists, spoke up, "Mr Watts, your family and the whole town has been so kind to us in our time of need. If you're ever in Charleston, please come stay with us as our guest."

"Hear, hear," Mr Carmichael said. "Same goes with us, if you're ever in Ripley, come stay with us. We'd love to have you."

"Mr and Mrs Beckett, Mr and Mrs Carmichael," Lynn said, "we got a couple of Christmas gifts for you. First is to remember your stay here in Chapman Grove during the blizzard of 1963." She hands each of them a toy snow shovel with an oversized red ribbon. A good gag gift. All thought it was funny.

Then Amy Watts adds, "And we have another gift for you to take home and enjoy on Christmas day." Amy hands them each a gift about the size of a shoebox.

Mr Watts says, "Folks, I'm so glad that you got to spend time here with us. I know you want to get home to be with family but you're welcome to stay till morning if you want."

"Thank you," said Mr Carmichael. "I'd like to get home. You folks have been so kind and we'll remember you all for this."

"I tend to agree with Mr Carmichael. We'd like to get home to family also. They'll be wondering if we can make it home. So we'd like to get back," agrees Mr Beckett.
Amy and Lynn packed snacks for along the way home and gave them some blankets to help them stay warm during the trip. The boys had arranged to bring the cars to the house from the garage, then they had loaded their guests' cars with their few items of luggage. The Carmichaels then the Becketts drove away, warmed by the hospitality of the little town of Chapman Grove that winter.

Chapter 7
I'll Be Home for Christmas

Tuesday, December 24ᵗʰ 1963

Tuesday came and all the boys were out with George. Some had old sleds. Others came from nearby with inner tubes. Out back of Mr Watts' house was always ideal for sled riding. But if there wasn't any traffic on Marshall Street the run could be extended clear down the road.

Susan and her mom came over to visit. Susan had an old snow shovel to use as a sled. Some of the other boys from nearby had old shovels too. Travis was a little bit big for the old sled but he took a shot at it anyway. Down the hill he went, like there was no tomorrow. He continued down the street which was a great run. The sheriff had put up detour signs, 'Children playing on the road.' Then Susan came up the with the snow shovel sled. She sat on it and pushed off. Maybe she pushed off too hard or maybe the shovel was just too slick, but she sped off like greased lightning, screaming all the way down.

Some of the adults glanced out of the window to see that they were alright just at the moment when Susan lost the little control she had and crashed into the snow bank. She came out laughing so hard she could hardly catch her breath, saying how much fun it was. Then one of the other neighborhood kids, on an inner tube, came down sitting in the hole, but turned around with his feet pointed uphill. So he had no idea which direction he was heading till he bashed into a tree, bouncing him off his ride.

Then came George's turn. George sized up the run, guessed how he should push off then then launched himself down the slope. George was doing pretty good until he got to the road. He hit the road a little too hard and at the wrong angle. Flip, he went as the sled continued a great run going down the road. George went sliding over the roadside up against the school wall. Many of the kids came running down to see he was alright. There was George, laughing up a storm. This went on for hours that day. But as the sun started going down, one by one kids started heading for home.

Mr Hill came by and picked up Mrs Hill and Susan. It had been a great day for sledding.

"Susan honey," Mrs Hill says, "you have a good day with your little friends?"

"Yes, Mom." Susan rolls her eyes at the 'little friend' comment.

"Well, Daddy is here to give us a lift home. So you thank Mr Watts for a good time."

With a glowing face, Susan looks at him and says, "Thank you Mr Watts, the sledding today was fun. Merry Christmas."

"You're welcome, Susan, and Merry Christmas to you too."

Mrs Hill and Susan head out the door to where Mr Hill is waiting, keeping the car warm.

George and a bunch of his future brothers come piling in the back door. Mr Watts says, "You all have a good time?"

"Sure did, sir."

"Yeah, when he didn't fall off the sled or crash into the school!" Travis commented.

"I only fell off one time that I remember," George says, laughing with the others. "This has been a great day and place for sledding." Rick, one of Mr Watts' adopted kids, came in. "George, haven't you ever seen snow before, let alone go sledding?"

"Hmm, 'course seen snow before, but not really on the sledding. We use to use anything we could find when we lived at Kaymoor. Sometimes a sheet of metal would make a great sled if you didn't get cut up on the sharp edges."

"You get cut any then, George?" Travis asked.

"Just about every year at least one time." George showed his hands and arms. All up and down his arms and on his hands were scars. It looked like dozens.

"Your dad must had a job bandaging these up. Dad, come look at all these."

Mr Watts came up and looked at all the scars and said, "George, you got to be more careful."

"Oh, I never told my dad anything. If he had seen any cuts he would beat me senseless for being careless."

"Well George," said Mr Watts, "that wouldn't happen here. If you have an accident let me know."

"Alright, sir." George felt warm inside, knowing Mr Watts cared. All that day, so many people had been coming and going. Any kids of Mr Watts, whom he expected to arrive at some time through the day, had indeed been arriving, staying a while and then leaving as others came in. And so it had gone on, busy all day.

Slowly, the family started heading into the living room where the lights on the Christmas tree had come on. Gathering all around the room were Lynn, Josh, Amy plus her four kids (her husband was in Korea), Gary, Travis, John and his wife and three kids, Jeff with his wife and two kids, Rick, Mike, Raymond, Charles and George. The TV had been on but nobody was watching it. It looked like Judy Garland Christmas Special. George turned the TV off.

Daddy (aka Mr Watts) sat down in his favorite chair with the big family Bible. His kids knew what was next so they sat down on the floor, followed by the sons-in-law and daughters-in-law, and the grandchildren. He opened up the huge family KJB Bible to the book of Luke, chapter 2: 1-7, and started reading out:

"'And it came to pass in those days that there went out a decree from Caesar Augustus that all the world should be taxed. (And this taxing was first made when Cyrenius was governor of Syria.) And all went to be taxed, every one into his own city.

And Joseph also went up from Galilee, out of the city of Nazareth, into Judea, unto the city of David, which is called Bethlehem; (because he was of the house and lineage of David) to be taxed with Mary his espoused wife, being great with child.

And so it was, that, while they were there, the days were accomplished that she should be delivered.

And she brought forth her firstborn son, and wrapped him in swaddling clothes, and laid him in a manger; because there was no room for them in the inn.

And there were in the same country shepherds abiding in the field, keeping watch over their flock by night.

And, lo, the angel of the Lord came upon them, and the glory of the Lord shone round about them: and they were sore afraid.

And the angel said unto them, Fear not: for, behold, I bring you

good tidings of great joy, which shall be to all people.
For unto you is born this day in the city of David a Savior, which is
Christ the Lord.
And this shall be a sign unto you; Ye shall find the babe wrapped in
swaddling clothes, lying in a manger.
And suddenly there was with the angel a multitude of the heavenly
host praising God, and saying, Glory to God in the highest, and on
earth peace, goodwill toward men.
And it came to pass, as the angels were gone away from them into
heaven, the shepherds said one to another, Let us now go even unto
Bethlehem, and see this thing which is come to pass, which the
Lord hath made known unto us.
And they came with haste, and found Mary, and Joseph, and the
babe lying in a manger.
And when they had seen it, they made known abroad the saying
which was told them concerning this child.
And all they that heard it wondered at those things which were told
them by the shepherds.
But Mary kept all these things, and pondered them in her heart.
And the shepherds returned, glorifying and praising God for all the
things that they had heard and seen, as it was told unto them.'"
George had sat there during the whole story and was still fascinated
by it even though he'd heard it at church. All the other adults just
sat and enjoyed their father reading the Christmas story to them as
he had done for more years than they could remember. It was so
familiar.

"Grandpa?"

"Yeah, Danny?"

"In spouse wife, is that a wife that stays in the house?"

"No Danny, Mary was great with child and..."

"The child was great or Mary was great? I don't understand,
Grandpa," asked Debbie.

"Well Debbie, Mary wasn't married yet..."

"SHE WASN'T MARRIED!" exclaimed Mark.

"No, she wasn't married yet, Mark, because the child wasn't..."

"So who was the father, Grandpa?" asked Albert.

Annie, one of the mothers, quickly ordered, "Alright kids, time for bed. Go and get changed, brush your teeth and I'll tuck you in."
"Same to mine," said Bonnie.
"That goes triple for mine," Amy said.
As they were heard scampering off to go to bed, one voice said, "Why wasn't there room at the inn, anyway? Just how big was this Mary and Joseph?"
"That's not the point. Mary was pregnant with the baby Jesus," came another voice.
"SO WHAT! There's always room here at Grandpa's house."
"Hey guys, hurry up and get to bed or Santa Claus won't come," called Amy.
"Who cares about Santa Claus, I want to hear more about this Mary, Joseph and Jesus." The voices trailed away as the children climbed the stairs and disappeared to the bathrooms and bedrooms.
"Dad, you okay?" asked Amy.
"I'll be alright, kids. You all need to have a talk with them about the Christmas story and the facts of life."
"Yes Dad, we do. But for now I'm turning in for the night. You going too?"
"Yes, it's been a nice long day, Amy."
So everyone in the Watts house headed off to bed. Late that night sleigh bells were heard outside. It woke George up, along with his roommate, Charles.
"George," whispered Charles, "you hear that? It sounds like Santa's sled coming through."
"You're pulling a fast one on me, Charles. It's not Santa."
Several of the younger kids came charging down the stairs, "It's Santa Claus, it's Santa Claus!" all of them sang out.
Mr Watts and their moms, Amy, Annie and Bonnie came out to see what the commotion was all about. Annie hollered, "What you kids doing out of bed? It's only 11:45 at night."
"It's Santa Claus, Mom. We heard the sleigh outside."
"Kids," Mr Watts shouted, "that's Mr Bowman moving his sleigh for sleigh rides tomorrow. Now you all listen to your moms and go back to bed."

"Sorry, Dad. They never saw an open sled like that before."

"It's alright, Bonnie, just have them go back to bed."

"Kids, tell your Grandpa you're sorry for waking him," Bonnie ordered.

"Sorry, Grandpa," they all said.

The moms marched all the kids back upstairs. Mr Watts, Charles and George went back to bed.

George tells Charles, "I told you so. No such thing as a man in a sleigh."

Charles just chuckles at George.

Wednesday, December 25th 1963

Morning came very early for the Watts house. And all the grand-kids were still in bed? Amy, Bonnie and Annie were slowly making their way to the kitchen, yawning with every step.

"Mornin' Dad," Annie said, yawning and staggering into the kitchen.

"Mornin' kids," Mr Watts said, "coffee's hot on the stove." Mr Watts yawns.

"Dad, how shall we start Christmas dinner?" asked Bonnie, sitting down to the table.

"Well girls, the turkey's in the right hand oven. We'll put all the potatoes, carrots and onions in later, after the turkey's done. In time, we can use the left oven for all the pies. Is there anything the grand-kids won't eat? Maybe can have a few substitutes."

Amy relied, "I've not found anything yet the kids will not eat. You know kids, Dad, they're eating machines."

"Yes, they are eating machines. I knew some first hand, girls." George and Charles, hearing all the talking going on, came into the kitchen.

"Good morning, George, Charles. You all sleep okay?" asked Mr Watts.

"Charles snores."

"No I don't, Dad, it's George that snores," Charles stated.

"Hush boys, you both were snoring when I came in the kitchen. I thought the dishwasher was running." Mr Watts ended that argument. "Can you two boys bring in a couple of armloads of firewood each? The fire will make it a nice homey place for when the little ones get up."

"Yes, Dad. You ready, George?"

"Yep, I'm ready, Charles and I still don't snore."

"You do, too!"

"BOYS!" Mr Watts hollers.

George and Charles head out the back door then both come back with an armload each, clear up to their chins. They took the wood into the living room and were back and out through the back door like a flash. Minutes later, here they come barreling back through with armloads, ready for the fireplace.

"Dad," Amy asked, "why have so much firewood? You have gas heating."

"Because it's seventy five percent cheaper. It heats the house better. The fuel grows on my own land. And it's more like home with the fireplace. I really don't like the smell of gas fire heat."

"Okay Dad, you win. Those are good reasons. I do like the open fireplace also."

All the kids and their families had finally gathered in the living room by the Christmas tree, and the fireplace gave the room a nice homey glow. Travis had started the record player and it was playing some nice Mel Tormé. Packages were under the Christmas tree and spilling out on the floor. You really couldn't see the base of the tree. The grand-kids got most of the usual gifts. Girls got dolls, Susie homemaker®, and Easy Bake Oven® while the older kids got sewing machines. Boys got footballs, model cars, Erector Set®, airplanes and boats. One boy even got a complete model rocket kit. Mr Watts' older kids got clothes, which was nice.

Robert, they heard, got a really nice slide ruler which he needed for college. John got a new lunch pail for working in the mines, and a new helmet with light. Lynn got a nice purse with lots of extras that went with it.

Then came George's gift. The wrapping was red and white shiny foil paper. It was tied with a nice wide green ribbon and bow. George never got a gift that was wrapped up so nicely before. He just sat there, looking and rubbing the paper, touching the ribbon and bow. He didn't know if he wanted to rip the wrappings and ribbons off, like the others had been doing, or try to save it all. A few tears started to come to George's eyes.

"You okay, George?" asked Mr Watts.

George didn't answer right away but continued admiring the packaging. "It's just that I never saw a gift wrapped so nice for me before."

George started by loosening the ribbon and saved it. Then he just RIPPED open the paper, tearing into as if his life depended on it. George thought that felt good. But the sensation was new to him. The wrapping revealed a box from an electronic company he had never heard of. What could it be? There already was a radio in his room. Besides, he thought it was too big for a radio. Can't be a TV 'cause one was in the house and they hardly ever watched it. And we surely had every book you could ever need. One wall alone …

"**GEORGE,** open your gift!" Everyone shouted, eager either to see what he got, or his reaction. Anyway, it startled George in a humorous way. George breaks open the box and looks inside to find it wasn't one gift, but many gifts inside. Right on top was a pouch of hand tools; screwdrivers, files, wrenches, a small hammer and other tools he'd never seen before. George set that aside, only to see another pouch. This one had an electronic soldering gun and another smaller one, two tins of flux and a variety of solders. It just doesn't get any better than this.

"Keep digging, George," Mr Watts said.

George looked puzzled, then looked in the box. Some paper packing was hiding more things. Many of them he'd never heard of. Linear amp he recalled from somewhere. But then he saw the grand prize. What looked to be a well thought of, outstanding gift; a build yourself amateur radio kit. As it came out of the box, tears started pouring down his face. "I love you all," George said in a trembling voice.

A number of them had gotten together, during Thanksgiving, and planned all this with their dad.

"We love you too, George!" they said, coming up to hug their future brother.

"George, Robert helped us get everything needed, we hope. Also, it hasn't come yet but the antenna has been ordered and we're still waiting on it. Robert said if he missed something, let us know."

George was still sitting there, crying. "Oh sir, one more gift. It's for you," George comments the best he can through his tears. "But there was no way it could be wrapped. Some of your other kids plus Mr McKee and many others helped in pulling this off."

"Okay," Mr Watts said, puzzled. "So how do I see it?"

"Come over here, Dad,"Amy said, and some of the kids grab hold of Dad and nearly drag him over to the wall next to the stairs. George moves some items that were hiding some wrapping paper taped to the wall.

"So what's this?" Mr Watts exclaimed, laughing. "If you were trying to gift wrap the house you needed lots more wrapping paper."

Josh spoke up, "Dad, this was all George's idea and he got our opinion and help to pull it off. So how about open your gift."

Mr Watts takes a step up and rips the wrapping off the wall. He looked at it and said, "It's a light switch. I don't get it."

"All through the house has light switches like this one," George informed him.

"But George, the whole house has lights already." They all laughed as their father wasn't catching on to the nature of the gift.

"Dad," Josh explained, "George had the fantastic idea of rewiring the whole house. But the power isn't coming from the electric company. In fact, if you look at your next bill they will be paying you."

Mr Watts was even more confused than ever.

"Put on your coat, sir, and see what we've done!"

Mr Watts and the rest of the family put their coats on and headed out to the garage. In the far back of the garage was George's magnetic motor with not only one, but two, four thousand watt generators hooked to both sides of it, twirling away.

"Mr Watts, this was the original plan of my science project to generate power. Your kids thought it be cool to just start with your

house."
Mr Watts just stood there, looking at the thoughtful gift everyone had worked on together.
"It wasn't easy, sir. Sometimes we had to get Mr McKee to think of ways to get you out of the house."
"That Tom is one okay guy."
"How about you throw the switch, right there, sir."
He reaches over and flips the switch. All the new lights came on in the once dimly lit garage. Outside, the Christmas lights on the house had been switched over to the new power.
"And Daddy, it's all better than current electrical code," Amy adds.
"You have four thousand watts of free power. And four thousand watts of backup."
Mr Watts starts hugging all the kids then comes to George.
"George, you're really something, you know that?"
George says nothing but just hugs him. In the afternoon, around 1:30, the family gathered in the kitchen for a nice Christmas meal together:

30 lb turkey with stuffing
10 lb ham
lots of mashed potatoes with gravy
a large pan of candied sweet potatoes
corn, green beans
cranberries
homemade dinner rolls
bread pudding
apple, pumpkin, sweet potato pies
apple cider and fruit juices

Amy and her little daughters (Amy, Tresa), Bonnie and her daughter Debbie, Annie and her daughter took over Christmas dinner this year, and it was a meal fit for a king. This Christmas, Dad was booted out of the kitchen and enjoyed being with the rest of the family. As the family started coming to the kitchen table they saw the girls had put on a grand feast. Dad looked over the table and said it was good. This time, Dad was served and treated to the best meal in a long time. In many families, the older ones sit at the main table and the younger ones are at a separate table. However, in the Watts home there's always room for everyone at the same table. Nobody is ever segregated to another table because of age. Christmas dinner in their home usually lasted an hour or two. If you left the table hungry it was always your own fault.

Just as in the past, everyone is full from a fantastic meal. No room for desserts. That was alright. In a few hours most would love desserts of pie, maybe topped with ice cream. Many prepared to head to the living room to chat. Some dozed off after a well planned meal.

"George?" Mr Watts asked. "What are you going to do now that your motor is running the electricity in the house?"

"I have plans to build a bigger one as a form of transportation."

"A form of transportation?" Mr Watts queried.

"Yes, sir. If we're going to go through time, we might as well do it in something safer. Not just hanging on."

"Sounds like a good improvement, George," Robert chipped in. "You ought to check out some community colleges up in Wheeling," he added.

"You mean start college now?" George blurted out.

"No George, there are night classes you can take part time. Maybe take classes they have that would interest you, like history," Travis explained.

"I'm interested in a welding class at the vocational school. Maybe a half semester. I love building stuff. Mr Watts, can I sign up for vocational classes next semester?"

"I don't see any reason why not. Your grades are exceptional. You almost have enough points to graduate in your junior year. Sure, go ahead if you still want to at the end of this term."

"Far out!" George shouted.

Four or five others that had dozed off woke with a fright. "Huh huh, what happened?" someone said in a panic. Everyone else burst out laughing.

Thursday, December 26th 1963

The sun was shining through a light fluffy snowfall the next morning. Some of the young ones were playing with their Christmas presents in the living room. George had gone into the kitchen to help a few of the girls to prepare breakfast. Annie, Jeff's wife, asked George if everybody in his family was this smart.

"I was an only child in my family. I barely remember Mom. Dad said she was a no-account and deserted when I was about two."

"George, I don't believe for a minute your mom was a no-account. She had you, didn't she?"

He turned his head and gave a thoughtful look.

Mr Watts came into the kitchen just then. "What's smelling so good in here, girls?"

"Girls and young man, Dad," Lynn commented. "George has been working on breakfast too, while we've been doing other items."

"Then I'll bet it will be incredible."

"Yes Dad, George is an excellent cook," Lynn replied.

"Then let's sit down and enjoy this incredible breakfast."

Then more of the adults came in and they all sat down to a nice breakfast with the sounds of the children playing in the next room.

Chapter 8
More Than Just Education

Thursday, January 2nd 1964

The year begins with George in his second half of junior year. He has been able to start going to a vocational school half the day and regular school the second half. The votech school was about five miles away but the school bus got the students there in minutes. It was a nice building made of red brick. His class was in welding, including arc welding, heliarc, brazing and acetylene usage. Mr Spradling, the teacher, was an old pro at this. Like many things, George grasped the welding skills instantly. He was turning out to be one of the smartest students that ever came out of the area. Some of the other students from school also attended vocational school but this was their second term.

Today, George learned about welding aluminum together. It took a special process, using helium, called heliarc. If one were to try to weld this metal using an arc welder it would just burn up the aluminum. Helium gas actually protects the soft metal. Some of the class content was in book learning and much was hands on experience. A twenty minute break in the class would come about halfway through. Most of the time George would want to keep at it. But the teacher wanted a break so all work had to stop. Near the end of the school term students would be able to build something of their choosing. George had a few things in mind.

"Mr Spradling?"

"Yes, George?"

"Is there any limits on what we can build for our passing grade?"

"George, it has to show good workmanship. Have a well thought out plan that you can follow. Once it's done it can be taken home by the student's mode of transportation or can be cut up for scrap."

"I don't think I could ever scrap things once I build them."

"That's good, George. I would hope what you'll learn to build in here will be taken home to be appreciated for years to come."

The bell rings to let class out for the day at the vocational school and the students pile into the bus to head back for regular classes.

When they'd get back to Chapman Grove High, they'd be in the middle of second lunch period. George worked it out that he could get his lunch in that time and could pick up an extra class. George's classes included Mr Snuffer's English, Mr Watts' science class and Mrs MacQueen's math class.

At the end of the day, walking home from school, Mr Watts asked George, "You ever have anything to do that's fun? All I see you do is chores, homework and school."

"But sir, I find your class fun. And I love going to the votech school. I like getting my hands onto stuff to build. I'm also building the amateur radio set I got for Christmas."

"But George, do you ever want to go out with your friends to the ball game or just hang out at the Dairy Queen®? Bet Susan would love to see more of you than just at school, or do something with the other guys. Maybe camping, fishing or hiking."

"You know something Mr Watts, it was kind of fun sleeping out next to the campfire at Fort Randolph and with Mr Chapman."

"Would you be interested in something like the Boy Scouts®, George? Our church sponsors Cub Scouts and Boy Scouts. They meet once a week and also go camping, hiking, fishing. You earn merit badges for things you learn and build."

"Building? Like what, sir?"

"Well George, I was never a boy scout, but I can tell you a few things they offer. There's wood working, wood carving, there's a reading merit badge."

"Oh you know me, I love to read."

"Yes, you do, George. But every now and then you should look up and see what's going on around you. Let's see, what else? Metalwork, automotive repair. Oh George, I can't think of them all. Just check them out the next time they meet. You can't possibly do everything they offer."

"But I sure can give it a try," George said, smiling.

"I bet you will, I bet you will. I'll give you the phone number of the scoutmaster. He's a member of the church and an all round swell guy."

Tuesday, January 7th 1964

Early the next morning George phoned the scoutmaster at his home. But he had already left for work, his wife said. She took down George's phone number then said, "Oh, are you George that's staying with the school teacher, Mr Watts?"

"Yep, that's me!"

"Mr Ritchie doesn't get in the door till 4:30. The troop meeting is tonight at the church and meets at 6 pm. He can call you or you can meet him at the church annex building. I'm sure he'd love to see you."

By 5:45 pm George is at the church annex building and the doors are already open. A few other scouts, whom George already knew, were there and welcomed him.

"George!" one of them called out. "I didn't think you would be interested in scouting." It was Timmy from school. They were in science and math classes together.

"Well Timmy, Mr Watts said I should check out other interest beside school and building stuff in the garage."

"That Mr Watts is one okay man. Mr Ritchie is in the back. Would you like to meet him?"

The two of them went to the back of the meeting hall where the kitchen was located. Mr Ritchie was talking to some of the other boys. Then he finishes and turns towards Timmy and George. "Hey Timmy, who's this?"

"This is George, from school. He's in a couple of classes with me. He might be interested in joining."

"That true, George? If it is, welcome aboard." Mr Ritchie gives him a handshake to welcome him. "George, to join you'll need to get permission from a parent or guardian."

George remembers the last time he had to get a permission paper signed, from his dad. He might or might not have had his permission to enter the school science fair. He would never know. George thought he had to put that behind him now.

"George, if you're definitely interested in joining the Scouts, go to this store up in Wheeling for these items." Mr Ritchie hands him a list for the store that carried scouting supplies. "If you're strapped for cash you can ask for help. The top item on the list is your handbook. It tells you everything you need to know."

George hung around to see what else happened at the meeting. In the beginning they lined up for inspection and answered scouting questions. Most of them had a sharp looking uniform. Some had what they could afford but were still in keeping with the regulations for scout attire. And one boy had regular clothes but still looked good. The reason was he hadn't yet been to the store. He was a small young boy that came up from the Webelos®.[17] The rest of the time they broke up into patrols. George made his way around to the different groups to see what they were doing. The Bear Patrol was planning a weekend camping trip, coming up soon. It was Navaho Patrol's turn to help in a community project of picking up litter in Chapman Grove. Fox Patrol was planning a hike on the old Kanawha Trace. Boone Patrol was currently covering their part of town, selling light bulbs as a fund raiser for the troop.

George approaches the patrol leader and says, "Can I join the Boone patrol?"

David, the patrol leader, replies, "If nobody objects I don't see why not."

None of the members of Boone Patrol had any objections. In fact they said they'd welcome him in, soon as his membership is submitted.

"I'd like to go ahead and help sell those light bulbs if I could now, anyway. Timmy can vouch for me. We know each other from school."

"George, how many do you think you can sell?"

"I don't know. How are they packaged?"

David points to the boxes. "There's four bulbs to the box. Most folks buy one box, maybe two. Can you sell sixteen boxes?"

"I think so, David, least I can try."

"Just do your best. Each box cost a dollar."

After the troop meeting George heads for home. When he gets in Mr Watts asked how it went.

"Great, sir, I got a membership application to fill out and return next meeting. Also, I'm in the Boone Patrol and we're selling light bulbs as a fund raiser. Would you like a box?"

"Well, George, I think we're all set for light bulbs. . ."

George's first try at selling light bulbs seemed to be failing and his heart sank a little until he heard, ". . . but I don't think we have any spares. What sizes do you have?"

"We got 40 watt and 100."

"Give me one of each."

"Yes, sir!" George hands him two bulbs, one of each strength as a joke, but Mr Watts is surprised and tells him, "No, George, I meant one box of each bulb!"

Very encouraged, George hands over two full boxes and Mr Watts pays him two dollars. His first sale. YES, George thought.

Wednesday, January 8th 1964

George went to school the next morning where he sold two more boxes of light bulbs to his welding instructor. Mr Spradling told him the Boy Scouts® are an excellent organization for a young man. It would teach you good morals and values.

When George got back to high school, another two boxes were sold to Mrs MacQueen. After class George went to the McKee's house and sold two more boxes. He was glad he had an even number of those particular sized bulbs as they seemed the most popular. And that made half of them sold in a twenty four hour period. By that weekend George had all his stock sold and was requesting more.

Saturday, January 11th 1963

Saturday morning came with a little skiff of snow on the ground. The temperature was a mighty bone chilling -12° Fahrenheit. The gas fire was having trouble keeping the house bearable. George went out to the back porch and got an armload of wood. This morning however, he seemed not to be able to light it.

"What's the matter, George?" Mr Watts said. "Having trouble rubbing two sticks together?"

"Huh?" George replied. "What you mean?"

"It's said boy scouts can start a fire by rubbing two sticks together."

"I'm not yet officially a boy scout, sir. So I've not learned anything yet about scouting. But I hope to."

"Yep George, you sure will, I know."

Mr Watts got some old newspapers and kindling, and showed George how to light the fire. Soon it was burning well and started taking the chill off the room. Mr Watts said, "George, when the fire is lit make sure the safety screen is in place. This is so sparks can't jump out and start a house fire."

"Yes, sir." George puts the screen on then gets a book, to read about building the radio set he got for Christmas. This way he could enjoy the fire and read. Some parts of his set he had already assembled and he could hear far off lands, like London in England, and the U.S.S.R. which had the strongest signals.

"Mr Watts?"

"Yes, George."

"I was thinking of working on my radio set in my room. Will the fire be okay with that screen on?"

"I think it will, but why not bring your work in here and be warm."

"Alright."

So George goes into his bedroom and brings everything he needs. Mr Watts comes with his Bible and reads while watching George work. George was meticulous at what he set his mind to do.

Sunday, January 12th 1964

Church bells could be heard throughout the town. George jumped up, thinking about church. Andy, his Sunday school teacher, made classes interesting.

That Sunday, Pastor Bess came to have lunch at the Watts place. It was in this way that he got to know the congregation better.

"So George, what have you been into?" Pastor Bess asked.

"Well Pastor, the usual; going to school, taking vocational classes, building a radio to hear all around the world, and when finished I can talk back to them also."

"Oh, a ham radio set. Have you thought of joining MARS?"

"Mars, the planet?"

"No, Military Affiliated Radio Service. They provide services of communications between service men, service women and their families."

"I've not heard of them. But I might look into them. I've also joined the Boy Scouts at church."

"They're a good bunch, George. Stick with them. What about this time travel you been doing?"

"It's really cool to be going into history, Pastor Bess. The first trip was an accident, going to Fort Randolph. But I found it great to meet John Chapman."

"John Chapman?"

"Yes, sir. Also known as Johnny Appleseed."

"I know who you're talking about. You planning any more time trips?"

"I just might. I'm building an all new machine. But right now I'm learning to weld to build its frame. I been doing the math for the journeys and how to drive it better. One trip, Mr Watts and I crashed into the side of the Washington Monument."

"Maybe you should watch a TV show from England. It's about a time traveler, called Doctor Who."

"Who?" George questioned.

"That's right, Doctor Who. He travels through time and space. Like you're trying to do."

"I'll see if we can get it, Pastor."

Just then Mr Watts came in and said lunch was served.

Chapter Nine
So Is This All There Is To life?

Monday, January 27ᵗʰ 1964
"Houston, this is Captain George. Doing tests of all electronics."
"All seems a-go for this first flight to the moon. You're looking good here, Captain George, all circuits are green."
"Houston, can you say again. You're breaking up." A few moments pass by. "Houston, we are good to go. Houston, can you hear us? How we going to get to the moon if we can't talk between a few buildings?" Then the silence is broken with blood curdling screams, **"Houston, we're on fire, we're on fire. We can't get out."**[7]
George wakes, out of breath, but it's still dark outside so he tries to go back to sleep.

Saturday, March 28ᵗʰ 1964
The sun came out to say it was going to be a bright sunny day. But George didn't feel the brightness that day. It was a year ago today that his dad died in the house fire. George left a note for Mr Watts that he needed some alone time then headed out the door. George first walked down the road into town. It was still quite early and many shops and stores weren't open yet. He continued on, just walking and thinking. Next thing he knew, he had come up the filthy road and ended up at his old home. The lot had been leveled now. No sign that there ever was a house there. He remembers the last conversation he had with his dad, about permission to enter the science fair at school, and how he felt afterward. How low he felt that day when Dad said he'll think about it. Then the next morning he wanted to get out of the house before Dad got home.
If he had waited for his dad to get back from his night shift, he would have seen him alive one last time.
George continued walking until he came upon a store that had just opened. He went inside, looking around. The next thing he knew, he'd bought some plastic flowers. As he comes out the store George turns and walks up the street and ends up at the city cemetery. The

grounds were well kept. Flowers were on other graves but none on his father's grave. The gravestone looked cheap. Name, year born and date died.

"So is this all there is to life?" George said to himself. "You're born, you live, you die." He pondered this with something tugging at his heart. He placed the flowers on the grave, thinking he wished he could have found better ones. But that was all the store had. George pulled the few weeds that had grown up next to the stone, stuck the flowers all together in a group then stepped back to look and see if it was alright.

"It looks mighty nice, George." A voice came from behind him. Coming up the hill was Mr Watts, also with flowers. "I thought I would find you here. Your dad's grave looks nice."

"The stone looks cheap, sir."

"That's what the insurance would pay for. Others from church pitched in also to get it this good."

"That was nice of them, Mr Watts. So why you come up here? Looking for me?"

"That and I wanted to put new flowers on Mrs Watts' grave."

They walked to another section of the cemetery. The whole cemetery was reasonably well kept.

"Is this it, sir?

"Yep!"

George picked up the old flowers and pulled out some of the weeds near the stone just as he did before. Then Mr Watts took the fresh flowers and placed them on her grave and stood up. The stone was very nice. It was a double stone. On one side of the stone was her name, Eileen Watts, placed alongside her picture and the words, Born 1916 Died 1960. Then it read, Will be missed by her loving husband, family, foster children, grandchildren and friends.

Next to her grave there was room for another grave sharing the same stone. Some graves just had cheap markers and others had none, just a rock, nothing to know who got buried. Tears fell from Mr Watts' eyes. They turned and headed back home, saying nothing along the way.

Sunday, March 29th 1964

George and Mr Watts woke up with their alarm clocks going off and the sun shining in the windows. The two of them made their way slowly to the kitchen and started breakfast. Eggs, bacon and toast was the norm. The two of them chatted about the weather and what church would be doing today.

At 11am the Easter Sunday service began with the choir singing He is Risen. Then Pastor Bess came up and read from the book of Matthew, chapter 28:1-10 and 16-20.

"'Now after the sabbath, toward the dawn of the first day of the week, Mary Magdalene and the other Mary went to the sepulcher. And behold, there was a great earthquake; for an angel of the Lord descended from heaven and came and rolled back the stone, and sat upon it. His appearance was like lightning, and his raiment white as snow. And for fear of him the guards trembled and became like dead men. But the angel said to the women, Do not be afraid; for I know that you seek Jesus who was crucified. He is not here; for he has risen, as he said. Come, see the place where he lay. Then go quickly and tell his disciples that he has risen from the dead, and behold, he is going before you to Galilee; there you will see him. Lo, I have told you.

So they departed quickly from the tomb with fear and great joy, and ran to tell the disciples. And behold, Jesus met them and said, Hail! And they came up and took hold of his feet and worshiped him. Then Jesus said to them, Do not be afraid; go and tell my brethren to go to Galilee, and there they will see me.

Now the eleven disciples went to Galilee, to the mountain to which Jesus had directed them. And when they saw him they worshiped him; but some doubted. And Jesus came and said to them, All authority in heaven and on earth has been given to me. Go therefore and make disciples of all nations, baptizing them in the name of the Father and of the Son and of the Holy Spirit, teaching them to observe all that I have commanded you; and lo, I am with you always, to the close of the age.'"

Then Pastor Bess continued, "Why are millions of posters with magnificent landscapes and little philosophic sayings sold each

year in America? Why did I feel happy when I looked at purple snapdragons and distant mountains on an Easter card this week? Why did George's dad die last year, apparently a non churchgoer? Why is there such a thing as stardom in the world of popular music and theater and sports? Why are scenic cruises and scenic tours and $25 coffee table scenic books a million dollar business. . ."
(Sermon courtesy of www.crosswalk.com)

George's mind began wandering and asking himself, why did Dad have to die? If I had stayed to see him come home he might not had died that day. What is the meaning of this? George's mind was confused. The pastor was a wonderful man but he couldn't hear him.

Tears were coming to George's eyes. A few of his friends saw his body trembling. One of them went to where Mr Watts was sitting and brought him over.

"George, you okay?" Mr Watts inquired in a whisper.

George didn't say anything. Friends were giving him a caring touch. Mr Watts took him to the pastor's study. After the service was over, Pastor Bess came in.

"Hello men, what might I do for you?" The pastor saw that George was upset and quite deep in thought.

"Pastor, why don't I wait outside while you have a chat with George. You know, just like you had with me about four years ago." Mr Watts gets up and leaves the room.

About forty or more minutes later the two of them come out and go to where Mr Watts was talking to the McKees. As they walk home, George keeps thinking about what the pastor said to him.

"George, I'm always here for you."

"I know."

"But if you feel more comfortable talking with Pastor Bess, he's a great person to speak to. I'm glad he was around when Mrs Watts passed away."

"It was just his message that sparked something. I would like to talk to Pastor Bess more. I hope I didn't embarrass you, sir."

"No, not at all. It was your friends that came and got me. They're good friends to have."

They got home before George knew they had been walking.

Chapter 10
An Unwanted Birthday Present

Wednesday, April 1ˢᵗ 1964

It was a sunny morning and George was another year older. He has been excelling in vocational school and his junior year in high school. The Boy Scouts® has turned George into a well rounded young man, earning awards and helping the community. But today was something special. Today is George's fifteenth birthday. George never knew what to expect for a birthday.

Mr Watts had been planning something nice to remember. He and George had a nice breakfast that morning. George loved a hot breakfast. He had all his homework by the front door ready to pick up when it was time to leave. They head out for school, into a warm bright day. When they get there, they have plenty of time before the bus leaves for votech.

Mr Biggarstaff was at the door. "George, report to my office!" George and Mr Watts get to the reception area and wait for Mr Biggarstaff. As he comes into the reception area, he barks at George, "In my office."

Mr Watts goes in with George.

"Watts, I didn't call for you!"

"Yes, you did. When you call George, I come too. And it's MISTER Watts."

"OKAY, MISTER WATTS. George, the reason I called you in here is, since you go to that so called votech school and have no homeroom time, it is my privilege to give you your birthday present. Bend over."

"Hold on there, Mr Biggarstaff, I don't do this in my homeroom class and don't believe in abusing children just because it's their birthday."

"Watts, eh, Mr Watts, it's been a tradition in schools since I went to school and it never did me any harm."

"Mr Biggarstaff, I beg to differ with you."

"And what does that mean?"

"Ever since you came to this school, students have looked at you like a big mean bully, and it stops now!"

"We'll see about that!" Mr Biggarstaff said forcefully.

"George has a bus to catch now. Come on, George." Mr Watts intervenes, and the two of them march out of the office.

There are dozens of students out in the hall. Many of them were cheering them on. A few of them were standing with their mouths dropped open. Just then the office door opens and Mr Biggarstaff steps out with a belligerent look and a firm grip on the paddle still in his hand. Students cleared the hallways in two seconds.

"George, don't you concern yourself with him. If he takes this to the school board he'll have a war on his hands. Now don't miss your bus."

George takes off out the door and just catches the bus. Many of the students on the the bus asked what happened in Biggarstaff's office.

"He wanted to paddle me for my birthday!"

Did it hurt, they asked.

"No, Mr Watts wouldn't allow it."

Thursday, April 9th 1964

Mr Watts gets a letter from the school board asking him to come to the next regular board meeting to answer charges of being insubordinate.

"George! Come in here would you, please."

"Yes, sir?"

"Read this."

George takes the letter and his mouth drops open. "THEY CAN'T DO THIS SIR! THEY'RE ALL WRONG. WHO WOULD SAY SUCH A THING?"

"George, calm down. It's not them saying it but they have to investigate it."

"But you're a great teacher. It's just wrong."

"Alright, let's get to school for now."

Tuesday, April 14th 1964

It's 7 pm at the Board of Education. Mr Watts and George squeeze into the boardroom.

"George, I've never seen so many people in here for a school board meeting in all my days."

"Word must have got around about the meeting."

"Hmm, I wonder how."

The chairman of the board calls the meeting to order. The secretary reads the minutes of the last meeting and they go over old business then new business. After that the chairman says, "On to special business. Mr Watts, thank you for coming. I have a report, from the principal of the school where you teach, that on the morning of April 1st 1964 you did willfully interfere with the disciplining of one student named George. What do you have to say about this?"

"Mr Chairman, I did interfere. But if I may continue, it wasn't a disciplining action on the part of the principal. You see, April 1st was George's birthday and Mr Biggarstaff took it on his part to invoke a traditional paddling just because it was his birthday."

"Mr Watts, you know this tradition has gone on for years. It was done even when I went to school."

"Well, Mr Chairman, it's about time it stops."

The crowd in the room gave a modest cheer for Mr Watts. A lady in the back said, "My little Susie got one of those TRADITIONAL whippings and with her health condition couldn't walk for a week after getting out of the hospital."

Another person said, "My son ran away from home because of this too, and you all wouldn't do a thing about it then either."

"My child's grades has fallen ever since she got into high school." The crowds were getting restless to near the point of getting violent themselves. The school board was going to have to do something, and now. Five minutes go by and they just sit there waiting for the crowd to calm down. Just then the sheriff walks in with Judge Hanson and they calmly take a seat.

Mr Biggarstaff stood and said, "Spare the rod you spoil the child."

"Mr Biggarstaff, you're taking the Bible out of context. It's he who spares the rod hates his child. You better read your Bible more if you want to quote it to me. Besides, the way you talk to kids you seem to hate them all!"

The room erupted with more loud cheering for Mr Watts.

"Folks, if you'll take your seats please, we can continue," the Chairman called out.

The sheriff and judge stood up.

"Hello, Sheriff Shamblin, Judge Hanson. You all got anything to add?"

Sheriff Shamblin speaks, "First off, Mr Watts never laid a hand on me as my foster dad and I think I turned out okay." The sheriff was standing next to where Mr Watts was now sitting. He places his hand on Mr Watts shoulder and continues, "As you can see, I've been elected many times to fill the post of sheriff. Nobody seems displeased with the work I've done. Mr Watts has not only adopted and raised me but he was one of my teachers. He's the best parent and teacher one could hope for." Bob Shamblin looks down, smiling at his dad who returns the smile.

A small group clap their hands in support of the sheriff's statements.

"Judge Hanson," the chairman says, "your turn."

"Mr Watts was my sister's husband till she died. They've raised so many kids I lost count of them. All of them are pillars, not only of Chapman Grove, but some are serving this country. I know all parties in question. George is a fine young man and has never been struck by anyone that I know of. He is also under the jurisdiction of my court. If I hear he's put through this barbaric TRADITION of the paddling for no better reason than what I caught wind of, this board will be answering to family court."

The crowded room cheered for Judge Hanson. It went on and on. When it finally died down, the Chairman and the rest of the board had made their final decision.

"Mr Watts, we made a ruling," the Chairman announces. "We have no doubt you're a superb teacher and parent. Your record shows you've been a teacher ever since the school opened its doors. Now it is clear that you have not interfered with the proper operations of Chapman Grove High School. If any existed. Mr Biggarstaff, this board is disturbed by what it has heard tonight. If this is brought up to the school board again, we will be filing charges for student abuse. This practice of the birthday paddling, as of this moment, will cease until we can review its practice. For now, if discipline is warranted for students, parents must be informed in writing and present at school before the discipline takes place. Meeting closed!"[5]

Mr Biggarstaff sneers at Mr Watts, "Well, Mr Watts, you got off this time. But just you wait till...." Judge Hanson and the sheriff come up behind Mr Watts, listening. Mr Biggarstaff turns and stomps off.

"Mr Watts!" calls out the Chairman. "Mr Biggarstaff is up for mandatory retirement soon and you might consider his position, if interested."

"No thanks, sir. I just love teaching kids and that would take me away from them."

"But the position is yours if you ever want it."

Friday, May 29th 1964

It was the last day of school. George was somewhat glad that he had passed his second year of high school. He had also passed votech welding class. He wished school could continue through the summer.

"George, what you going to do now that school's out for the summer?" Mr Watts asked.

"Hoping for school to start back up again, or something. Always got the project in the garage to get put together. I hope it flies real good too."

"I'll bet it will. You know, George, you can go to summer school for half the day during the summer months, if you want."

"Summer school? I thought that was only for kids that failed a grade."

"No, many kids can get ahead. Some take extra classes to get ahead. Others go to votech to learn new skills. It lasts most the time sixty days."

"Mr Watts? May I go to the votech during the summer?"

"Yes, you may. But you might miss out on some of the things the Boy Scouts® do in the summer months."

"I know, but I can go on hikes and summer camps later. After I graduate that will be the end. Besides, learning is fun to me."

"Yes, you do kind of get engrossed in a good book. I guess you can if your heart's really set on it. What class do you have in mind?"

"I was thinking about electronics. I've learned lots from building my radio. But I get a feeling there's more out there to know."

"You're not going to turn into some mad scientist, are you?"

"No sir, not me. I want to be a good scientist. Help people. It makes me feel good to help people."

"Okay George, the bus will be waiting on you all to go to votech and enroll in summer school classes in the morning. Why don't you go on over tomorrow?"

Next morning George is up and ready to go, eager to enroll for his electronics class at votech. At the high school, where the bus for votech is waiting, he and Mr Watts part.

"Have a good day."

George gives Mr Watts a hug then runs for the bus. A few more kids get on then the bus drives away.

"I think George has turned out to be a fine young man," Mr Watts says aloud to himself. He goes inside to prepare for teaching his summer class soon.

Chapter 11
A Weekend Trip

Thursday, June 4th 1964
Summer school was less than a week away and George could
hardly wait. He was always busy; mowing lawns, doing odd jobs
around the house, reading or tinkering on projects in the garage.
The scout troop was planning an early trip to the boy scout camp in
Greenbrier county. They had planned this as a pioneering trip. No
eating at the dining hall or other conveniences, just roughing it by
whatever they can carry on their backs.
So that day they set off in the bus loaned to them by the church. By
6 pm they finally arrived at Buckskin Council's Dilly's Mill just on
the other side of the small town of Marlington, WV. Mr Ritchie
parked the church bus on the gravel parking lot. All the scouts
swung packs up on their backs and headed out to the pioneer camp
area. Passing the lake, George asked, "Mr Ritchie, will we be doing
any swimming here?"
"I think it could be arranged."
George moved over closer to the scoutmaster. "Mr Ritchie? I never
been swimming before, sir."
"You don't know how to swim?"
"No, sir." George's heart was sinking.
"Well, George, if we go swimming let's see what you can do then
we'll take it from there."
"Okay, Mr Ritchie." But George still felt a little embarrassed.
They got up to the camp site and set up the tents for shelter and
sleeping; four tents for sleeping and four scouts to a tent. Another
tent was set up mainly as a kitchen and eating area but at other
times would be used for crafts and projects. The stillness of the
night at dusk was incredible; no sounds of cars going by, people
walking down the street, church bells ringing or trains going by.
Nothing like that. Off in the distance an owl was calling, then
another, as if they were talking to each other. Then it was still for a
moment. George and the others turned in for the night, listening to
the distant sounds of nature. Then, starting off like the sound of a

whistle, came a loud noise just outside the tents. Then the strange sound came again, "whip-poor-will, whip-poor-will, whip-poor-will"

"What's that outside?" George asked.

"That's a bird. Listen to the sound it makes," David, the patrol leader, said.

A moment of silence then, "whip-poor-will, whip-poor-will, whip-poor-will"

"A whip-poor-will?" George commented.

"Yep," from David.

After the longest time of listening, George fell asleep.

Friday, June 5th 1964

Most of the time George wakes up with the sun. But this morning he seemed to have slept in. One of the other scouts came and woke him up. "George, wake up! The day is starting."

George looks out the tent flap and the sun wasn't even up yet and the crickets were still singing. "The sun ain't even up yet," George complained.

"Yes, but we are, George. We got only two and a half days so we have to make the most of it. Come on George, you'll not regret it."

George starts to drag himself out of his sleeping bag, somewhat grumbling. Coming up to the tent for the kitchen, George starts assisting the older boys at getting breakfast. Everybody ate and the kitchen was put back in order. Food cooked over an open campfire tasted great, just something about the flavor.

Next thing on the list was heading down to the archery range, something most of them wanted and needed. So that meant heading down the trail past the lake and down to the face of the dam.

First, they met the archery instructor, Mike. He gave the rules for safety then went over the basics. Most of them did well. Some, including George, took a while to get the arrow near the target, and longer to hit the target. However, none of them quit till their goal was done. Every one of them earned their archery merit badge that morning.

A lifeguard and instructors had arrived so they all rushed over to

the roped off area for swimming at the lake. George had never ever even been near a lake. He was as nervous as he could be. The instructor was speaking about coming into the lake swimming area. "When you come in, take your name tag and move it to the 'In' section on the board." He also demonstrates. "And when you leave, move your tag to the 'Out' section on the board. This way we will know who's out and in. When you hear this whistle," (he blows it) "everyone out of the water. Does EVERYBODY have a partner?" All the scouts held up their hands, holding their swimming partner's hand.
"Very good. Who doesn't know how to swim whatsoever?"
George slowly starts to raise his hand, but not too high.
"Was your name George?"
"Yes, sir," George said in a muffled voice. "Never been swimming, ever."
"George, it's alright. There's a first time for everything."
One of the other instructors came up to George and his partner.
"Hi guys, my name is Joe. So you never been swimming?"
George doesn't say a word but shakes his head, no.
"Okay then, we'll start in the beginner section."
The beginner section was easy. George's partner was quite good at swimming as he'd been before. He turned out to be an excellent partner to be with. One time George started to panic but he was right there to help. After a while, George was more comfortable in the water and was moved to the deeper section which was about four foot deep. George, with the help of his partner, had his swimming strokes quite well. There was just one problem George seemed to have; he could make distance fine but he'd seem to slowly sink until he'd finally have to come up for air. George would try again and again. After a while George was getting too tired. Then the whistle blew for everyone to get out of the water. They had been at it until almost noon so the instructor said it was time to break for lunch. George didn't want to stop. He wanted to keep trying until he could do it!
"George, you can come back after 4 o'clock. You're trying too hard."

So all of them headed back up to the campground. As they passed the lake George looked back at it, thinking, 'I'm going to conquer that lake yet.' All of them get back to the campground where they make lunch of hamburgers with chips and drinks.

"Hey, George!" called out the patrol leader. "You're doing fine. You're just trying too hard. Relax. You'll do it."

George thought it was great to have people believe in you. He wasn't going to quit.

After lunch a nature hike had been planned for around Dilly's Mill. The only items taken were: canteen, a few snacks, camera and binoculars. Many kinds of birds, mammals, snakes, lizards and many insects were seen. George and a few of the others brought guide books for identifying most of the wildlife. They just didn't have a clue what some creatures were. Cameras were very handy. Many things done on the hike applied to the following merit badges: insect, wildlife management, reptile study, bird study and hiking. George achieved the bird study merit badge.

About 4 o'clock the instructors and lifeguard were back at the lake, and so was George. Some of the others came just for the fun of swimming. But George came to learn swimming. Time after time he would launch out in the water, arms and legs trying to swim. George realized he could float, but when trying to swim he'd still begin to sink. About an hour and a half later he was starting to get the hang of it. The instructor checked him off as finally earning his merit badge for swimming. With that accomplished George went on to canoeing. Since the swimming had just been done, it was applied to the requirements for canoeing. This was a breeze. When it was starting to get dark, all canoes had to report back in and George earned the canoeing merit badge.

They all headed back to camp. George felt very pleased with himself for having learned to swim. Back home there were no swimming pools or lakes to swim in. All they had was the Ohio river. No way was he going to swim in that chemical infested river. It was just too polluted.

Everybody met back at camp. Some of the others had started making supper of baked beans and cornbread. Later that night, by the camp fire, the time was used for storytelling.

"George, did you really travel back in time?"

"Yep, I sure did. First time scared the heck out of me as I didn't know what had happened."

"Where'd you go?"

"A place called Fort Randolph. Today it's in a place called Point Pleasant. I was in the room where Chief Cornstalk was killed. You know of his curse? It's said that the land wouldn't be prosperous and evil spirits would haunt."

"Aw, you're making this up," someone else said.

David, the patrol leader, said, "I heard of an Indian bride that was captured by travelers. She was the prettiest of all. But the Indian warrior wasn't going to let the travelers take his bride without a fight. So he got all the others to mount an all out attack. The tribe wiped out all the white men. But before the attack, they hid the Indian bride out in the wilderness. So the brave Indian warrior mounted his horse to go and search for the bride he loved so much. To this day he still searches for her. All over this countryside you can see highway signs saying, watch out for Falling Rock."

A moment of silence follows, then all the scouts burst out laughing at the joke.

Saturday, June 6th 1964

Another sunny morning came. Well, as soon as the sun came up. This time George was up, and they were on the ball. After breakfast, activities included rifle range, geology and more swimming then lunch followed by another nature hike and back in time to make supper before the bonfire. Later that night the sky was clear to do stargazing for astronomy merit badge. No city lights to drown out the stars. It was like you could reach up and pick one.

Sunday, June 7th 1964

It was their last day at camp. It was a bit hectic since camp was only for the weekend. But all good things come to an end. All the younger scouts had earned the swimming merit badge, archery, rifle, cooking, and bird study badges. They had also started on camping, insect life, reptile study and wildlife management merit badges.

The church bell down by the lake was ringing and many were making their way there. It wasn't only the scouts from Chapman Grove who had been there that weekend, but a few other scouts from various troops were there preparing the campground for the regular summer camp season.

So they made it to church by the lake on time. Some fellow they'd never seen before gave a message that was very short indeed. Was this for real or what, George thought. Why, it took longer to walk down to church than the message lasted! George felt like he left the service hungry.

David announced, "Patrol, listen up. We need to break down camp and get everything stacked next to the trail. Then let's walk the whole area, and then some, to make sure not a scrap of trash remains. Even if it's not our trash, pick it up. Let's leave the place better than when we got here."

After all this was done the patrol slung their packs on and started hiking down to the church bus for the long journey home.

When they reached Chapman Grove some of the boys' parents were there, having driven up to the church to give them a ride home. Mr Watts was there but he had walked.

"Welcome home, George. You smell a campfire somewhere?"

George sniffs the air and says, "I don't smell anything, sir."

Mr Watts chuckles a little as George gives him a puzzled look.

Monday, June 8th 1964

In the morning Mr Watts had to wake George. He'd had a productive weekend of learning and it was enjoyable too.

"GEORGE, WAKE UP!" Mr Watts had to shout for the first time ever to wake George. "George, you had a good weekend but the bus for the votech will be leaving soon. Come on, breakfast is ready."

George gets out of bed, has breakfast, tells Mr Watts bye, sorry to oversleep, and rushes out the door. He gets on the bus at the high school just in time.

George gets in the door of the votech school. It's a new term but he'd been there last term so he has an idea where the classrooms are.

"Students, I'm your electronics teacher, Mr Absher. In the next forty days, if you apply yourself and work hard, you can do anything in this class that you set your mind to."

Mr Absher hands out the text books for the class and they begin lessons. There seemed to be a lot of math needed for electronics. So this was a cinch for George. The teacher gave them Chapter One in the text book to read and then the questions at the end. So the class was mostly silent for that ninety minute task until break time. But forty minutes later George takes his paper up to Mr Absher's desk and hands it in.

"Are you sure, you still have lots of time till break."

"I'm done, sir. Can I do the next chapter?"

The teacher looks over his paper and sees he's got a grasp of this subject. "Yes, you may do Chapter Two."

George turns and goes back to his desk, smiling. This time he was a little bit slower getting through.

Then the bell rang for break. Lots of them started charging out the door, hurrying as the break was only twenty minutes. Not much time for anything but bathroom, drinks and chips.

After break, the class started getting down to the business of hands on electronics until the end of that subject period.

Chapter 12
FIRE!

Wednesday, June 10th 1964
The day went well in votech school and now George was back at home. But trouble was brewing in Chapman Grove. A group bent on causing mischief had been filtering down from the larger towns, and residents were getting unsettled.
It started out as what seemed to be silly little pranks; trash cans turned over, making street lights turn off with a spotlight, detour signs changed to make traffic go down side roads, but nothing really serious.

Saturday, June 20th 1964
The biggest birthday celebration Chapman Grove ever knew, came on this day. Many went up to Independence Hall at Wheeling. Yes, West Virginia was a hundred and one years old today. Activities for the day's celebrations in Chapman Grove included music, carnival rides, reenactors, and various food stands. It was just a grand old time.

Monday, June 22nd 1964
Monday was trash pickup day in Chapman Grove. Many of the residents either put the trash out the night before or in the morning, to be collected. Most folks do this then head off to work. Some of the kids head out to summer school or summer jobs. Most folks were gone for the day, working or shopping. When the trash truck came by to collect, here is what they mostly found: trash strung out on back streets, sometimes set on fire. Other times the trash had been set on fire in the trash can itself, a total of some hundred in all. The fire department shrugged it off as the actions of some kids with nothing better to do than play pranks during their summer break. However, since this was still odd for Chapman Grove it was reported to the sheriff and he reported it to the fire marshal, who did nothing.

Saturday, July 4th 1964

Chapman Grove had a grand scale Fourth of July celebration going on. All day long, in the huge field behind the McKees' house, was food, music, hay wagon rides, more food, games, a ferris wheel, merry go round and more food. About ninety percent of the town was there. It's the biggest event of the year, starting out with a marching band from the high school parading through town, veterans marching down the street, other civic groups doing the same, and each group displaying banners. The parade ended at the fairgrounds. All events were free for the community to enjoy. George, Susan and their friends were all hanging out together playing the games, riding the rides and eating the food which was about the only thing not free. But that was alright for they had saved up, looking forward to this event.

Later that night a fantastic fireworks show would light up the sky. It would be seen for miles. So everybody found a good spot when it was near show time. A sudden **BOOM** was heard throughout the whole Ohio river valley, startling Susan who grabbed hold of George's arm. Then the real show began; shooting rockets, spiraling streamers, star bursts and others they didn't know what to call, in a rainbow of colors. This went on for at least twenty minutes.

People were mesmerized until the fire engines started pulling out to go on a fire call. Some turned to watch as they pulled out, to see which way they were going. To the south was a huge fire-red glow. "Hey, look everybody! What's that burning?" someone cried out. Whatever was burning, it was BIG. Big really wasn't the right word for it. Many of the fair goers started getting in their cars and heading to where the flames were coming from, like moths heading to the light. As they got closer they could see it was the lumber mill, fully engulfed in flames.

The brave volunteer firefighters had their hands full with this fire. All the chief could direct the men to do, was to attempt to protect the exposures of the nearby homes. The chief called Glen Grove Volunteer Fire Department from the south, and Ben Dale from the north, for assistance. Minutes seemed like hours but Ben Dale got there super fast. They must have been ready for prompt action, back at the firehouse.

"Ben Dale engine company, this is Chief Jones of Chapman Grove Fire Department. Can you all catch the hydrant at the intersection of Route 2 and Twelfth Street, lay a supply line up behind those houses and protect them best you can. We've done the same."

"Roger, Chief. We got your back door." Seconds later, here came Glen Dale.

"Glen Grove, can you lay us another supply line from Garfield and Twelfth Street?"

"We're on it now, Chief."

"Chief to dispatch, call the railroad and tell them the situation, hoses across the track."

"Acknowledged."

It was all the three engine companies could do to protect the homes. Some homes were scorched but with no further damage. Many of the residents were out there too, supplying food and drinks to the brave firefighters that had worked throughout the night. The fire was still burning, deep in the lumber mill. However, the danger had been beaten back to within the mill boundaries. It would be days before the fire would be out and it would be possible to begin an investigation in order to determine the exact cause of the fire. Residents and the firefighters packed up all the hoses which were lying out like huge snakes all over the road. It seemed as if there were miles of hose that would never be folded back onto the fire engines, but at last it was done. This fire would be a terrible blow for so many residents whose jobs were now lost along with the loss of the lumber mill which had been there for what felt like forever.

Chapter 13
A New Ship

Friday, July 31ˢᵗ 1964
The last day of summer school arrived and it was well worth it, not only from what he learned but because he applied it to the time machine. It was ready for its maiden voyage into time. George had added all the hoots and whistles he could think of.
The top and bottom were round. Eight struts came down from the top to a center shelf in one inverted V of an octagon shape then came down to the base in the same V pattern. This made the whole structure very flexible and strong; press on one part and other sections pressed back. In the back was the door, hydraulically operated. The inside and outside wall, including the framework, was constructed of a strong aluminum; the best that could be found. Inside and between the wall struts were housed all the electronics. Two seats mounted inside would make the ride the most comfortable one could enjoy. The right seat was for the pilot, left seat the co-pilot. The top half gave a clear view through the plexiglass windows. And yes, it also included seat belts. All of this was built for less than four hundred dollars; money earned from mowing lawns, delivering groceries and doing odd jobs.
But a decision had to be made. Where should they go? George thought about it. Should they go into the future and see what happens or explore history?
"MR WATTS!"
"Yes, George, you hollered?"
"I'm at a dilemma. Should we go into the future or the past? I have no idea what range we have now. It might not get off the ground, but then it could take us clean around the world."
"In eighty days?"
"Huh?"
"That was a joke, George. Jules Verne wrote 'Around the World in 80 Days.' I'm surprised you've not read that book yet. I thought you'd read every book in the library."
"That one slipped past me. Is it in the quantum engineering

section?"

"No, I don't think..." Mr Watts pauses for a second, "George, you ever read just for fun? Jules Verne wrote stories. This one was about traveling around the world in eighty days so he could marry Glenda May. He meets all kinds of people during his journey."

"OH, a love story."

"Not really, George, it just has a little bit of romance in it."

"I'm not sure I get you, sir."

"You will when you read it, maybe when you're a bit older. But for now, whereabouts do you want to go? No place dangerous, mind you. The judge would be very unhappy with me."

"How about you pick a place, sir. Your turn."

"Gee, I'm not sure. Any place without shooting."

Mr Watts and George climb into the new, well built craft, able to launch them into history. George glances at the clock before he writes down on a notepad their current date and time; Friday July 31st 1964, 14:28. George turns on the battery, gives the rotor a little spin then presses down on the start pedal. A needle on a gauge starts climbing, indicating how many rpm the motor is spinning. Then a second gauge started indicating how much power they had. George flipped a lever behind him and the back door closed. George and Mr Watts took their seats, putting on the seat belts. A green light came on.

"We're ready, sir."

"Remember I'm an old man, George. Go easy on me. You know how to drive this one?"

"I'll tell you in a minute, sir." George pulls up on a green lever to the left of his seat. The whole machine rises up and hits the ceiling in the garage. "Oops, sorry about that."

"George, the garage is old too."

The direction is controlled almost like a helicopter. George gently pushes the stick in his right hand forward a tiny bit. Moving forward went well until they started drifting sideways, knocking cans and other stuff off the shelf. George panics a little and moves the ship left, banging into the car. "Sorry, sir."

"I hope you get the hang of this soon. The car insurance might not cover being hit by time machines."

"Me too, sir."

The ship is slowly coaxed out into the open without any other incidents. "Where to, sir?

"Clarksburg, West Virginia!"

"And the date?"

"Let's head for the year 1779."

"Any reason for the selection?"

"Visit family."

George gives the ship more altitude, sets the compass for Clarksburg then tugs on the red lever and the ship's gone, faster than you can blink, into a spiraling vortex. Then, as fast as it took off, it came to a HALT!

Sometime in Fall of 1779

Hovering high above the trees, George and Mr Watts survey the land.

"Is this Clarksburg, sir?"

"It will be someday, George. Right now it's part of two other counties."

"So whereabouts are we in relation to our time?"

"We'll have to look around and see if we recognize landmarks, George. Try heading west."

George turns the ship a full about face until the compass is pointing west. A river appeared and George made the ship hover there.

"How about that, sir? This looks familiar."

"I think we're near to what will become Parkersburg. Well done, George. Go back east to where we were and that..."

Zoom, George takes the ship back. To say Mr Watts is a little dizzy would be an understatement.

"George, slow down for this old man."

"Sorry. So whereabouts are we?"

Mr Watts glances around. "Hmm, that stream looks right. The hills too. I think we're in the right place."

"So where's the family?"

"We'll have to circle around the area to find him."

"And who are we looking for?"

"Jesse Hughes.[4] Pioneer, scout, Indian fighter."

"Another Indian killer?"

"Yep, afraid so. When Jesse was ten years old, Indians killed his brother. From then on he swore to kill every Indian he could."

"Sounds very vengeful."

"Yep, but he is family. Not a word about who we are or where we came from, though. We have a lot of land to cover so let's make big gentle circles from this spot."

George started big slow circles from that location. Lots of wildlife could be seen from the air for most the day, but no sign of people. Then close to sunset, smoke was seen to the north of them.

"George, see if you can slowly creep up towards the source of the smoke."

"Yes, sir." George slowly inched his way up to the area. Up ahead they saw some settlers making camp.

"George, can you set her down over there behind the bushes?"

He turns the ship around and heads to hide behind the bushes.

"Is this good here? I don't think anyone saw us."

"This will do, George. No one saw us, I hope."

George secures the ship and the two of them head out.

"Mr Watts, I was thinking we're a little out of our time dressed like this. Maybe we should remember this next time."

"Maybe you're right, George."

The two of them keep walking until they come to a small clearing then Mr Watts hollers out, "HELLO!"

The people in the clearing stand up, looking at them. A few of them pick up rifles to be ready. George and Mr Watts slow their pace and Mr Watts raises his hand to wave. The settlers just stare at them, keeping their rifles at the ready.

"Hello!" he calls out again, waving.

"Strangers, you be lost?" a large man inquired.

"We're not sure. We're looking for a man named Jesse Hughes. Have you seen him?"

"Last I heard he was up at Prickett's Fort. But he might be heading down the West Fork, for home. You folks friends of his?"[9]

"No, we just heard of him from people talking to a David Morgan about the Stroud family that was tortured and killed. I'm Mike Watts and this is George."

"Yep, Jesse and a Captain White went after that bunch of savages. I never heard what happened then. That was seven years ago. Now if you two want to find Jesse you go this direction," he points past the Clarksburg courthouse. "Keep going till you get to a large stream. That should be the West Fork. If you see no sign he's been there, you can wait and he'll turn up. But I might suggest you keep moving. Anyway, at the West Fork head south till you come along a branch with a large cornfield; that will be Hacker's creek. The Hacker family lives there. If you find them, tell them I sent you looking for Jesse."

"I'm not sure I caught your name," Mr Watts said.

"John Simpson, you can call me Trapper John. Why you folks looking for him anyhow?"

"We want to write stories about people opening up the land and we been trying to catch up with him for weeks."

"You folks have some way to defend yourself?"

Mr Watts opens up his coat and pulls out two pistols. George's eyes get bugged out.

"Well, those will never do," Trapper John says.

"All we had."

"Here, you take this rifle, shot and powder. Took it off an Indian I shot, who was coming after me."

They thank Trapper John for the directions and the rifle then head out in the direction he pointed out. As soon as they were out of sight they headed for the time machine.

"Mr Watts? Were all Indians cold blooded killers?"

"No George, many of them were kind decent people that lived in harmony with nature. It wasn't till we came and started raping the land and stealing it that they started getting violent. Remember when Eddy Gulch was harassing you?"

"Yep."

"You finally punched his lights out and gave him a bloody nose. But that didn't mean you're a cold blooded killer."

"No, sir. I need to think about what you said. Well, here we are, back at the ship. Should we look around the West Fork river or head on to Hacker's creek?"

"Let's look around the West Fork, if nothing seen we'll head on to Hacker's creek."

"By the way sir, where on earth did you get those old guns?" Mr Watts points them at George, pulls the trigger and he gets squirted with water. "Heck's toy department."

They laugh as the two of them lift off and head for West Fork. It was very pretty up there with the leaves changing into their autumn colors. Just about then an arrow came shooting up in front of them.

"George, is this thing arrow proof?"

"I've never really tested it for that. Let's get out of here."

Then some more arrows came and cracked the side window as the ship sped off.

"That was too close, sir."

Then gunshots were heard. Looking down, they saw that on the ground some settlers were having a shootout with Indians.

"Careful George, don't get too close. In fact, how about back off some more."

George gains some more altitude and does as he's asked, backing off a short distance.

"Wonder who that was, shooting down there."

"Whoever it was, George, they chased the Indians clean over the hills. Follow them. But be careful."

"Yes, sir!"

The two of them race off in the direction they saw them heading. But it was no use. With them trying to keep a safe distance, not being seen, and dodging tree branches, George and Mr Watts lost sight of them.

"George, this is no good. Let's just go on to Hacker's creek and wait there."

"Right, sir. Eh, which way?"

"Turn right here...."

Zoom, went George. "Oops, sorry sir, I forgot."

"Yes George, gently."

Slowly and gently the two of them headed south. At a large flowing creek they started descending and looking around for signs of people. Nothing seen, they made their way upstream.

"Sure looks different without houses and roads."

"Yes sir, it does."

The two of them continued upstream until it seemed the creek was disappearing.

"I don't think anybody's up this way. Let's head back downstream."

"Right you are, sir."

 Turning around in mid-flight they start heading back downstream. After some time, a clearing way up ahead comes into view. It was getting late in the day. But they slowed down even more and descended until a good hiding place was found.

"Over there, George. That looks like a good landing spot. Just enough cover to hide the time machine but we'd still be able to find it. We can walk from here."

"Right!"

The two of them land and get out. George goes around to the side that was hit with an arrow. Stuck in the seal for the window was a broken off arrow head.

"Man, I just built this too. Lookie what they did. Cracked the new window and dented the frame."

"Aw George, I'm sorry that happened. Are we still safe for time travel?"

"I think so. But I guess no use crying over spilled milk. Let's see who we found."

The two of them walk some distance. Up ahead they could see a man working in a cornfield.

"HELLO!" Mr Watts called out.

The man, startled a little at first, looks up then waves his arm in friendship.

"Hello, we be looking for the Hughes farm. Are we heading the right way?" Mr Watts asks.

"Aye, you be heading the right way. If you keep following the stream their farm will be on the .... which Hughes?"

"Jesse."

"The first farm you come to across the creek is his daddy's place. Now if you keep going, Jesse and Grace Hughes' farm will be on this side of the creek. Why you folks lookin' for Jesse?"
Mr Watts explains, "I write stories for newspapers. Right now I was in this area and heard about Jesse Hughes the Indian fighter. These stories need to be told and preserved for generations to come before they're lost or not told right. Trapper John said Jesse lived down this way."
"You met Trapper John? Well, he sent you the right direction. But if you head the way I told ya you'll find the Hughes farms. But I'm not sure if Jesse is home. Grace should be home."
"I be thankin' you so much Mister er..."
"Hacker, John Hacker."
"I'm Mike Watts, and my son George."
They all shake hands then Mr Watts and George set off for the Hughes farms. As they walked, George was standing tall.
"You called me your son."
"Yes, I did. You're getting to be like a son to me so why not start announcing it to the world."
George just stands taller and smiles. In the distance a farm was visible. Out in the field was a man and a younger man picking corn faster than a storm.
"HELLO!" George shouted this time as they walked across a footbridge.
All the work stopped and the older man approached.
"Can I hep you folks?"
"Yes, you can. We be lookin' fer a Jesse Hughes," Mr Watts replied.
"Well, I be his pa. His place is just up the way a little bit more. But he's not home. Out escorting settlers to new homesteads. But the wife should be home with the younguns. This be my son Tom, he'll walk with ya. Can't never tell, Grace might take a potshot at strangers."
As they walked Tom asked, "You folks ain't from around here are ya? Talk funny."
"No, we came a long distance, to write stories."
"Y'all put words on paper? Don't sound like much work. And

people pay ya fer this?" He pronounced 'don't' as 'dud'n'.

"Yep, they sure do. Newspapers and book publishers."

"Only book we read is the Bible. That's the only book fer me."

"It's what we call the good book," comments Mr Watts.

"Us too," agreed Tom. "Well there ya be. That's Grace taking in the laundry."

Tom waves an arm at Grace, and Grace waves back.

"Y'all got it from here. Pa be waitin' fer me. Got lots more chores needin' done before dark."

Mr Watts, George and Tom Hacker shake hands and part company. As they approached Grace, Mr Watts put the rifle up to his shoulder with the butt up in the air. In those days, this was a sign it was unloaded, or so he hopes.

"Greetings, strangers. Who mite you be?" Grace spoke the dialect too.

"Hello, I'm Mike Watts and this is my boy, George. We came to visit with Jesse Hughes."

"Well, yer in the right place. But he ain't home at the moment. Don't know when he might be back. I'm Grace, his wife."

"Well ma'am, I'm pleased to make yer acquaintance. We're from Philadelphia. I write stories and send them to newspapers, book publishers and so forth. This is still a new country and these stories will be told fer generations to come."

"Well Mr Watts, have I got some stories fer ya. Let's have a seat out here till dark. It too nice a day to be inside."

"Right y'are, ma'am."

Just then some kids came around.

"Mr Watts, this here's my boy Jesse junior, and his older sisters Massie and Martha. They just love hearing about their pa. Now let me tell ya the first story I heard about Jesse."

As she began, George took out a notepad and pencil to start taking notes as the kids sat round listening to every word their ma said. She tells the first one and she blends into another without anyone ever noticing. She must have told hundreds of stories while they sat listening to every word. George, using the front and back of each page, took notes of all the stories. Night was then falling and the kids just couldn't stay awake much longer.

"Then yer pa went to sleep in a nice warm cabin," Grace finished her storytelling, seeing the kids were almost asleep.

Mr Watts and George looked around and even Jessie junior was sleepy.

"Get thee ready fer bed. I'll be in, in a minute. Mr Watts, yer welcome to stay in the hayloft of the barn."

"A hayloft? I ain't been in a nice hayloft since I was a wee lad on my pappy's farm in Lancaster. I would like that."

The two of them head to the barn, climb up in the hayloft and George takes a couple of apples out of a poke then hands one to Mr Watts.

"Mr Watts, what's happened to Jesse? Is he alright?"

"He's fine, George. Just a busy man escorting settlers to new frontiers. He'll live to the ripe old age of seventy nine. How much you got empty in that notebook?"

"Two and a half pages, sir."

"Oh dearie me. Oh no, that will never do now. Here's another notepad." Mr Watts hands George a notepad like those that secretaries use to take shorthand.[18]

"Thank you, sir."

"No, thank YOU, for writing all this down."

"Too bad Jesse wasn't here."

"Yes, but Grace is family also. Good night, George."

"Good night."

Next morning, still fall of 1779

That morning (or so they called it, the sun wasn't even showing) Grace Hughes had the whole family out tending the chickens, milking the cows, slopping the hogs and splitting firewood. Mr Watts and George got up and joined them.

"Sorry we overslept, Mrs Hughes, can we help?"

"Naw, we about finished here. Come have something to eat. The younguns will hep pickin' beans in the garden."

"Well, I know how to do that, we'll help. It's our thank you for the use of the barn and the stories."

"Then come on out to the garden when yer ready. We'll be out there."

The two of them got some corn pone and a quick drink then raced out to join the Hughes. They stayed close to Grace, talking as they worked.

"Mrs Hughes?" Mr Watts begins to dig a bit deeper into the Jesse Hughes legends.

"Please, call me Grace. Mrs Hughes is Jesse's ma."

"Grace, then. I just want to understand Jesse. Does he shoot all Indians?"

"Naw, it started out when he was a boy. See, Indians scalped his brother. Something just kept gnawing at him since then. He's a good man inside. He's just got a war with Shawnee. Not all Indians are bad. Like not all whites are good."

As they talked, Mr Watts kept on picking beans faster than a running jack rabbit. George did the same when he could but he wrote notes down too. Just then Grace grabs a rifle, pulls back the hammer and lets it go, BANG! The kids keep working like nothing happened. Grace puts the rifle down and walks to the edge of the clearing. What did she shoot? Was it an Indian? She reaches down and picks up a nice size turkey. Grace hands it to Massie.

"Here Massie, how about ya clean this fer supper. Yer pa be hungry when he gets back."

"When be that, ma?"

"Don't rightly know, child. As I was saying, Jesse a good man. Give ya the shirt off his back."

About mid-day the family took a break for corn pone, apples and cider.

"The land provides well fer us. Apples from the grove over there, Mr Chapman helped us plant."

"John Chapman?" George exclaimed. "We know him."

"How is Mr Chapman? Ain't seen him in donkey years."

"He's doing good. Last we saw him he was over by the Ohio river planting apple trees and seeds."

"That be him, sir. That man, short of the Lord, eats and sleeps apples. He's a folk hero in his day."

"Well Grace, we need to be getting on. What you told us about Jesse will be a fine story to come."

"Please remember, Jesse can be a tender hearted man."

"I think Jesse will be remembered till after his dying days. I'll try to paint a picture of the real man who his wife and children have grown to love."

The two of them depart, heading back to the time machine hidden out near John Hacker's place.

"George, you got a lot of notes written down?"

"Yes, and I'm getting an understanding about shooting. If someone came and shot you I would be terribly upset. Maybe even angry. I still have to think about it awhile."

They headed back the way they came, passing Thomas Hughes and their kids working out in the field. Waving at them, they waved back and Mr Hughes asked, "Y'all see Jesse yet?"

"No, but Grace told us stories till all hours of the night. Let us sleep in the hayloft and fed us good. She told us all we needed to know and then some," Mt Watts replied.

"Bet all them younguns sat around listening too."

"Yep, till they was falling asleep."

"That sounds like them. Didn't get a bit of their chores done did they?"

"We made up fer it, picked beans all morning while talking to Grace. She was a wealth of information. She ought to write them all down on paper."

"Maybe she will. Where y'all heading now?"

"Up ta Clarksburg. Send all our notes back ta Philly. Then head on ta Wheeling."

"Will ya be back this way again?"

"Maybe not. Got so much ta do, I think we need ta call in more writers. You folks living a good life here. People want ta read about it."

"Y'all have a good journey."

They passed the Hacker farm but no one was in sight. Continuing their walk until they were sure they were out of sight, they then hunted for the exact spot where they had left the time machine. It was well hidden in the brush.

"George, you sure it's here?"

"Yes, sir. See the way those trees are growing over there? That's my landmark."

About fifteen minutes later they finally find it.

"Gosh Mr Watts, I thought we'd never find it. Need a better way to hide or find it."

"George, I hope this is not poison ivy we hid it in."

"Me too. I get it something awful."

George opens the door and the two of them board the ship and take their seats.

"You enjoy yourself, sir?"

"Yes. Grace was my great-great-grandmother on my mom's side of the family. According to my dad."

"You ought to make a family tree on paper."

"I just might."

George had the motor picking up speed. As it started lifting off, he gave it a little more power. They cleared the top of the trees and George aimed it for home. "Ready for Chapman Grove, Mr Watts?"

"Let her rip, George."

Z O O M!

Chapter 14
The Prowler

Sunday, August 2ⁿᵈ 1964

Rain was pouring all night and into the morning at Chapman Grove but that never stops the Watts household from attending church. George was up and singing in the kitchen while making a hot breakfast.

"MR WATTS, BREAKFAST READY!"

"Sorry George, I was on the phone with Bonnie. You remember her? Anyway, someone dropped a baby girl off at the church and she now has her at the foster home. A crib is needed and her old man has a few. So after breakfast let's carry one down to the church."

"Why would anyone want to abandon a baby? That doesn't sound right."

"I know, George. It happens sometimes, so it's up to us to step in." The two of them eat up then get the crib that was left upstairs from last winter. They cover it up with a plastic trash bag then head out the door, crib in tow, to church where Bonnie will meet them. As they get to the front of the church, Bonnie is already there. Just then the rain ends.

"DAD, over here."

There in the church parking lot, with her car ready to take the crib back to the home, was Bonnie. "Oh Dad, thanks for the crib. I need it bad."

"Anything else you need?"

"Take the baby for an hour? She been crying all night."

"Sure, daughter. I know how to hold a baby," says Mr Watts loudly, above the cries of the baby.

Bonnie hands the little baby over, and she screams even louder. George comes over to look at her and she calms down a little.

"George? Would you like to hold her? Now put her head up on your arm like this to support her head."

The little girl stops the screaming completely.

Bonnie says, "George, I think she likes you. Would you like to watch her during church?"

"Yes, I would love to."

George wanders off into the church with one content baby that slept all though Sunday school and church service. But after church George handed the pretty little one back to Bonnie and...

"WAAAGHAA!" bawled the little one, screaming her lungs out.

"George, please hold her again," asked Bonnie, nearly in tears.

George takes her and she calms right down.

"George, can you come help me? You're the only one she wants."

"May I, Mr Watts?"

"Go ahead, George."

Susan comes out of the church. "George, have you another girl?" she says in a teasing voice.

"I think so! Would you like to hold her?"

Susan holds the little one.

"WAAAGHAA!"

"Oh George, what's wrong?" Susan looks worried.

George takes the baby back and, as before, she calms down and smiles.

"She'll not have anybody but George," Mr Watts says.

So George, Bonnie and baby make three, drive up to the foster home.

Monday, August 3rd 1964

It was morning and the baby had enjoyed a very nice sleep. George was getting ready for another school day. Bonnie gave George a ride to school, and as soon as he got out of the car the bawling began again, WAAAGHAA! Bonnie just waved George to go and catch his bus to votech. George walked off with a WAAAGHAA echoing in his mind.

George gets back from votech at noon to find that Bonnie is in the parking lot. George comes up and takes hold of the baby who is still bawling, then she calms right down.

"George, I don't know what gives with her. She'll not let anyone touch her but you."

"Did she sleep any today, Bonnie?"

"Yes, but when I try to feed her or pick her up, well you know."
Bonnie hands the baby bottle to George. He takes it and gives it to
the baby who accepts it, looking very happy. Moments later the bell
rings for class. The principal, Mr Biggarstaff, comes charging out
the door.

"GEORGE get to class! Bonnie Watts! Get that screaming brat
outta here. It has no business at a place of learning. Is that baby
George's? I knew all along he was no good."

"MR BIGGARSTAFF!" Bonnie screams. Then she adds with
emphasis, "Why do you have to be so hateful? You trying out for
the meanest man on the planet? Congratulations, you won! And, by
the way, George is NOT the father but he'd make a great one."

Mr Biggarstaff points for her to get out of there, then he stomps off
back into the school.

"Thank you, George." Bonnie looks at him gratefully, her attitude
completely changed.

"You're welcome, Bonnie. See you after school."

George turns and heads into class, having spent his lunchtime
feeding the little baby.

Later that day the bell rings for school to let out. Mr Watts and
George come out the door to find Bonnie holding a screaming
baby. George just takes the little one, knowing she'll calm down.
And she does.

"Bonnie, where did you park your car?" Mr Watts inquired.

"It's at your house. I thought maybe a walk would help. It didn't."

"Bonnie, if the sheriff hasn't found out yet who the mother is you
need to inform Judge Hanson about the baby."

"I've already phoned Aunt Mary. She said just keep her informed."

They reach the house and put the baby down in a crib for a nap.
They all then head for the kitchen. George raids the refrigerator for
a snack of pickled beets.

"Dad, what can I do with that little baby? She seems to hate
everyone but George." Just then Bonnie's eye catches slight
movement outside. "Dad! Who's that looking in the window?"

Outside there was some kid staring into the house. The three of
them go out and the kid takes off, running. George blasts off after

him.

"Dad, I don't like this. Who was that boy?"

"I don't know, daughter."

A few hours later George comes back all hot, sweaty and exhausted.

"Gosh, that kid can run fast. I lost him somewhere near Fourteenth Street. But he outran me big time."

"Go inside, George, and cool off. I reported this to the sheriff's office."

Thursday, August 6th 1963

Evening came and Bonnie and Mr Watts were out on the front porch, enjoying the cool breeze. George was inside, feeding the little baby. Then he comes out to enjoy the sun as it sets.

"Where's the baby, George?"

"I put her down in her crib, Bonnie. Boy, a baby can be a lot of work."

"Yes they can, George," Mr Watts agreed.

After a while Bonnie gets up to look in on the baby.

"Don't wake her, Bonnie. I just fed her," George said in a joking way.

"I'm just going to look and see that she's okay." Bonnie goes inside.

"What's going to become of that baby?"

"Well, if after a length of time the parents are never found, she'll live at Bonnie's foster home till adoption can be arranged."

"DAD, come quick!"

Both of them go charging in to see Bonnie crying and holding the baby. "Daddy the baby needs to go to the hospital, she might have scarlet fever or diphtheria." Bonnie cries uncontrollably. "Oh Daddy, why is the baby deserving this? She's a good baby."

"Burp," the baby says.

Mr Watts goes up to the baby and looks at her as Bonnie continues her wailing. **"Bonnie! Calm down.** She's not got scarlet fever or diphtheria."

"Burp," goes the baby again.

"How do you know, Dad?"

"'cause I'll bet George fed her my pickled sugar beets."
Bonnie takes a better look at her.
"Burp."
"It's pickled beet juice on her face, honey."
"Yes Bonnie, I let her taste one when she was watching me eat them. It's just the juice staining her face. I'm sorry," admits George, relieved.
"Bonnie? You hear the baby?" Dad interrupts Bonnie's thoughts.
"No..." her voice comes softly, her tone curious.
"She's not crying."
"No, she's not, is she? Wonder why," observes Bonnie with surprise on her face.
"She might feel safe in your arms, Bonnie," Mr Watts suggests.
"You feel safe in my arms, girl?"
"Burp," and a little laugh.
"You ready to come home with me?"
"Giggle."
Bonnie, holding the baby, starts heading for the door. George, who was sitting, gets a kiss on the top of his head as she passes him on her way out. "Thanks, George."
A few moments later Bonnie comes back. "Dad, there was that kid spying through the window again when I went out. He's gone now."
George says, "I'm not going to chase him. He's too fast for me."
"I'll just call Bob and tell him he showed up again," Mr Watts reassures them.
"Dad, I don't like this. It's creepy having people spying through windows like that."
"I know that, daughter, but if George can't catch him, who can?"
"Well, this little one and I are going home before he comes back."
"You want George to go with you for safety?"
"No Dad, I think this kid is long gone."

Sunday, August 9ᵗʰ 1964

It's a hot Sunday and being at church has its advantages. Inside, out of the sweltering sun, the ceiling fans make it seem cooler. But the humidity is really high so most folks stay inside by a fan, out on a porch or in a cool basement. After church, lots of kids enjoy a fire hydrant opened by the fire department. All the kids from the neighborhood are having a blast.

Later that day some of the kids started going home to get ready for evening service at church. All of them were soaked to the bone and had a great time. George got home only to find Mr Watts, the sheriff, Bonnie and even that speedy kid were there. He was sitting at the table, surrounded.

"So," George said, "you finally got caught didn't you? Well, serves you right, sneaking around scaring people, and me trying to catch you."

"George, shh," Mr Watts signals him to keep quiet.

"First off, you have a name?" the sheriff questions the boy.

"Jacob Hacker, Sheriff. You going to lock me away?"

"I'll ask the questions, Jacob Hacker. Whereabouts are you from?"

"Hacker's Creek."

"You trying to be funny?"

"NO SIR."

"Bob, there's Hackers in Hacker's Creek, West Virginia," Mr Watts informed him.

"That's true, Sheriff," George comments. "We been there recently I think, or was it a long time ago...."

"Oh, one of them time voyages. So, Jacob, why were you shoplifting down at the grocery store?"

"Because I was hungry."

"And why are you here in Chapman Grove?"

"I been searching for my mother. She left home to look for work when Dad died."

"How'd your dad die, Jacob?" Bonnie asks gently.

Jacob just shrugs his shoulders.

The sheriff continues, "So your name is?"

"Jacob Hacker."

"From?"

"Hacker's Creek."

"Street address?"

"Route 1, Box 879, Hacker's Creek Road."

"And the town or nearest city?"

"We're south of Fairmont in a place called Colfax."

"Oh good, now we're getting somewhere. So who did you stay with while your mother went to look for work?"

"Nobody. I took care of things while Mom was away. When food was getting scarce I started looking for her. She wouldn't leave me alone for weeks unless something happened. She drove for the town; she heard about a job. That's the direction I headed for. Nobody would help us there, not even the sheriff."

"So where did you set out for?"

"Moundsville."

"So you mean to say you walked all the way from Fairmont to Moundsville all by yourself?"

"No sir, my sister was with me."

"Well, first off, you missed Moundsville...."

"I know, she wasn't to be found there..."

"... and in the second place there was no girls hanging around you when you got caught."

"No, my sister is at the foster home."

"The only one in the foster home is a baby girl," Bonnie comments, realizing who he means.

"That's her!"

"Can you prove it?" the sheriff demands.

"She's got black hair and brown eyes. She has a birth mark on her right hip. Every time a stranger holds her she'll scream to the high heaven. She loves pickled vegetables more than baby food. And she loves to burp."

"That's her, Sheriff," Bonnie said, totally convinced.

"You going to lock me away now, Sheriff?"

"No, but I am going to put you in Bonnie's care till we can find your mother. I'm going to go check out that sheriff, see what gives to not help find a missing mother. So why did you abandon your sister on the doorstep of the baptist church?"

"I didn't totally abandon her. I was watching from a distance till someone found her. It was getting harder to get food for her so if she was cared for I could look for Mom faster. But I ain't found her yet."

"I'll start the search." The sheriff picks up his hand radio. "Sheriff to Kyra."

"Go ahead."

"Call all the hospitals and see if, in the last month, they've gotten any woman, maybe in her twenties or thirties, last name Hacker."

"All hospitals?"

"Yes. Start in Moundsville and work your way back to the Fairmont area. Also check up in the Wheeling area."

"You know how many that is?"

"Many. So get started. We need to reunite a baby and young man with their mother. Also put out an APB."

"Will do."

"Jacob, for now you stay with Bonnie and take care of your sister. I'll do some detective work myself and notify Judge Hanson. Maybe she'll have some suggestions."

Bonnie and Jacob start to leave for the foster home, Bonnie saying humorously, "Now, no teaching the baby how to burp. By the way what's her name?"

"Molly. Besides, she learned that on her own."

"My goodness, what kind of kids have we got these days?"

Mr Watts asks the sheriff, "Bob, what could have happened to Jacob Hacker's mother?"

"I'm not sure, Dad, but I'll not leave one stone unturned till I find out. I'd also like to have a word with that sheriff who couldn't be bothered."

Saturday, August 29th 1964

Helen came up that morning, from Charleston, investigating the whereabouts of any family of George's. Helen asks, "George, you have anything I can go on to find your mother? Anything at all?"

"All I have is a picture, and that nearly got burned in the fire. I'll go get it."

George leaps from the kitchen table and heads for his room. Seconds later he comes back with a dirty yellow four by five picture frame with a somewhat faded picture of a pretty young lady, and hands it to Helen. She looks at it then hands it to Dad. "Yes, I've seen it before."

"Dad, you don't remember her? Follow me."

They all get up from the kitchen table and head to the wall with all the pictures of the kids, except one is missing. Helen takes the picture and way up on the top row she hangs it in an empty spot. "Now do you remember her?"

Mr Watts stares at it, thinking hard, trying to remember.

Helen prompts him, "Leann? Leann Brown. Went to the college in Beckley. Always in trouble with Mr Biggarstaff. She tee-peed his whole office. That was so funny."

"Leann Thomas Brown? How you know it really was her that did that?" asked Mr Watts.

"Because I helped her carry the toilet paper that morning. I was wondering what she was planning till I saw it. Anyway, after high school she wanted to go to college. Beckley was the only one that would give her a chance. Then she met that guy that worked at Kaymoor, named Herbert. Anyway, they got married. Had one child named George. Herbert started in drinking, smoking then beating on her. She just barely escaped only to die in Statts Hospital from her injuries."

"How you know it was her that died?"

"I was there when she died, Dad." A few tears trickled down her face. "She begged me never to tell you. She thought you'd be ashamed of her. I knew she had a child but never found out where Herbert went when he left Kaymoor."[6]

"I loved all you kids. I could never be ashamed of any of you."

"Yes Dad, I know and I told her that."

"Where did she get buried?"

"At the old city cemetery between Charleston's west side and North Charleston. It's been my secret till now."

"No other kids? No grandparents, cousins, aunts or uncles?"

"None I could ever find, Dad. In a way, you're his grandfather."
"So, George, it looks like both your parents are gone. I see now it was the same Herbert, your dad, who died in the house fire. If you still want me, I want you."
George had stood there this whole time, sad and shocked to finally know the truth about his mom and his past. But he loves Mr Watts and would like to have a dad like him.
 "George? It's in your ballpark now." Helen's voice pulls his thoughts back to his present situation.
George, with tears in his eyes, replied, "I want to call you Dad. But I'd like to keep my name. Not change any of it. Kind of use to it."
"George, I'll draw up the petition and send it to Aunt Mary. Sorry, I mean Judge Hanson."

Monday, October 12th 1964
Early that morning was typical in the Watts kitchen with the aroma of bacon, eggs, sausage and toast. Just then, in through the back door burst some of the older Watts kids.
"KIDS!" Mr Watts shouted. "Why are you all here?"
"We came to welcome our new brother into the family. Rest of the family is outside," Josh announced.
"How many of the others came?"
"Except Barbara and Judy, who are still on active duty at who knows where, all of us plus their families."
George's mouth had dropped open and he was totally bug eyed.
"If anybody's hungry, they better rush in here and grab a snack 'cause it's time to go," called out Mr Watts.
Many of them grab biscuits, slice them, and put sausage or egg or both in the biscuits then rush out the door. That really cleaned off the table. It looked like a crowd going down the sidewalk. But as the Watts family crowd went on their way, it kept on getting bigger and bigger. George never knew the family was this big. Where were they all coming from, he thought. Then he saw Pastor Bess, Susan Hill and her parents, and even lots of church members and classmates. Was this the whole town? What gives?
Then they get to the courthouse and squeeze their way into Judge

Hanson's courtroom. It was very crowded indeed.

After a few moments, the bailiff comes in, staring, and his voice bellows out, "ALL RISE. This court is now in session. The honorable Judge Hanson in and for the family court of Marshall county for the state of West Virginia. You may be seated."

Judge Hanson, still standing, looks around her courtroom and says, "I'm pretty sure Mr Watts does not have this big a family. So if the immediate family would take the seats to my right and the rest of you find another place. PLEASE." What a mob to get sorted, Judge Hanson thought. She rolled her eyes and shook her head at the situation. "Miss Watts, I have your report on George and I see it dates back quite a while. You knew his mother?"

"Yes, Aunt Mary. Sorry, I mean Your Honor." Some of the crowd chuckled. "His mom and I were both adopted by my dad, Mike Watts. So you could say we are his family. But if it pleases the court, could we make it official?"

"I don't see why not. All your research, documents and paperwork seem in order. There seems to be the matter of a fifty dollar court fee."

Just then all the Watts kids held up a dollar each and a bunch of the townspeople held up cash too.

"Just fifty!" shouts the judge, smiling. She signs the petition and gives it to Mr McKee, the clerk.

George had sat there all this time in anticipation, smiling. He knew it would be a done deal.

"Okay George, you may go home with your family."

"Thanks, Aunt Mary."

She gives him a stern but indulgent look. The whole family gets up and takes their new brother home.

"George," Mr Watts speaks, "now that you're my son, if you want, I'm Dad."

"Yes sir, Dad. I like that."

"Also, the funds you've been getting each month will be ending. You're no longer a ward of the court or state. So whatever you have in the bank is yours. Spend it wisely."

"I think I have, with the bank's help."

"You have? How does it look? You need an allowance?"

"No sir," George takes the bank book out of his wallet and reads. "Six hundred and nine thousand, four hundred and forty three dollars and ninety two cents."

They keep walking, Mr Watts with a stunned look on his face. "Did I just hear you say $609,443?"

"And ninety two cents. You okay, Dad?"

"George, **I** might be inclined to ask **you** for an allowance, but I'm real proud of you. You handle your money very wisely."

"Really?"

"Yep, in the Bible, Mathew 25:15 I think it was, a man gave his servants money according to their abilities till he returned. The first one took the money and invested it and doubled his money."

"WOW!"

"The second servant did the same with the smaller sum he had been given."

"Good for him, for trying."

"But the third that received a little, took it and buried the money."

"Like a buried treasure?"

"Yes, but burying money in the ground doesn't do any good."

"I guess not, sir."

"Then the man came back. The first servant came and said, 'Master I have taken your money and invested it. I have more than doubled it.'"

"'Well done,' says the master?" George interrupts.

"Yes, he was very pleased and gave him a large reward. Then the second servant came. 'Master, here is your money plus a little bit more.' So he got a nice reward but not as much."

"So what about the third servant?"

"He came up and handed him the money he had and said, 'Master I was afraid and hid your money away. Now I bring it back to you.'"

"Sounds alright."

"Yes, but the master said, 'You wicked servant! You know that I harvest not where I have not sown, and gather where I have not scattered seed. You could have put it in a bank to make interest.' Then you know what the master did?"

George shakes his head, no.

"The master cast out the unprofitable servant into the outer darkness."

"Wow," George thought aloud, "so that's what I've done?"

"Yep, and I'm proud of you. But why did you think to invest your money?"

"I have things I want to do; go to college, start a business, have a family of my own."

"Yep, all that takes money."

Finally they reach home with his new brothers and sisters. There in the back yard, tables were set up with lots of food for a great big cookout, celebrating George being added to the family. Not only the Watts family were there but the community as well.

Tuesday, November 3rd 1964

It was election day in America and also in Chapman Grove. On the ballot for Chapman Grove were:

David Ripple or David Masters for Mayor
Bob Shamblin, Sheriff
Tom McKee or George Warner for City Clerk
Mary Hanson or Helen Goldman for Family Court Judge
Harry Wheeler, Judge
Erma Gulch, City Council
Ron Biggarstaff, City Council
Allen Miller or Jack Hall for Animal Control

Since the election poll was being held at the high school as it was the largest public building, no school that day. People were slowly coming in to the polls all day. Sometimes a few spurts of people would come. But it was a typical small town holding an election, not only for the country but for their town as well.

About 2 pm would you believe what hit the fan. Six of West Virginia's finest State Police quietly drove in. The Secretary of State got out of one car, came in and handed a warrant to the head of the election poll, saying, "I'm Jay Rockefeller, Secretary of State, and this is a warrant for my office to take charge of this election poll. Also for the arrest of David Masters, George Warner,

Helen Goldman, Erma Gulch, Ronald Biggarstaff and Jack Hall for election fraud with intent to overthrow government, vote buying, voter intimidation, arson, manslaughter, falsifying income taxes, renting out substandard houses. Officers, collect the rest of the people that you've been instructed to arrest."
Mrs Gulch yells, "This isn't over yet, Chapman Grove!"
"OH, yes it is, Erma Gulch," Jay announced. "We have so much evidence on all of you, court will just be a formality. You all know Mr Hill from the garage and Mr Lawson from the barber shop. Well, they really work out of my office. They been collecting information almost four years now."
Mr Hill and Mr Lawson come up in suits and ties.
"You see, they didn't even know each other was undercover here in Chapman Grove. So the evidence we've got about the plot to destroy this nice little town is more than enough to ensure that particular game is at its end."
About then a truck backs up, ready to take the big voting machines and drop off four other machines. Jay continues, "Officers, could you be so kind as to show these people the way to the local jail while these machines are picked up. Also, please go to each home and hand out these papers; the residents need to re-vote for honest candidates here and not worry about anything. We the people are in charge now. Sheriff Shamblin, thank you for so much assistance in this."
Sheriff Bob Shamblin just gives a sharp snappy salute.
On the new election ballot were:

David Ripple for Mayor

Bob Shamblin, Sheriff

Tom McKee for City Clerk

Mary Hanson for Family Court Judge

Harry Wheeler, Judge

Write-in candidate, City Council

Write-in candidate, City Council

Allen Miller for Animal Control

A little bit later one of the state troopers came back and told the truancy officer she wasn't able to catch Eddy Gulch.

"He must have seen us coming and took off. Pruntytown will have their hands full with this one."

About then Jacob says, "Pruntytown! That's where they wanted to send Molly and me."

The state trooper came up to him and asked, "And who are you?"

Trembling, out came the reply, "I'm Jacob Hacker, ma'am."

"Oh, we been searching for your mom. We found three women in hospitals matching your mother's description. They been in auto accidents and aren't able to speak right now. So you just hang tight at the foster home until we know something more."

"Thanks, officer. We're treated good here. Thank you very much."

So David Ripple was elected Mayor and Bob Shamblin, Sheriff. Tom McKee got City Clerk position. Mary Hanson for Family Court Judge and Harry Wheeler, circuit court Judge. And Allen Miller for Animal Control manager.

Write-in candidate for City Council was 542 for Mike Watts; 491 for Andy Brown; 280 for Clifford Bowman. So Mike Watts and Andy Brown won city council and Harry Wheeler, Animal Control.

Wednesday, November 4th 1964

All had heard what happened to the principal, Mr Biggarstaff. News travels fast in a small town like Chapman Grove. Just as the students were about to start for the day, the voice of the vice principal, Mr Sidebottom, came over the PA system.

"May I have your attention, please. This is Mr Sidebottom, your vice principal. As most of you have heard, Mr Biggarstaff is no longer employed with us."

Just then a roar of cheering students and teachers came thundering throughout the whole school. It lasted what seemed like forever.

"I would like to apply for the position as your new principal but..."

Then another roar came again throughout the school.

"AS I WAS GOING TO SAY, I would like to know what you all think. If you want me, I'd like to be your next principal."

With the cheering roar we would think Mr Sidebottom was honored by the school and applied for the position as Principal.

Monday, November 9th 1964

The whole school was called into the main auditorium that morning. Mr Sidebottom addressed them, "Good morning, everybody. In past years Chapman Grove High School has been, what you might say, at the bottom of the ladder. Our average test scores stink. When our school plays sports with other schools we'd do better by not showing up. The building and grounds are simply atrocious.

You might be thinking, that teacher never gave me an 'A.' No, they didn't. As of now everybody in the school has an 'A.' It will be up to YOU to hold on to it. Study hard. If you're having trouble in a subject, ask for help! Teachers, you are to help ALL your students. It will be a challenge, I know. I'll be helping too. If need be, students can tutor others. Study halls will be places where students will study. Now for extra activities: sports, band and any other events. I want to see the losing streak end. We are going to raise money for new sports equipment, uniforms and instruments to make us feel proud. Look out West Virginia, Chapman Grove is going to be on the move!

Now get out of here and show me what Chapman Grove is made of!"

The students head out of the auditorium, to go to class with a new sense of pride. Others went to the buses to head to votech.

Wednesday, January 27 1965

"Houston, this is Captain George. Doing test of all electronics."

"All seems a go of this first step to the moon. You're looking good here, Captain George, all circuits are green."

"Roger, Houston. But how can we go to the moon if we can't talk between a few buildings? You're breaking up here."

A few moment pass by. "Houston, we are good to go." Then the silence is broken with blood curdling screams, **"Houston, we're on fire, we're on fire. We can't get out."**

George wakes, nearly jumping out of bed onto the floor, trembling violently and out of breath. To say George was getting tired of that dream would be an understatement.

Saturday, April 3rd 1965
George's birthday was officially Thursday. But since it was a school day he elected to have it on Saturday. This way, many of the family and friends could enjoy the day. Some brought presents but George wanted to give rides to everybody over Chapman Grove in his time machine, staying in this time period of course. A nice gift to everyone else, he thought. All kinds of food was being served; hot dogs, hamburgers, baked beans, coleslaw, cake and ice cream. It was a beautiful day for flying too. No sooner than George would land in a set up landing zone and let his passengers disembark, he'd take on three more passengers. He could take two more than before because he had added two small fold down seats, one to the left and one to the right of the door. All got to have a ride that day so George offered to take anyone that wanted a second trip.
After about the fourth flight, George saw the sheriff waving his arms frantically. He zoomed by to show that he saw him. Bob then motioned George to head for home which he did instantly. George came up to the landing area about the same time as the sheriff pulled up in the driveway.
"Hi Sheriff, you want a ride too?"
Another person gets out of the sheriff's car. He was stuffy looking, with a suit and tie on in the warm weather. George then knew something was up.
"George, where's Dad?"
"I think he's in the house."
Bob, George and the man went in the house.
"DAD!"
"Bob, what are you doing here, and who's your friend?"
"I'm Charles Mallet, Federal Aviation Administration." He shows a picture ID. "I'm here to investigate reports of an unregistered aircraft flying over this area."
"Well, we haven't seen any but we'll be glad to keep a look out for it."
"Dad, he's referring to George's time machine."
"That's not an aircraft, it's a time machine."
"Yes Dad, I had this same conversation with Mr Mallet."

"Yes sir," Mr Mallet continued. "George's vehicle flies but it's an unregistered vehicle that's in this air space. Can I see George's pilot license?"

"I never knew I had to have one."

"Well, I need you and your father to come with me."

The four of them start heading out the door when a young boy comes running up to Mr Mallet and says, "GRANDPA, I'm so glad to see you! What you doing here?"

"Just working."

The little boy starts to look worried. "You're not arresting my friend and Mr Watts are you?" His little face looked like it was about to burst into tears.

No way could he disappoint a face like that. Mr Mallet started pondering in his heart how not to be a big bad villain to his grandson. "No, I guess not. I'm just here to inspect, is all." And he mumbled to himself, "Grand-kids can really get to your heart." They stop by the time machine and he takes out a notepad and starts taking notes. He climbs on top. He measures everything. He lies on the ground to inspect the underside. He taps at the windows. He goes inside. All this time he writes in the notepad. Then he comes back and says, "It's a very well built aircraft. But where is its propulsion? The motor, the propeller?"

So George showed Mr Mallet its power. Standing outside but reaching in, George raised a panel in the floor. "There you are, Mr Mallet."

Mr Mallet looked puzzled at what he saw. Under the well built floor was unbelievable; a system of electromagnets fixed on a rotating spoke and electromagnets in a fixed position. Underneath that was another system that looked exactly the same, except larger. Still looking puzzled, Mr Mallet asked, "What is it?"

"THAT is the magnetic rotor motor. I built the first one years ago as something to tinker with but it got ruined in a house fire. It was going to be in the science fair. So I built another one a little better."

"Is this it?"

"Oh no, it's in the garage running the lights in the house. Come on in and see."

The two of them go in the garage to see and hear a whirling motor running two generators.

"You did all this? It's brilliant."

"Heck, no. I just built the power. Lots of people helped me hook the generators up for the house."

"It's absolutely brilliant. I'm glad I got to meet you, George, and glad my grandson talked me into this."

"More like blackmailed you into it."

They laughed.

"Yes, they are good at that, George. Let's go back out to your creation. I want to have another look."

So they go back out, George grabbing a lantern. Every so often Mr Mallet asked a question like what's this do or how does that work.

"George, you know what time it is?" Mr Watts came up to those two who were acting like kids at Christmas time enjoying a new toy.

"Hi Dad. No, is it getting late?"

"I should say so, it's 10:30. We got church in the morning. Mr Mallet, you're welcome to spend the night here, sir. We have plenty of room and you're invited to come to church in the morning."

"Thank you, Mr Watts. I'll take you up on that. I need to call Mrs Mallet and tell her I'm spending the night here."

Sunday, April 4th 1965

That morning the sun came out to play. Mr Mallet had shared George's room. After being up late and then talking until they fell asleep, the two of them weren't too lively. In the kitchen, Mr Watts was making breakfast and singing.

"♪Good morning, ♪ good morning, ♪ it's fun to say good morning ♪ to you ♪ and you. Good morning, sleepy heads."

George and Mr Mallet came staggering out to the kitchen. Both could hardly get their eyes open. Yes, they both looked like they'd been up most of the night.

"Have a seat both of you. Mr Mallet, like a strong hot cup of coffee?"

He just nods his head as he tries to take a seat without falling.

"I could hear you two talking last night till 2am. George always enjoys company. Well now, after breakfast George and I will be going to church. If you'd still like to come with us, we'll be leaving in about forty five minutes."

"Yes, I would like that."

They all ate up breakfast of eggs, toast and sausage then went off to get ready for church and headed out the door.

Pastor Bess was at the main church door greeting everyone, shaking hands and chatting.

"Pastor, this is Charles Mallet with the FAA. He's a guest at our house. He's been inspecting George's time machine. They might not appear too lively. They were up all hours of the night chattering like you wouldn't believe."

"I know George and I'd believe it."

George scampers off to Sunday school class and the adults stay in the main worship area for their class. After class most of the kids came back for the regular service which lasted twenty to forty minutes. After service the folks just head out the church door to go home. Nothing is open on a Sunday in Chapman Grove.

"Pastor," Mr Watts says, "you're welcome to come to visit if you and Mrs Bess wants."

"I like that. I bet Mrs Bess would too. If we're free, we'll be up to your house soon."

"Hope to see ya then."

The three of them walk back to the house and the adults relax on the front porch, Mr Mallet admiring the view.

"Mr Watts, you all have a nice town here. When I first came here to investigate this UFO, I was on the verge of arresting the two of you. Glad I didn't. I would have never met so many good people. And to my grandson I'm still the greatest grandpa who ever lived. Until George makes the changes to his ship and gets his pilot license, he's grounded. Except for testing he must not go any higher than ten feet. Here, give this 'to do' list to George later. Have him call us when he's finished and ready to certify. Bet he'll have his license faster than you can shake a stick at it. He's been flying since the 18th century. So I'm not sure if that's a few time travel seconds

or almost a hundred years."
Mr Watts thinks about it for a second until Mr Mallet starts
laughing then Mr Watts realizes it's a joke.
"So what must we do to get his ship airworthy?"
"Well, first off, the plastic windows aren't good enough. Maybe go
with arrow proof. Can't tell when an Indian attack might happen."
"I know what you mean, Mr Mallet."
"And call me Charles."
"Charles, what else?"
"George could use some more guidance instruments."
"Like what?"
"Compass, altimeter, speedometer, artificial horizon gauge, but the
big thing he should invest in is a two way radio."
"He has a shortwave radio in his room."
"Yes, I saw that but it works on AC current and is kind of big for a
tiny ship. What kind of power does the ship have?"
"Well, George told me but it was over my head what he said. Then
he said it runs off the earth's magnetic waves. About all I think I
understood."
"He's a very bright young man."
"Yes, and very kind too. Will help anybody at the drop of a hat.
You know that was his birthday party yesterday? He put it on for
his friends."
"Yesterday was his birthday?"
"No, it was on the first. He had it Saturday so more could come and
enjoy."
"Yes, very kind young man. He needs to have a fenced off concrete
landing pad also."
"That can be arranged, Charles."
The two of them continued sitting out on the front porch, chatting
and waving at folks driving by. George brought out some snacks
for lunch. Later they were joined by Susan. They were all just
enjoying the day until church that night.

Friday, May 28th 1965
It was the last day of school. Most kids are pleased on the last day. But George is more interested in keeping busy, taking a summer class, working more or seeing Susan and his friends. At the school lunchroom George and Susan were talking about summer plans with other classmates. George had finally decided for a more advanced electronics class.

"So Susan, what's your summer plans? Like to do anything special?"

"George, next week Dad says we're moving back to Charleston. It's where his office is. His work here is done. Dad just hung on till I finished this school year." Tears were rolling down her face as she continued breaking the news to George. "Dad just told me this morning. The last school day dance is tonight and he said I can go since you asked him if you can take me."

"Then we'll make tonight a grand night. Pick you up at six? Then we can walk over together."

"That sounds nice."

That night, about five minutes till six, George knocks on the door of the Hills over in the shantytown. Mr Hill opens the door and invites George to come in and have a seat. The house looked run down but was kept clean. It was one of the Gulch's rental houses they took as part of being under cover.

"Susan will be ready soon. You know girls, they got to change three times before they're satisfied."

"I think she's pretty no matter what she wears."

"Hmm," Mr Hill said. "So George, what's your plans for this summer and when you graduate high school?"

"I been thinking about going on to college. Some colleges has been checking up on me. But I'm not sure what to take. I'd love to take everything needed to become a college teacher. Electronic engineering seems most likely."

"That's a good one to choose. I have a few friends that work at some of the universities. A Mr Morag at Georgia Tech. I can put in a good word for you, if you like."

"I'd like that, sir."

Just then Susan and her mom entered the room and George stood up. Susan was pretty as a picture and dressed like a queen.

"I'm ready, George."

George was admiring how pretty she was.

"George? You okay? I'm ready."

George walks up to Susan and gives her a corsage. Her mom helps pin it to her dress. Then the two of them walk out as her dad says,

"Have her home by 10:45, young man."

"Yes, sir."

The two of them walk, holding hands and talking.

"Susan, is this a permanent move?"

"I'm afraid so, George. Not unless Mr Rockefeller sends Dad somewhere else."

"Maybe I can come visit you. I have a sister now that works at the Capitol."

"That would be nice, George."

They finally get to the high school and go to the main auditorium where the dance was being held. The faculty started this year to put on dances for the students as a reward for making it through another school year, this time with improved scores throughout the whole school. Many were dancing to the music of a local band. Some were enjoying the punch being served. After the walk there, George and Susan enjoyed a glass of punch then mingled with other classmates. A little bit later they danced to the music, cheek to cheek.

"George, I'm going to miss you when I'm gone." Tears trickled down her face.

"Your family is great Susan, saving the town from corruption."

They just danced the night away. About 10:30 George starts taking Susan home. They get back to her house at 10:43. Dad, being the protective father, peeked out the window only to hear Mom say,

"She's home now. Come away from the window and leave the kids alone."

George and Susan sit on the porch swing, watching the moon go behind the hills across the river in Ohio. George kisses Susan goodnight and she kisses back.

184

Chapter 15
A Dying Town?

Monday, May 31ˢᵗ 1965

She's gone. Susan, her mom and dad left very early that morning. The old shantytown house was looking sad without someone living there. For the last four years it had been a home to a wonderful family. George had a great few years with Susan. Maybe in about a week he would go and visit her by staying with his sister Helen in Charleston. This would give them time to settle back in.

George then turned away from the shantytown house and headed back home. His dad was reading the local paper.

"Hi George," he said. "You see this in the paper? More families are moving out of Chapman Grove since the lumber mill burned to the ground. Seems they can't pay the rent. Anyway, the property is about to be yanked out from them because the taxes aren't paid. Lots of those old shanty houses need fixed up or torn down."

"Hmm. That's too bad, Dad."

"Anyway George, if something isn't done soon this town will die. Just become a wide place in the road."

"I'm going to step out, Dad. Walk down to the bank."

"Going to go count your money, are you?" Mr Watts laughs a little at his own comment.

George heads out down the street and goes into the bank. He walks over to Mrs Harper's desk to find her with a stressed look on her face. As she looks up to see him, some of the stress leaves her.

"Hi George, what can I do for you today?"

George just smiles and says, "We need to talk. You got the time? I think you'll like my idea."

George and Mrs Harper talked for a long time. Then she made a phone call. They talked more. More phone calls. Mrs Harper's secretary came by and took the notes to type up. Then the branch president came by with more documents. George and Mrs Harper had talked for hours. Then Mr Watts came into the bank looking for George.

"George, you still here?"

"Yes, Mr Watts. Your boy is still here. Have a seat. George has a great idea but he's still under age and we need your signature on this for his permission to do this project."

Mr Watts reads over the documents. "George, you know you can be getting in over your head on this?"

"Mr Watts, just before George came in another customer closed their account to move out of state. If this keeps up, this branch of the bank will have to close. George's idea could help. We've talked about the risks."

Mr Watts signs the permission then hands it back to Mrs Harper. They all shake hands, smiling, then the two of them head out the door.

"George, you think your plan might work?"

"I hope so. I've grown to love this little town."

"They love you too, George. By the way, Mr Sidebottom called. He wants you to contact him asap."

"Am I in trouble?"

"Not one bit. He would like you to start a math club. Then start helping the others to get their math grades up. He's dead serious about turning the school around to be number one. Or in the top ten in the state."

"Think he might still be there? Could stop on the way home."

"We could try," his dad says.

Just as they get to the school, Mr Sidebottom is heading out the door.

"George, my fine fellow! I was talking to your dad today. You be interested in starting a math club?"

"I like math, sir. But what's a math club? What would we do?"

"They're like any other club. They have gatherings, plan events. But I'd like to see them set up tutoring programs. Our ball players' grades are just barley passing. Think you could work this out in the summer?"

"I think so. Maybe set the club up to meet in the school library? Then you send the players our way, we'll see what we can do? Can we use the school library this summer?"

"You just tell me when and I'll have the key ready. What's your first

step?"
"I think I'll telephone a few of my friends that's good at math. Wow, I was just thinking. We hardly ever had clubs here before. I'd be interested in doing an electronics club too."
"Well then, George, get with it. Time's a wasting."
"Thank you, sir. Thank you very much."
"No, thank you George, for helping."
Mr Sidebottom was finished locking up the school for the day when Mr Watts said, "Mr. Sidebottom, would you and your wife like to come over for supper? Maybe you and George could talk some more about plans for the school."
"Thank you kindly, Mr Watts, but we've been invited down to my sister's and her family for supper."
"Well, maybe next time then."
"Yep, next time."

Thursday, June 3rd 1965
On Thursday night George and some of his friends were hanging out at the Dairy Queen® when George hit them with some ideas.
"A math club!" Ginger said, not believing it.
"Yes, a math club. Look at it this way; we got a great principal now and he's asking for our help."
"But a math club?" Brian commented.
"What would we do? Spout off numbers during meetings?" Ann remarked.
"No, silly. The first project is to help others improve their math scores. Mr Sidebottom said the ball players are just on the edge of failing. If any player fails, they can't play."
"Well, none of them is good enough to win anyway," Sally says caustically.
"Well nothing. Winning ball games is the coach's department. Ours would be keeping them on the team by helping them in math. Let's be team players for this school. Mr Sidebottom is asking for our help. All we can do is try. Anyone that doesn't think it's worth trying can leave now and the others are to not think anything less of you."

Two of the ten that had showed up to the meeting got up and left. George just thanked them for coming and invited them to come back anytime, they will be welcomed.

"Anybody know how to get started?"

The others just laughed. They got down to business. Wrote out a mission statement. Rules for the club. Then elected their officers. George was made President. Amber, Vice President. Ann, Secretary/Treasurer.

Monday, June 7th 1965

George and Mr. Watts went to the school. Mr Watts, to close out the books for his class for another year. George went to see Mr. Sidebottom. He stepped in the front office where Mrs Harless was typing away. She looks up and says be with him in a minute. She kept typing while George had a seat.

Use to be every time he was in the office it was because he was in trouble; not this time, he thought.

"George, follow me please," said Mrs Harless.

The two of them walk down an inner hallway to Mr Sidebottom's office. Mr Biggarstaff's office was right next to his but he was gone.

"Here are the contracts you wanted typed up, Richard. George is here to see you."

"Good, send him in," Mr Sidebottom responds with his usual cheerfulness and also with a note of great enthusiasm, anticipating this get together with such a fine young man as he knows George has become.

George comes right in and stands in front of his desk. On the wall are awards, plaques and photographs. On top of the bookshelf were tons of trophies.

"Have a seat, George. Take a load off your feet. So what brings you in here? School's out for the summer."

"This." George hands him the documents for the math club.

Mr. Sidebottom takes them and starts reading. Every now and then he goes hmm, hmm hmm. Then he picks up his pen and signs it.

"Approved. Mrs Harless!" She comes in. "Would you make three

copies of this and give one of the copies back to George."
"Yes, sir," she replies then leaves the room.
"Mr. Sidebottom, you win all these awards?"
"Some of them, George. Many was a team effort."
"One problem with our team is they're malnourished. They come to school without a breakfast. Some eat lunch of a sandwich and maybe an apple and water. This summer will be the same. And with work getting more scarce it's only going to get worse. They can't think on an empty stomach never mind play ball."
"You get the math club going and I'll investigate this."
"Sir, if you see what I say is true, I have some ideas that might help."

Monday, June 14th 1965

Mr Sidebottom was in the lunchroom chatting with many of the students while they were eating their lunch. Summer school had just started last week and Mr Sidebottom didn't like what he saw. Some students had purchased their lunch there but many others brought their own. Just like George had said, these kids were malnourished, and it wasn't confined to just the ball players. It was nothing that their parents did wrong; they just didn't have the money for a decent meal. He watched as many of the kids saved the wrappings and the tattered brown bag their lunch came in, to reuse. Then he got mad. Real mad. He was about to blow his top. He was madder than a wet hornet. He stomped off to the office.
"MRS HARLESS! Come in my office now. And bring your notepad."
She followed him into the office and closed the door. He could be heard talking on the phone. It sounded like the board of education he was speaking to, and getting transferred to different departments. That went on for what seemed like forever. Even with the double walls of Mr Sidebottom's office he could still be heard a long way down the hall.
"Mrs Harless!" She had been sitting there listening to every word and taking shorthand. "Take this letter. Address it to the board of education. Dear Sir, First paragraph. Further to my telephone call

this morning, during which I was redirected to every department before finally having a conversation with you, please note and consider the following. New paragraph. I described my concerns, as I had just come from the lunchroom where I told you I had witnessed the very obvious hunger, to the point of malnourishment, of many students. This is a horrible atrocity. New paragraph. How do you expect students to learn when they are thinking about an empty stomach? How could you people at the Board of Education be so heartless, voting yourselves a raise when students go hungry? Last paragraph. It is the responsibility of the Board of Education to address the dire situation of some of our poorer students and to put some kind of aid in place for them. Signed Richard Sidebottom, Principal, Chapman Grove High School. Type that up, Mrs Harless. ASAP. I want it out in yesterday's mail!"

"YES, SIR! RIGHT AWAY." Mrs Harless starts to hustle out the door with a big smile on her face.

"Mrs Harless?"

"Yes, sir?"

"What's happening out there in the yard?"

They look out his window and see a big, older student stopping younger ones as they enter the schoolyard.

"I'm not sure. My window doesn't face that way so I've never got to see."

"Call the sheriff." Mr Sidebottom heads out to investigate and confirm his suspicions of what is taking place. Before he could get to them, the big boy walks into another part of the school building. He follows, careful to remain undetected.

"Hey, kid. Nice shiny quarter you got there. Here, let me hold it for you so it be safe."

Mr Sidebottom walks up behind him and gives a few hard raps on the bully's shoulder.

"Hey dude, what's up?"

"You are."

Mr Sidebottom grabs him by the shirt collar and belt. Money falls out of his pockets all over the floor, mostly quarters. Mr Sidebottom comes up to the door, still holding on to the bully, and uses the big boy's head to open the door. More quarters come falling out of mister money bags' pockets. The sheriff is just pulling in as he throws the big bully out onto the sidewalk.

"Hey sheriff, you see what he did! He assaulted me."

"Come along, Brad. You can tell me all about it."

The sheriff slaps on the cuffs. More quarters fall out. The sheriff drives away. Mr Sidebottom starts picking up the quarters.

A few nearby kids help him. "Here's your money, Mr Sidebottom."

This gives him an idea. "It's not mine! It must be yours."

"No, sir."

He took the money into the office and put it in a big jar. There must have been at least twenty dollars.

"Where did that come from, Mr. Sidebottom?"

"Santa Claus."

Translation, Don't ask.

Tuesday, June 15th 1965

One morning Mr. Sidebottom was at the main entrance door. He directed everybody into the cafeteria. They would know what to do when they got there. As the students come in they are directed to the food serving area. The cooks just started handing out breakfast consisting of cereal with milk, toast and jelly, juice and an apple or orange.

Mr Sidebottom comes into the cafeteria. Many of the students are munching away but then start to think, Where did this food come from? Who paid for it?

"Mr Sidebottom," says a young girl. "I can't pay for this."

"It's already been paid for by your parents' tax dollars to run this school, honey. Kind of like leftovers. If we don't serve it up it will get thrown out. So eat up and enjoy before we have to toss it."

She smiles and accepts the answer.

George comes up behind Mr Sidebottom and whispers, "And how long are these leftovers going to last, sir?"

"Until I can think of something else, George."

"If the parents think this is welfare, they will be mad. They don't like beholding to no one."

"Keep this quiet and think of plan B for me, George."

Monday, June 28th 1965

Mr Sidebottom's scheme to feed the students has been going quite well. But he knew it was time for plan B. He had figured out which students could and could not afford breakfast and lunch. These past few weeks he had been paying for it himself. But he now starts on plan B. One at a time, he would call a student to his office and ask them if they would they like to work to pay for their breakfast and lunch.

"What kind of work you want me to do?" was the big question.

"Well, I want this school to always look great. Can you sweep the hallway after school each weekday?"

"You bet I can!"

"Then go get breakfast. I'll contact your parents and make sure it's alright with them."

"Yes, sir. Right away, sir." A young boy runs out the door, excited to have his first job ever.

Mrs Harless comes in. "Richard, just how many kids are you going to employ?"

"Until I can't think of any other chores. Tell the janitor he's got an easy summer ahead of him."

She just smiles and leaves the room.

Saturday July 3rd 1965

No money for fireworks this year, the town just didn't have it. The mayor took a drastic seventy five percent pay cut and was working part time up in Wheeling. City council members were volunteer jobs now. Animal control was still low paid. Sheriff was county paid.

"Dad, what's going to happen to this town?"

"If things don't shape up soon I think it will just become a wide place in the road."

"Let's see if Mr McKee would go in with us to have a Fourth of July party behind his house. Maybe it will pick the spirit of the town up."

"I hope so, George. I need some pick up too."

"YOU?"

"Yes, I've been here so long and it hurts to see the town like it is now. Kind of like a child or a pet dying. But you got a great idea. We can ask people to come just like last time. Some can bring music or food to share. Just have a big time. Put our worries in the Lord's hands. I'll phone everybody that still has a phone and you can run to everybody else's houses. Maybe Jacob up at the foster home can help."

"Great, Dad, we're on it." George shot out like a light.

The first thing Mr Watts did was call Mr McKee. "Tom? This is Mike. Let's plan a party for tomorrow after church."

Sunday, July 4th 1965

Church attendance was way down. Many that used to go there had moved away or had to take whatever work they could get. Sometimes it meant working on Sunday. Pastor Bess was way past retirement age so he gets a pension and social security from his full time job. From the church, he is paid ten percent of what is collected during service. At the end of today's service he makes an announcement.

"I got a phone call from Mr Watts yesterday about celebrating the Fourth of July behind the McKees' home. Everybody is welcome to attend. You can bring a covered dish, bowl or barrel of whatever you want to share. Others can bring in the entertainment of music or talent.

A few of the kids, while canvassing the neighborhood telling as many as they could, got a man to set up a hot air balloon to ride. This will be to tethered to the ground so you'll not just float away. See Chapman Grove from the air! Hay rides will also be given by Mr Bowman, a farmer in the area. Sounds like lots of good fun."

Church let out and many folks rushed home to get ready for all the fun. People were tired of the gloom of the town dying. Chapman Grove wasn't giving up without a fight.

Many came early to help get the grounds ready, set up tables or whatever else. A billowing ball of smoke came out of the McKees' grill. But people were arriving long before that. About a third of the town wasn't there anymore to celebrate with them this year. Maybe they would come back someday.

Then a surprise guest arrived. It was Charles Mallet from the FAA. He came because his grandson invited him.

"GRANDPA! You came! I love you." His little grandson put an arm lock on so tight he couldn't move anymore.

"Hey, little buddy. I wouldn't miss you for the world. I got good news for you too."

"What!"

"Your grandma and I are purchasing a house here in Chapman Grove. It seems for some reason the bank has some homes for sale. It was a deal we just couldn't pass up. Oh, by the way, your grandma is right over there."

The little guy shot off like greased lightning, nearly knocking over George, and did the same to his grandma as he had done to his grandpa, hugging the stuffing out of her. George just smiles to see such a happy kid and goes up to Mr. Mallet.

"Good evening, Mr Mallet. Come to join the fun?"

"Yep. Our grandson invited us. I also heard of the balloon rides. Just thought I'd make one trip do several things."

"Oh, really?"

"Yep. We just purchased a nice little house here. Was a great price too."

"Is that so," George said, smiling.

"After the bank does the paperwork, we will be moving nearer our grandson."

"Well, he'll be pleased."

"Also, I have something to hand you." Mr. Mallet hands him an envelope.

George looks puzzled. He's not flown since being grounded, just made the improvements he was told to do. George opens the envelope. Inside was his pilot license, subject to solo fight, AND certification for his ship, now designated XT-1.

"DAD! DAD, COME LOOK AT THIS! I GOT IT! I REALLY GOT IT!"

"What you got, George? It's not catching, is it? I can hear you clean across the yard."

"Look!"

Mr. Watts takes the paper and looks it over. Tears come to his eyes. "George, I'm so proud of you." Mr Watts was out of breath, maybe because he had run to see what was up. He was such a proud dad again. He gave George such a hug, George had a hard time breathing.

"Charles, would you like to stay with us tonight? Nobody's ever turned away."

"Mrs Mallet and I?"

"Always."

"Thank you, Mike. But I better go rescue Mrs Mallet from the grip of the grandson."

They smile.

"George, this was a good idea. A nice gathering."

"And Dad, did you hear they are moving to Chapman Grove? They purchased a house for sale here."

"Really!" The two of them share a knowing smile.

Tuesday, July 6th 1965

The Fourth of July fell on a Sunday so school was out on Monday. On Tuesday Mr Sidebottom was outside, putting up signs around the campus. They read, NOTICE Only faculty, students, school personnel and bus drivers permitted. All others must sign in at the office.

Students were walking by, going to class. "Good morning, Mr Sidebottom," they'd say, smiling.

He'd reply, "Good morning, kids."

The school had entrances in various parts of the building. The faculty couldn't guard all the doors from thugs that wanted to come in. So here's what they did: a notice was placed on each entrance door informing everybody that the first point of entry for all was the front entrance which must be used on their first visit. At each entrance where one or two classrooms were located, Mr. Sidebottom selected big students as part of the summer work program. They were each allocated a seat just inside each classroom, allowing easy views of anybody trying to come in by those doors, and they were instructed to challenge them. No thugs were permitted on the grounds ever again. In this way the students were provided with a safe environment in which to learn. Thugs started hearing that Chapman Grove High School was off limits. They were not welcomed.

Across the way, a moving van was going up to one of the newly remodeled houses. It was the Mallets moving in. George hoped more people would either move back or new people would come. It was a nice little town.

Chapter 16
The Wright Stuff

Friday, July 30th 1965

Summer school let out for another week. George wanted to go exploring this weekend. As George and his new dad were walking home, he mentioned it to him.

"Dad, not much is happening this summer. The most excitement is going to school."

"All work and no play makes Jack a dull boy, huh."

"Who's Jack?"

"That was just an expression. I got lots of school papers to grade this weekend."

"So, are you Jack now?"

"I'm afraid so. Why not welcome Mr Mallet to the neighborhood with a ride?"

"Can we go time traveling?"

"I think so. He seems a good man. Help him get away from the grip of his grandson for a bit."

"He sure loves his grandpa."

That evening after supper George went down to the Mallets' place. Mrs Mallet came to the door. "Why hello George, won't you come in and have a seat in the den. Mr Mallet is in there."

George goes in and finds Mr Mallet sitting, reading a text book.

"Hello, Mr Mallet. It's the weekend, time to put the school books away."

"Well, I would if I could George, but I'm teaching a class Monday and I got to have my facts right."

"What's the subject?"

"The early design and development of the Wright Flier."

"How to build the right airplane?"

"Not the right airplane, but the Wright brothers' flying machine."

"Oh, Wilbur and Orville Wright! Would you like firsthand information?"

"Not unless you can... wait a minute, you suggesting we go meet them?"

"Yep."

"I'll check with the wife and see." He jumps up to go to the kitchen, but at that same moment Mrs Mallet was coming out with cold drinks for them all. "Mary, George has invited me to go with him to visit the Wright brothers."

"Oh, really?"

"Thing is dear, his ship only holds two people comfortably."

"It will hold four, Mr Mallet," George reminds him.

"No, honey. You go and have a good time with your friend. I got a quilting circle in the morning at church."

"Mrs Mallet, we should be back within a few hours."

"That's fine, George. Whereabouts you two heading, Charles?"

"I think first stop will be Dayton, Ohio. Then North Carolina."

"And you say you'll be back in a few hours?" She looked puzzled.

"Yes ma'am."

She still looks puzzled.

"Mr Mallet...."

"When I'm not at work call me Charles."

"Charles, you want to pack a bag? Camera, couple of notepads. We could be gone days, to us."

"I thought you said be a few hours, honey?" Mrs Mallet looks at her husband for a sensible answer.

George explains as best he can, "It will be a few hours here to you, Mrs Mallet. Days to us."

"I'm not going to even ask. Have a good time, honey."

Charles packs a small backpack with a change of clothes and the other items they'd need, puts some apples and other foods on top.

"You think this will do, George?"

"I hope so. You can never tell what is needed on a journey."

Mr Mallet kisses his wife goodbye then the two of them head out the door. On the walk home George tells him what he and Mr Watts have learned about time travel, especially Rule 1 for any trip; never tell people in the past who you really are.

"How can we tell if we disrupt history?" asks Charles.

"I think we would be the only ones to know it. Ah, here we are. Come on in and let me pack something and tell Dad we're leaving.

Dad, I'm back! Mr Mallet, I mean Charles is going with me," George calls over his shoulder as he runs for his room to pack his bag.

"Hello, Charles. Whereabouts you all heading?"

"I believe head to North Carolina. About the year 1900," replies Charles.

"But the Wright brothers flew in 1903."

"Yes, but they developed gliders long before that. It will be good for the class I'm teaching Monday."

"You file a flight plan yet?"

"I was going to call it in, but not sure if it's needed."

"Phone's right over there. Help yourself."

"It will be long distance."

"That's fine."

Charles goes to the phone and dials the number. His side of the conversation ended like this:

"Hello? Hello? I think they hung up on me."

"Something wrong, Charles?"

"I was calling in our flight plan and right after I told them our ETA they hung up."

"Call them back."

"I will." Mr. Mallet dials the number again and says, "This is Charles Mallet, special agent of the FAA. I'd like to speak to the supervisor." A few minutes go by. "Hello, Phillip? This is Charles. I got a really weird flight plan to file. The aircraft is the XT1. Taking off from Chapman Grove. Huh? Yes, I know there's no airport runways here. This vehicle doesn't need a runway. Kind of like a hovercraft. Yeah... Huh huh. This the part that got me hung up on. Promise you'll not hang up. We'll be leaving in thirty minutes and get this, the ETA is, hold on to your hat, about 1900. No, not the time 19:00, the year. No, I not been dipping into the sauce. It's a new aircraft. Phillip! Just give me clearance. I mean it Phillip. Watch the radar and you'll see us take off and then disappear in flight. Fine! Thanks, Phillip."

"Charles, you all set?" asks Mr Watts.

"I hope so. Boys at the airport going to think I'm nuts."

"I'm packed and ready. You file our flight plan?" George asks, coming back with his bag packed.

"I hope so, George. Let's take off. Bye Mike, I think we'll be back soon."

"I understand."

George and Mr Mallet board the XT1 and stow their packs away.

"Now Charles, I push down on this foot starter for reverse time travel. It gets the rotor going. This gauge shows the rpm and this one shows power. The rest you know, as any plane has them. The rpm are up and we have full power. This black lever on my left will make us gain altitude. And the stick in front of me is direction and attitude control."

The XT1 rises higher above Chapman Grove.

"Control tower, this is the XT1." George smiles at Charles. This is the first flight since it's been rebuilt.

"XT1, this is control. You have clearance. I think."

"Roger, control." George moves the stick forward and twists it a little. They are now aimed for North Carolina, having decided that it would be best to go straight there.

"So, when do we leave?" asks Mr Mallet.

"We'll be there before we even leave. This white lever does it!"

"Huh?"

George pulls up on the white lever and they are gone!

1900, North Carolina

Then George lets go of the lever, stopping them at the point in time they were aiming for, and time ticks by at a normal pace once more.

"So, are we there yet?"

"I hope so, Charles."

"What you mean, you hope so. Are we or are we not?"

"We are over North Carolina. As to the exact time, I'm sure we're close. Time travel is more than rocket science."

"So, how do we tell if it's the right year? Go down and ask?"

"Something like that, but we got to sneak in. Can't have Charles and George first flight. It's got to be Wilbur and Orville, just like history planned it. So whereabouts is Kitty Hawk?"

"It's near the Atlantic coast."

So the two of them headed east in the ship to the Atlantic coast then turned north until a small coastal town appeared. George sits the XT1 just out of sight behind a weather battered barn that looked like it had not been used in years and was about ready to collapse.

"From here, Charles, we walk."

They get out and George shuts the door, showing Mr Mallet how it operates. Then they head for the little town that looks no bigger than a minute. The roads were nothing like those they knew back home, just muddy trails. People stared at them as they walked by.

"I think we're still a little out of time, Charles."

"I think you're right, George. But nothing we can do about it now. Let's head on over to that place over there. Looks like the blacksmith shop."

As they enter, Charles says, "Hello, I was wondering if we could get some directions."

"I look like a map to you? Git on out of here. I'm busy." The blacksmith spits on the hot iron then continues hammering it into shape.

"Thanks just the same." They turn and leave.

"Oh gosh, Charles, he was rude and nasty."

"We're not in Chapman Grove anymore."

"You said it!"

They continued on down the mid part of town. At the sheriff's office, the sheriff was out on the porch, sound asleep in a chair. At least he looked like a sheriff. Across from his office there was a building with Saloon on the front. On down the street, if you can call it that, was a store. A man was out in front, sweeping the wooden sidewalk.

"Hello," George greets him.

The man looks up and just walks back in.

"This is not a very friendly town, is it, George?"

Across the street was a building that looked like either a print shop, newspaper or both. They cross over and walk in. It was noisy. Then the noise stops just for a second, but long enough for Mr Mallet to holler, "Hello!"

The printer looks up and smiles, the first friendly face they've seen here. He stops the press, wipes his hands and walks over to the front desk. "Greetings, strangers. Can I help you?"

"Could you give us directions to Kitty Hawk and sell us a newspaper?"

"Directions are free. Paper's a nickel." Mr. Mallet hands him a nickel. "Now, Kitty Hawk is on the coast. You can't miss it. Right now you're near Chesapeake, Virginia. Head down the coast till you get to the sound. That's Albemurle sound. Follow the peninsula to its tip and you'll find the ferry that takes you right over to Kitty Hawk. But not much there. Why you folks heading there anyway?"

"Looking for some guys flying kites and gliders."

"OH, they might be at Kill Devil Hills. It's near the beach at Kitty Hawk."

"Thank you, sir. We should be able to find it now. You are very kind and helpful," Mr Mallet commented.

The two of them head towards the shore but as soon as they think they're out of sight they sneak off back to the XT1.

"Charles, why is it so many folks seemed snooty?"

"I don't know, George. Maybe they just don't trust strangers coming to town. What's the date on the paper?"

"October 3rd 1900."

"Hmm. They were testing gliders back then, or now I mean."

"Here's the XT1. Shall we go to 1903 or what?"

"Let's just fly down to Kitty Hawk and see what's happening."

George opens the door and the two of them climb aboard. Pushing down on the foot starter got the rotor going. Mr Mallet shut the door and they were off, faster this time, out to the coast and then turned south. Seconds later they sighted Kitty Hawk with a few people gathered there.

"George, be careful and don't be spotted."

"Yes, sir. We should be hard to see, being silver. But I'll set us down quickly behind that sand dune."

George went down a little too fast and hit the sandy beach quite hard, skidding to a stop.

"George, you need to work on your landing."

"Yes, but we can still walk away from it."

"Hmm. Let's just go see if we found Wilbur and Orville."

Walking around the sand dune then down the beach, they came upon the men. It had to be them. Who else would be flying a kite like a plane? As they get closer one of the men says, "Who are you all? And what you doing here?"

"Let me do the talking and play along with me, George. Sorry to bother you, gents. We were just walking along the beach and saw your incredible kite. It's so huge. Anyway, I'm Charles and this is my son, George. We're just enjoying the day. Wow, this is one big kite."

"Well, it's not a kite. It's a glider."

"Sorry, glider. I never saw one before. The boy and I love flying kites back home in West Virginia."

"Y'all from West Virginia? We just came here from Dayton, Ohio. Nice to meet you. I'm Orville and this here's my brother, Wilbur. We just come down here cause it's a nice steady wind to test our gliders."

"I heard about some people making gliders you can fly with," George mentions.

"Yes, a Frenchman did it, hanging onto the bottom. But we want to ride in it and steer it."

"WOW," came from George. "Did you all have a bicycle shop?"

"Why yes, we do," Orville says proudly.

"Dad, these are the men that built my bicycle. Grandpa bought it for Christmas. It's a grand bicycle, sirs."

"Well, thank you. Glad you like it," Wilbur mutters his words with a suspicious look.

Orville continues, "What we want to do is have a powered controlled flight. Not just hang on or glide. Someday we might go long distances. People will travel in airplanes high up in the sky, maybe even cross the Atlantic."

George and Charles stood there, mesmerized by the dreams coming from the Wright brothers.

Orville adds, "Our problem right now is getting enough people to pull the glider. We could throw a sandbag on the glider to simulate a person riding while we pull. But a sandbag or weight just lays there. It don't control it."

"Say, Mr Wright. How about have George fly the glider and us three pull it into the air? Just show George how to steer it."

"Hmm, what do you think, Wilbur?"

"Sounds like a plan, Orville. Can't hurt none to try."

"George, you see this control? It bends the wings to steer the glider. We call it wing warping. All you need to do is guide it while up in the air. Ready to try?"

"Ready when you are, Mr Wright."

The four of them drag the glider up a small sand dune. Way off in the distance, George could see the XT1. It was like it was just sitting there waiting on their return. Good thing Wilbur and Orville didn't notice it. How could they explain it?

"You all ready? Mr Mallet and George?"

George gives a thumbs up, smiling, and jumps in. Just think, he was going to get to fly for the Wright brothers. Just then George feels a hard yank as the men pull for all they're worth. The glider then caught a breeze and went soaring high in the air. At least twenty five feet. It was incredible. Then the front wing went up without warning, the glider stalled, then crashed backwards into the beach.

"OH, I'm sorry Mr Wright!"

"That's okay, kid. I done that a few times myself. You're a natural born flier. Want to try it again?"

"Yes sir!"

So they dragged it up to another sand dune and attempted another flight. As George flew, Wilbur and Orville took notes. He also saw Mr Mallet taking pictures. What a grand day this is. Then the wing dipped and the glider crashed.

"George, don't worry about crashing. You're getting better each time. Let's do it one more time. We have a dream that this will work."

"I'm ready to go for it."

One more time they dragged the glider up the sand dune. As before, the men pulled even harder to get George off the ground. Off George went like a bird flying, more than he ever knew could be done. Then he made a nice gentle banking turn and came back. If he had been high enough, George could have gone on a lot longer. But he came down in a somewhat controlled landing. George and the others cheered.

 "THAT WAS INCREDIBLE!" they all yelled in unison.
"George, Wilbur and I want to thank you in a special way." He hands him a paper. On it is written, We the undersigned do hereby certify that George knows how to fly. Wilbur & Orville Wright.
"And when we're ready to fly with an engine, please come and be our guest."
"We'll be here, sir." George and Mr Mallet walk off proudly, knowing how they helped history; gave it a push when it needed it. George opens the door, the two of them climb into the XT1 and start heading forward in time. Then George stops.

December, 13th 1903
"Why'd we stop, George? Don't tell me we're broken down."
"Nope. Look off in the distance."
It was the Wright brothers at it again.
"It's that day they make their famous flight. Look at all the photographers."
"Let's go watch."
So they get out and head for the scene. As they got closer, Wilbur and Orville waved. But they were very busy setting up.
"WOW, they used an idea I told them to try."
"What did you tell them, George? You got to be careful introducing information in the past."
"It's the weight on that tower, see it? That weight will help them get started."
"Hmm, that might be alright."
George and Mr Mallet secretly take cameras out of their jackets. As the weight drops, the airplane launches into the history books. George and Mr Mallet snap the cameras as fast as they can. When that flight was over, the Wrights set up for another flight going

even farther. The press swarmed around the Wrights. It was their claim to fame at this point. The two time voyagers wave, smiling, then walk away.

"Charles, what happened after this? Did they continue flying?"

"They went to France and showed up a Frenchman that tried to steal their thunder by claiming he flew before them. Let's go home. The year 1965 is waiting for us."

They reach the spot where the XT1 is hidden and climb in once more. George presses the forward pedal for the return trip. Then ZOOM!

Friday, July 30th 1965 (about 40 minutes later, local time)

"Back in Chapman Grove, Charles. Shall I drop you off at your house?"

Before he can answer, the radio interrupts, "Control tower to XT1. You still here? You've been given clearance. What's your delay?"

"Control tower, this is FAA agent Mallet, all is okay. Cancel flight plan. 10-36?"[12]

"Time is 20:32."

George drops Mr Mallet off at his home and then he lands the XT1, secures it, and goes into the house. Mr Watts is still reading the paper.

"DAD, I'm home."

"You just left!"

"Well, you know how it is. We're back now. I dropped Charles of at his house. He also certified my solo flight."

"He did?"

"Yep, after I flew for the Wright brothers and they gave me a pilot's license."

"Well done! I'm ready to turn in. Good night, George."

"Good night, Dad."

Chapter 17
The Longest Voyage Yet!

Monday, August 9ᵗʰ 1965

Summer school was over once again. Two weeks break had passed. Students were either walking to school, as George does with Mr Watts, or riding in on the bus or arriving by other means.

George was now in the eleventh grade. Junior year, some call it. It's also the year that colleges, universities and businesses start watching for that special student they want, rather like a bunch of wolves pouncing in a pack. George and his dad were just coming in and Mr Sidebottom was at the front door, greeting everybody.

"Good morning, Mr Sidebottom."

"Good morning, you two. You all ready to hit the books?"

"You bet, sir!"

"I'd like to see you sometime today, George, when you have a minute."

"I want to see you too, sir, about some ideas."

George hustled to his locker and put away what he didn't need, then raced back out to the school bus to go to votech.

"Slow down, George," Mr Sidebottom shouted. "The school will still be there when you get there. That boy is too full of energy, Mr Watts."

"Yes, he is. He's going places. And not just votech either."

This year at votech, George was taking the most advanced electronics class that could be offered. Of course, George excelled at all classes, anything he set his mind to. By this time, George only needed two points to graduate from high school. His schedule was like this:

Electronics in the morning at votech

Lunch upon returning

College math

English

Science

Wood Shop: Building for the Community

George gets back from votech, has a quick snack then heads to Mr

Sidebottom's office. Mrs Harless is at the front desk, selling lunch tickets. And some are picking up lunch/work tickets. George likes seeing the plan in action, providing for the students.
"Mrs Harless, is Mr Sidebottom in?"
"Yes, he's been waiting for you."
"Thank you, ma'am."
George walks down to the office where he finds him on the phone. He waves him to come in and have a seat while mumbling into the receiver, "Yes, huh huh, yes." This goes on for a few minutes. "I think that will work. I have a student with me now, got to go. Thank you, we'll talk again later." He hangs up and turns to greet his favorite young student. "George! We wanted to see each other, didn't we?"
"I believe so, sir. I'd like to see us set up a program to create more clubs in the school."
"Yes, we talked about this before, some time ago. How so?"
"If a group of students has an interest and wants to start a club I think it be great for the school spirit. Also, we need a school mascot. A symbol for the students."
"What kind of clubs?"
"How about French club, Spanish club; electronics club would be my favorite along with a science club. School spirit club, book club. Anything they want."
"Within reason of course, George."
"Yes, like we did for the math club. What they do is write out their mission statement, rules that they run by. Then get approval from you. And also have a teacher as a counselor. Kind of like guide them. Keep them out of trouble."
"So let's ask the student council, George."
After school, Mr Sidebottom, George, the student council and the faculty got together and discussed the proposition at a meeting. A minority among the teachers were outraged to be even asked to participate as counselors. Some felt it wasn't in their job description. Some said they'll think about it. But the rest said they'd like to try.

Tuesday, August 10th 1965

George didn't hear the announcements each morning because he was on the bus heading to votech. But when he got back, many students were in the lunch room, library or other places, planning club organizations. At the end of the school day, a line was forming into the office. Many students liked the idea of creating their own club. They just had to get Mr Sidebottom to approve the club description. The clubs that got instant approval included Electronics Club, Science and Technology Club, Book Club, Glee Club, Garden Club, French Club, Spanish Club and many others.

Friday, September 10th 1965

Friday was a faculty day. School was out to all students so teachers could go to meetings and in-service. But it only lasted until 2pm. So after that, the day was free.

George and his dad went shopping for food. The local store was what was called a mom and pop operation. This meant it was privately owned, most often by a couple. They carried food from local farmers, a variety of brands not carried by the bigger name stores up in Wheeling or down in Moundsville. As the two of them came up to the store, wagon in tow, a sign on the door caught their eye; NOTICE Absher's going out of business. Everything must go!

"Dad? Why are they going out of business? I thought they were doing good."

"I don't know, George. Let's go in and ask."

The two of them entered the store and saw that many of the shelves had been stripped bare of products; meats, breads, dairy products, sugar, some condiments. Other shelves still had lots of stock like flour, cornmeal, spices and other condiments.

"Dad, looks like most the stuff on our list is gone!"

"Yes, it does. We can get flour and make our own bread. Mrs Watts use to have the whole area smelling of fresh homemade bread. Mmm, it was so good. Get the huge bag of self-rising flour. You ever have cornbread?"

"I had it at scout camp, and something like cornbread. down at the McKee's gathering. Tasted pretty good. I liked it with the baked pork and beans."

"Get a huge bag of that cornmeal too."

The two of them gathered up all they could get on their list and a few things that were not on the list then headed to the checkout.

"George, do you think this is going to be enough?" Mr Watts said in a humorous way.

"Fifty two dollars and fifty nine cents, Mr Watts," the checker said.

"Maybe not, Dad. I could go back and get another shopping cart full."

"Hold on George, I was just kidding."

"Mr Watts, you might want to consider that. The store is shutting down totally. Nobody wants to move in to take our place."

"Well, our wagon won't hold more than one shopping cart load."

"Mr Absher, I'm sure, would let you borrow a cart today," the checker said helpfully.

"George, take the list and get what you can. Shall I wait for you?"

"Please. I like the company."

George went back and got two of everything; flour, cornmeal and anything else he thought they could want. He just went up and down each lane then came back to the checkout and whipped out his check book.

"George, starting your own store?" joked Mr Watts.

"I think I just bought the store."

"Hope we got room for it and can get it home."

The checker rang it up, "Seventy five, eighty."

George wrote the check and told the checker, "I'll have the cart back asap!"

"George, we have enough for a month of eating. After this we'll have to go out of town for food. What's in those boxes?" Mr Watts indicates a pile of boxes he's never bought from the store before.

"Pizza making kits, Dad."

"Hmm. Never made pizza before."

"Me neither, but I like it from the drive in."

Back up the street the two of them went, wagon and shopping cart banging on the bumpy sidewalk. Going round to the back door, which was the kitchen door, they unloaded the wagon first as it went right in without a problem. The shopping cart was too wide so they hand carried all their plunder into the kitchen.

"That ought to hold us out George, till we need to go to Wheeling."

"What about the other things on the list that we couldn't substitute? Bread, cheese, sugar and other things."

"Guess we'll have to go to Wheeling then. I remember Mrs Watts baking bread. The smell of her bread would come all the way down to the school."

Saturday, September 11ᵗʰ 1965

Mr Watts and George got up the next morning, ate breakfast and headed to Kroger's® in Wheeling.

"Dad, wonder if the McKees need anything? They don't drive well in big cities."

"I got a shopping list from them last night and a signed check from them. I'll get theirs and you can get ours."

Heading up WV State Route 2 they got to Kroger's in Wheeling. Finding a parking spot was atrocious. They went around and around that Kroger parking lot. Just when they'd see a spot opening up, someone would race in and grab it.

"George, we're not getting anything done today. I'm about ready to call it quits."

"Why don't I go in and shop for us. Bring it out to wherever you're at. Then go do the McKees' shopping and bring it out. Then leave."

"George, you got one level head on your shoulders."

George jumps out and runs into the store like a shot. Mr Watts almost had a parking spot but someone butted into it again. Then George came out and loaded his purchases into the car.

"Dad, I had to pay cash. They wanted an ID card. It's a madhouse in there today. I'll go in and get the McKees' things now. I might have enough to pay for it myself."

"Here's another twenty dollars, George. This should cover it."

Back in he went. Then another cartload came out with George just as Mr Watts got a parking spot.

"Perfect timing, Dad."

"Very funny, son. Let's hurry home with all this milk and stuff. It's

going to be a pain getting milk. We got to get just enough to get by a week. Any more and it would go bad."
"Didn't farmers use to have a milk route?"
"Yes, but government regulations ran those out of business. Let's go home."

Tuesday, November 9th 1965

George was walking around the shantytown that evening, looking at a few of the houses that had been fixed up nicely. They weren't selling off as fast as he hoped. But he was still managing. He walked over to the bank to chat with Mrs Harper about the homes.
"Mrs Harper, these are nice little homes. And I'm sure if more people knew about them they'd want them."
"I think a real estate agent needs to be called in George, or you're going to lose your shirt over this one. Shall I call someone in?"
"If you think that be best, Mrs Harper. You've done great for me so far."
"Good. I have a friend who knows a realtor. Let me get them in here tomorrow after you get out of school." She picks up the phone and dials a number. "Hello, Mary? This is Barbara. Oh, I'm doing fine. Say, listen, you know that realtor that sold your home? Can I have his number? No, it's bank business. Got a young man that needs to move some homes. Oh, thank you. You're a life saver. Bye bye."
Pushing the cut off button, she doesn't hang up the receiver but addresses George as she starts to dial another number. "George, just one moment. Let me call Rick DeVil private agent."
George can hear the phone ringing, then a recording comes on: Hello, you've reached DeVil private real estate agent for the greater Moundsville area. Can't sell your home? Or are you looking to buy? Well, I can help. Just leave your name and number and I'll get back to you as soon as possible. Beep.
"Hello Mr DeVil, this is Mrs Harper at the bank in Chapman Grove. I have a customer that has quite a few little homes to sell. Please call me here at the bank before 5:30pm." She gives the number. "Well George, only thing to do is wait. Call me after

school and I can tell you if we have a meeting with him here."
"Okay, Mrs Harper."
George walks out smiling, knowing Mrs Harper cares about all her customers. Even the kids. George has talked many of his classmates into opening up a savings account. Anyway, George heads for home where he finds Mr Watts is on the front porch, enjoying the breeze.
"Hi, Dad."
"Hello George, been to the bank?"
"How'd you know?"
"Mrs Harper at the bank called. You all have an appointment with Mr DeVil tomorrow at four o'clock. I have some suits that might fit you to make you look sharp."
"Cool. Thanks, Dad."
Later on that night all the power went out in Chapman Grove. It just died. The only lights on were flashlights and those powered by generators. But they just kept on chatting together, unaffected by the power outage.

Wednesday, November 10th 1965

After school George raced home and changed into the new threads. He looked at himself in the mirror, thinking, You're one cool looking dude.
Dad gave him a small briefcase for all his papers. He went out the door walking tall, heading for the bank.
"Hey, good looking!" some of the girls from school shouted.
George smiled bigger. He reached the bank, walking up to Mrs Harper's desk at two minutes till four. Mr DeVil was already there.
"Hello, Mrs Harper."
"Hey kid," Mr DeVil says. "We're conducting some business here."
"Yes, I know."
"YOU'RE the house owner!"
"Yes, I am."
"Mrs Harper, I am not amused. I thought I was going to have a real meeting with a real client, not some brat dressed up in a monkey suit." Mr DeVil gets up and storms out the door.

George was extremely put down by the rude behavior of this realtor, more like a fly-by-night crook.

"George, just put that creep out of your mind. I thought he was going to be good. Guess I was wrong. Let's do it this way. I will call every realtor in the area, tell them we want a concept bid for the job to sell those houses."

"A concept bid?"

"Yes. We tell them what WE want and they will have to bid for it. You go on home, George, and I'll call you when a meeting is planned. Oh, by the way George, you look sharp."

George left, feeling a little bit better for being told he looked sharp. He gets home to find Dad cooking.

"George! Are we celebrating today?"

"No, the guy turned out to be a creep."

"Oh, I'm sorry to hear that. Anyway, today is fried chicken, smashed potatoes with gravy, corn on the cob and dinner rolls."

The two of them sat down to a great supper, chatting about the day and the meeting.

Monday, November 22ⁿᵈ 1965

The real estate market in Chapman Grove was still really depressed, very slow to recover since the mill burned to the ground. George was thinking it was amazing how one action can have a chain reaction of events.

How far can one go back in history to see how they changed things? Sometimes for the better, too. Most the time it can turn into a great life just by an act of random kindness. "Hmm, act of random kindness?" George says to himself. "Like Mr Watts adopted me."

George runs into the house and sees Dad reading the paper.

"Dad, yesterday in Sunday school we read about how Moses built an ark."

"Huh huh. That's nice, George." Mr Watts is not fully listening and keeps reading the paper.

"Anyway, I think it be great to go see it being built. But I'm not sure what year."

"What year? It's 1965."

"Dad, I think the garage is on fire."

"Uh huh."

Hmm, George thinks, he ain't listening. George goes to the telephone and calls Pastor Bess. "Hello, Pastor Bess? This is George."

"Hello, George. How are you doing this fine day?"

"George? The pastor here?" Mr Watts asks.

"No, Dad. I'm on the phone."

"Oh."

"Pastor, I have a question. When or what year did Noah build the ark?"

"Well George, that's a different question than I'm use to. I think I'm going to have to call you back on that one. Right now I don't rightly know."

"Thanks Pastor, it's for a journey. Bye." George hangs up and sees his dad still reading the paper.

"So how is the pastor, George?"

"He's fine. Just got excommunicated is all. Nothing major."

"That's good." A silence goes over the whole house. Then Mr Watts puts the paper down. "Huh?"

George is just standing there, staring at him with arms crossed.

"I'm sorry George, I'm in the twilight zone when reading the paper. The wife use to scold me when I did that. Now I'm doing it to you." Mr Watts folds up the paper and shoves it under the coffee table stand. "Now, what were you saying, George? My mind was totally in the story I was reading."

"How about a trip to see Noah building the ark?"

"Gosh, that's a long long trip, George. Centuries ago!"

"We can be there in minutes if I knew the year. But what year to aim for is another matter."

"AND we'd be heading into an evil culture. They spoke an ancient language, they dressed differently. I don't know about this, George."

"Scared?"

"No George, I'm not..."

"I think you are."

"George, we got to plan this trip."

George starts making chicken sounds at his dad and laughing a little while flapping his arms like a chicken.

"GEORGE, WE'LL GO. I swear, George, you're a bad influence on me."

George just smiles that he got his way. Mr Watts goes off to get ready, grumbling. George goes to the phone to call in his flight plan. He talks for a few minutes then hangs up. "Oh man! DAD! Hold off on packing. We might not be able to go yet."

"How come?" he shouts from a back room.

"We got to have passports."

"They didn't have passports back then, George."

"Yes, but for safety I was thinking of flying to England. Service the XT1. Then go on to.... when and whereabouts did he build the ark, Dad?"

"George, every day you teach me. I need to read the Bible more. I learn something new all the time. But this takes the cake. Let's call the pastor. He'll know."

"Ah, I already did."

"What did he say?"

"He'll get back to us."

"Well then, let's get all our ducks in a row before we set out on this journey. We need passports. We got to learn a little bit of the language. Find some clothes for the time period. Oh George, wouldn't you be just as happy to visit Susan? I read something in the paper about her. It seems SHE won the regional science fair in Charleston."

Mr Watts gets the paper he had shoved under the coffee table.

"Here it is. Susan Hill of Charleston High School won the regional science fair with an electronic language translator that could be programmed for many languages and maybe even learn new languages on its own in the future. Her project was very innovative and ahead of its time. See there, that's one smart cookie. Look, got her picture in there too. Want to cut it out and put it under your pillow?"

"DAD." George does take the paper. "Until we can go, Dad, I'd like
to go visit Susan. Maybe stay with Helen?"
"Me too. Visit Helen I mean."

Friday, December 10th 1965
This is the first visit to the Hills. It's been what seems like forever
to young people when they're apart. So George went to visit them
alone. They had a nice place up Bridge Road near Sunrise. Helen
drops George off at the Hills, saying to call her when ready to
leave. He goes up to the door with a nice little bouquet of flowers
and dressed up nicely. He rings the bell. He could hear Mr Hill
saying he'd get it. The door opens. Mr Hill motions George in.
"SUSAN, it's for you!"
Susan comes in squawking, "If that's Rachel, Dad, please tell her I
got company coming and I can't be....."
She stops in mid sentence and leaps for George, hugging the
stuffing out of him. Dad just heads out of the living room and goes
back to his study. The two of them sit on the couch, holding each
other like there's no tomorrow, talking about what's been happening
and how school is going. Then Mom comes in with some drinks.
Susan has an apple juice and George a brisk cold ice tea. Hours go
by and Mom comes back.
"George, would you like to stay for dinner? It's nothing special.
Just a left over pot roast."
"Yes, ma'am. That sounds very nice. I like that. Susan, I saw you
won the regional science fair. Congratulations. You going for the
state?"
"Yes I am, George. What about you? Got something to enter?"
"I always have something to enter."
"So what did you put in the regional, George?"
"I put in a new and improved version of the magnetic motor. I had
to fix it till no one could break it or even touch it."
"How on earth do you do that?"
"Simple. I made a clear plastic case over it and put a padlock on it.
Then chained it to the table. Can't have people stealing something
that can travel back in time. OH, I was thinking about your

translator, can I build one for the XT1? I need it for a trip we're planning."

"Sure, George. Anything for you. What language you need it for?"

"I'm still researching that. It could be Aramaic, Hebrew, Syrian." Susan looks at him, puzzled, as he continues, "I'm still waiting on pastor Bess to let me know. I just didn't see it in my Bible."

"George? Are you talking about visiting someone in the Bible?"

"Dad said 'yes' to the way I planned it, but of course got to plan this carefully. Don't want to make God angry. Was thinking about seeing the ark built."

"George, you remember WHY God had Noah build the ark?"

"Because a big flood is coming."

"WHY is a big flood coming, George?"

"Because... the world had became so evil. But Dad and the pastor is going with me. You want to come too? One empty seat left."

"I don't know about this, George. I'll have to think about it and ask Mom and Dad. But here's the plans for the translator. Keep them private. Don't show them to everybody."

"I always try to keep promises."

"Dinner's ready, kids."

"Great, Mrs Hill! I always like to eat."

"Then come on. Mr Hill likes to eat too, you know."

During dinner Susan tells Mom and Dad, "George has asked if I'd like to take a ride in the XT1. I told him I have to think about it and ask you two."

"I don't see any harm in a joy ride. George is a responsible pilot, good head on his shoulders. Where you want to go?" Mr Hill asks.

"It will be either Israel or Turkey," Susan adds.

"No, Susan. That's too far away," Mrs Hill says, frowning.

"My Dad will be going."

"It might be alright for a weekend trip. What you all want to do there?" Mr Hill wants to know.

"See Noah build the ark, Dad."

Mr and Mrs Hill sit there, rather stunned expressions on their faces. George and Susan remain silent until Mr Hill asks, "Who else is going on this voyage?"

"Pastor Bess of our church, as a consultant. I think he wanted to go for the journey anyway."

"Can you fly to there from here? That's a LONG voyage."

"Was planning to fly to London first for a short servicing stop then continue on from there. Mr Mallet of the FAA has certified the XT1 for the flight. The flight from here to there wouldn't take long at all."

"Honey?" Mrs Hill addresses Mr Hill, "I see no problem. George has been planning this quite well. What do you think?"

"Long as they have Mr Watts and Pastor Bess going, you're okay with it, then it's okay with me. Susan, at this time you may go."

"Dad? I haven't said I want to go yet. I was thinking about it."

"Daughter, why didn't you say so?" Mr Hill sounds a little exasperated.

"I did, Dad."

"She did at that, honey. Anyway Susan, if you want to go this time, you may."

"Parents!" Susan says.

"Yep," George says with a smile.

Saturday, December 11th 1965

Next morning George and Susan went up to the Charleston airport. He showed her all the changes and improvements made since she rode in the XT1 last time, giving her a rough idea about its basic propulsion system. It's not certain she understood it but she kept going huh huh, as if she did.

"George, you ought to write all this down. It's a great piece of work."

"You really like it?"

"Yes, you're so smart, George."

"You want to go for a ride?"

"Huh huh, please."

As the two of them board the XT1, George pushes down on the starter, then gets on the radio. "Charleston tower, this is XT1."

"Go ahead, XT1."

"Charleston tower, XT1 requesting clearance for take off. Be cruising over Kanawha valley with a passenger."

"XT1, you have clearance."

The XT1 rose slowly and went out to the runway then picked up speed. Down the runway they went.

"George, couldn't you just go the way you wanted instead of going down the runway?"

"Yes, I could, but this is standard procedure for all aircraft." The XT1 climbs fast in altitude. "Look off to your right."

"OH George, it's my home. It looks so tiny from up here. Look George, that's the state Capitol on the left and there's the glass factory in Kanawha City on the right."

Then George turned around and headed down the Kanawha river. They passed all those sights again, from the east this time. Cruising on downstream, they passed the chemical plants, a college and lots of homes dotting the landscape. Upon reaching the John Amos power plant, George turned the XT1 and started heading for the airport.

"George, I had a wonderful time. Thank you for taking me flying. This was fun."

Landing back at Charleston airport, they were met by his sister Helen and Dad.

"Susan, need a ride home?" asked Helen. She just stood looking at George as they kissed goodbye.

"Yes Helen, I would. George, soon as Dad gets me a passport I want to go."

"That sounds nice. I think we'll have a great time."

They kiss again as Mr Watts and Helen pretend to not notice. Then Mr Watts says, "George, whenever you're ready, we need to get home and feed the dog."

The kids just kiss again then part company. Susan leaves with Helen, occasionally looking back at George as he leaves with his dad.

"Dad? We don't have a dog."

"Yes George, I know."

Saturday, December 25th 1965

Many of the kids and grandkids came for Christmas this year. As always the whole house was decked out, inside and out. A nice little snow had covered the ground during the night. You could hardly see where all the kids had been sled riding the day before. Christmas had been a grand time this year. But Barbara and Judy were still posted somewhere out in the world; hadn't heard from them in months and this made Mr Watts sad.

"DAD!" George shouted from his bedroom. "Can you and everybody come in here!"

"You going for a world record? How many can fit in a bedroom?"

"No, but I do have someone that wants to talk with you on the shortwave radio!"

Mr Watts, then all the family, crowded into George's bedroom. And you bet it did set a world record. How many foster family members of the same house can you crowd into a teenager's bedroom?!

"George, who would want to talk with me?"

"Go ahead Essex, your party is here."[10]

Through the static of the shortwave receiver some voices were heard, "Dad? Dad, can you hear us? We miss you, Dad. Merry Christmas! Barbara and I are here. We love you, Dad."

"I love you too, girls. I'm real proud of you all." Tears were streaming down his face. He could hardly talk.

"Dad, we can tell you're crying. We are too."

"MERRY CHRISTMAS JUDY AND BARBARA!"

"George, have you got the whole family in that little bedroom of yours? OH! Our time's up, we love you all."

"We all love you, girls," Mr Watts called back.

Nothing else was heard from them except the background noise. When time's up, it's up.

"Merry Christmas, Dad," came from George.

The whole family piled out of George's bedroom to the kitchen table which had been set fit for a king. Mr Watts and the whole family held hands as he gave the blessing for the food.

That night, Mr Watts had another reading treat for all the grandkids. He had found it in a dusty old book. As he sits down in

his easy chair, some of the kids start looking to see what he had.
"What you got there, Grandpa?" Bobby inquires as he climbs up in his lap.
"It's just an old poem I use to read to your dad when he was a little boy, maybe about your age."
"Read it to me?" he asked.
"Well, you get the others and I will."
"HEY EVERYBODY, GRANDPA GOING TO READ TO US!"
"Oh gee, why didn't I think of that, Bobby?"
"I don't know, Grandpa."
All the grandkids came charging in and surrounded Mr Watts. Then came the rest of the family. George was last, with lots of bags of popcorn to pass around as Mr Watts begins to read. [11]
"'Twas the night before Christmas and all through the house, not a creature was stirring, not even a mouse.
 The stockings were hung by the chimney with care, in hopes that Saint Nicholas would soon be there.
The children were nestled all snug in their beds, while visions of sugar plums danced in their heads.
With Mommie in her dressing gown and I in my cap, had settled our brain for a long winter's nap.
When out on the lawn there arose such a clatter, I sprang from my bed to see what was the matter.
Away to the window I flew like a flash, tore open the shutters and threw up the sash.
The moon on the breast of the new fallen snow, gave the luster of mid-day to objects below.
When what to my wondering eyes should appear but a miniature sleigh and eight tiny reindeer.
With a little old driver so lively and quick, I knew in a moment it must be Saint Nick.
More rapid than eagles his coursers they came, he whistled and shouted and called them by name.
Now Dasher! Now Dancer! Now Prancer and Vixen. On Comet! On Cupid! On Donner and Blitzen!
To the top of the porch, to the top of the wall! Now dash away,

dash away, dash away all.

As he rose out of sight you could hear him shout, merry Christmas to all, and to all a good night.

Grandpa looked up to see most of the littlest grandchildren had fallen asleep. The older ones were not far behind either. Their mothers and fathers, and uncles and aunts start getting them to their feet, with some needing carried. Then they turned in themselves for a long night's nap.

Note to reader: Time Voyagers: A Christmas Journey is a book being written and should be available for Christmas season 2014.

Friday, December 31st 1965

The day finally came. Everyone had a passport in hand. Flight plans had been filed. Each person had a small day bag packed and all the gear had been stowed away.

"Are we all ready? Dad? Pastor Bess? Susan? Susan?"

"She's hugging and kissing her mom and dad goodbye, George," Mr Watts noticed.

They just stood there waiting, and waiting, and waiting. George clears his throat rather loudly. Then the Hills let their little daughter go. She and the others climb aboard the tiny little ship. Once again it rises for this special task it loves to do. Then it taxied out to the runway, with them being third in line.

"Everybody fastened their seat belts? Because here we go."

"George, remember you got two old men now."

"Who you calling old, Mike? Floor it, George!" Pastor Bess commands.

George pulls up with his left hand on the throttle and forward on the stick. The XT1 races down the runway like a speeding bullet. Climbing to fifteen hundred feet, it then aims for West Virginia's eastern panhandle.

"Next stop Stansted airport, London, England!"

"Why there, George?" asked Pastor Bess.

"Less air traffic, sir. We can be in and out in less than an hour. And our ETA is about forty minutes."

"Forty minutes, George! I've known us to get places in seconds,"

Mr Watts boasted.

"That's in America, Dad. Our British cousins aren't use to this aircraft. This is as fast as we dare go. England's airports will be in shock at the speed we're going now. But they been told about us."

Forty minutes later

"XT1, this is London Heathrow air control."

"XT1 to Heathrow control, go ahead."

"XT1, minor course change. Please come in to a more southern approach to Stansted. Air traffic getting heavy. Turning you over to Stansted air control at this time."

"Roger. XT1 to Stansted control, we're ten minutes ahead of schedule, coming in at a more southern route due to air traffic."

"XT1, you will be in a holding pattern at your present altitude, reduce your speed to 200 mph."

"That's a copy, Stansted."

They were in that holding pattern for a good thirty minutes. Then Susan says, "I hope we land soon, I need the ladies room."

"Me too," says Mr Watts.

"You need the ladies room, Mike?"

They all laugh.

"Stansted to XT1, you are cleared to land on runway 31. You will park at gate 16A."

George comes down to runway 31 then turns to taxi to their gate.

"Ah, anyone see gate 16A?" George peers outside.

"Well, I see gate 34C," Pastor Bess says.

"Look George, the numbers seem to get smaller going that way," Susan points out.

So George turns around and heads that way.

"Ground control to XT1, are you lost?"

"Kind of. Are we heading the right way?"

"You'll get to 16A but you're taking the long way. Go back the direction you were heading."

"Thank you."

"Sorry, George."

"That's alright Susan, I might have done the same thing. Anyone here speak British English?"

"Not us," Mr Watts says.

"Then we'll get by. If we just proceeding on, wonder if we need to go through customs?"

Just then a couple of official looking people came out to the gate.

"We'd like to see your license, flight plan and passports. Also stand by for inspection."

George hands him the requested items. The other official inspects the XT1.

"Anything to declare?"

"No, just some cameras, toiletries and clothes, sir."

The other inspector says, "The aircraft is alright. But for the life of me, I don't see how it flies." He turns and asks Mr Watts, "Sir! What makes this thing go?"

"Ask the boy. He built it."

"The lad?" The inspector's face is astonished as he looks at George. "Well, in a nutshell, it works on the principle of magnetic rotation. This causes a local interruption of the gravity and magnetic waves of the earth and the ship rises. Control is controlled with a counter rotation of a secondary rotor and...."

"Stop! Here's your clearance."

"Thank you, sir. Whereabouts might we get a few refreshments?"

"Follow us."

"Susan, would you go with them and get our canteens filled with water? Here's some British pounds. This should be plenty."

"George? This doesn't feel like one pound. It's more like a few ounces."

"Hah ha."

Susan walks behind the inspectors, smiling at the joke. George goes to the XT1 and services the rotors, the heart of the whole system. It was looking good but he gave it a shot of grease anyway. The total inspection took less time with Dad and Pastor Bess helping.

"Where's Susan?" asks George. "She been gone a long time."

"I'll go see if I can find her. Be back in about thirty minutes," Mr Watts said, going off to search.

Thirty minutes goes by and then he comes back alone.

"Well Dad, no sign of her?"

"No, but I found a few law enforcement officers and they're looking for her. "

An hour goes by then here she comes, with the police. They're smiling very kindly with Susan.

"You have a nice flight, young lady."

"Thank you for helping me." She hugs them. Then Susan runs to join the rest.

"I was worried about you, Susan. What happened?" said George.

"Nobody wanted to fill our canteens. I looked around and couldn't even fill at a water cooler because there weren't any. Then the police found me. Thank you, Mr Watts, for sending in the rescue."

"It was George that alerted us to how long you were gone."

"I love you, George. Anyway, that constable helped us to get water."

"Excellent. Great job, Susan," George praised her efforts.

The four of them load up and get on board. George starts up and the XT1 rises, rotates and starts heading out.

"XT1 to Stansted control."

"Stansted, go ahead XT1."

"We're ready to depart. Waiting on instructions."

"XT1, make a U turn. Head to taxi way 16 behind TWA."

"Roger, Stansted."

George gets in line behind TWA. Then they wait what seems like forever. Then TWA moves off and is gone down the runway.

"Gosh, it's slow," Pastor Bess said. "Let's show TWA get up and go!"

"Pastor, be nice. Stansted control, we're ready for take off. Also if we disappear off the radar screen, that's normal. No need for search rescue unless you see us crash."

"XT1, we know how to handle air space. You're cleared for take off."

"Punch it, George," Pastor Bess says, enjoying the adventure immensely.

George pulls hard on the left lever and full forward on the stick.

ZOOM, off like a rocket.

"HERE WE GO! NEXT STOP ISRAEL!" George pulls up on lever two.

"XT1, this is Stansted air control."

Nothing is heard in response.

"XT1? XT1?"

"TWA Flight 17 to Stansted. You missing an aircraft? Something just zoomed past us then disappeared. I think it was the XT1."

"Thanks, TWA."

Back on the XT1, the crew is watching an amazing vortex of lights and sparks.

2427 BC or around that time

George eases off the time lever and comes out over the coast of Israel. "Let's see if we're in the right place and time. XT1 to Israel air control. XT1 to Israel air control."

All they heard was static.

"Well, it's getting dark. Let's land and see if we're in the right place and time."

"So whereabouts are we, George?" Susan wonders.

"I was aiming for 2427 BC. Let's land and get a star reading."

All of them got out and began setting up a camp. George took a telescope, sextant, compass and maps. Hours go by. Mr Watts brings George some food cooked on an open fire. It always tasted best that way.

"Dad, the way it looks over the next two mountains, that way we'll find Noah."

" Hope so, George, we came a long way. How about let's get some sleep and start out in the morning."

"Yes, I'm tired," he mumbles as he yawns. "There seems to be a few stars out of line or I didn't do my astronomy merit badge right in the Boy Scouts."

George lies down on his bedroll between Susan and Pastor Bess.

Next Morning, 2427 BC

The next morning Susan was cuddling up beside George, and he was awakened with her high pitched, blood curdling scream in his ear. Everybody jumps to see a poor camel running scared out of its wits and Susan clinging to George for her life.

"SUSAN!" Mr Watts' voice jerks her wide awake. "You're okay. You scared it off."

"Dad, I have a ringing in my ear. But it sounds more like a scream."

"You'll be alright in a few hours, George."

George walks around, rubbing his ear canal with a finger. A few hours later they pack up, climb into the XT1 and go in the direction of Shiloh, a place George thinks Noah will be. The others keep a lookout for people while George creeps the ship over each mountain.

"WOW!" Susan exclaims. "There it is. It's got to be it."

Down in the valley, near the town of Shiloh, was the ark; a huge ship of incredible size.

"Dad, look at that thing! It's really real. That's one BIG ship."

"Hey George, look over there. Go down that valley to the ark and I'll bet we can hide."

"Alright, Pastor."

George creeps the ship down the mountainside into the valley then heads towards the ark which seemed to grow as they got closer.

"George, better not get too close. Not too many people have seen a time machine before."

"Right!"

George lands behind some old building that looks as if it's not been used in centuries.

"Let's change into the right clothes. Susan, honey, you can change in the XT1. George will not peek."

"Thank you, Mr Watts."

"Dad, I got some gadgets that might help us. Something Susan invented in high school and I added to it."

"What is it?"

"A communicator translator."

He hands the two of them a weird looking thing that hooked over the ear. They try it out.

"Hello? Hello?"

"Hey, George," Mr Watts says. "This works great. The box that's attached to it with a wire, what's it for?"

"The box is most the electronics. The wire is the speaker cable and acts like an antenna."

Just then Susan comes out and laughs at the men as they looked ridiculous. "You all look so funny!"

"You seen yourself in the mirror lately?" George said, laughing. "Here Susan, clip this to your ear and hide this under your robe. Now listen everybody, I hope this will pick up what all is saying around us and translate into English. Oh another thing, if you get lost just touch the side of your earpiece. When you hear a beep the homing beacon is on. Just turn till you hear a steady tone. You're heading right back to the ship."

"Then let's get going," says the Pastor. "I hear it might rain."

The four of them walk through the village. For the longest time all they heard was garbled voices. Then a few words would come through. By the time they got to the ark, all kinds of translated words were coming through. But there were still a few the translator just couldn't cope with.

Some big brutish looking fat man was the loudest, "What is more -------- than building a ship on the land? Building it so big you can't get it to the water that's not even in sight!"

A roaring laugh floods the area.

"HEY NOAH, GOING ON A FISHING TRIP?"

More laughter roars though.

"Hey Noah, does this float your boat? When's the rain coming? There's not even a cloud in the sky."

It seemed like one man and his three sons were the butt of the villagers' jokes. The time voyagers just slowly crept up to the ark. Some people glanced at them, nudging them as if to share the joke about the ridiculous boat so far from water, and continued laughing. A few others were looking at the travelers as if thinking them to be eerie people from a strange land. After a while the

people started wandering off, tired of heckling the builders.
"Noah?" Pastor Bess spoke and Noah heard him in his own language.
"I am he."
"The Lord is pleased with your work."
"Will the rains come soon?"
"It will come in the Lord's time. The animals you shall carry will be here soon, just as He commands."
 "Come inside with me and have a meal with the wife and family."
"We would like that."
Noah led the way. The door was located dead center along the length of the ark. It was huge inside. Torches lit the way. A third of the way in, a hallway went the length of the ark from bow to stern with a narrow connecting hallway to the other side, completing the corridor across the width of the ark from the entrance door. That corridor also connected to a second hallway running the length of the ark, just like the first one from bow to stern. Each long hallway was lined down both sides with stalls for the animals. In the travelers' measurements the ark was about seventy five foot wide, four hundred and fifty foot long, and forty foot high at least. Ramps were placed for access to what seemed to be upper levels.
"Did the Lord send you to inspect the work? For I feel it's ready."
"No," George said. "Michael sent us."
"The archangel Michael? Very good then. The ark is ready for you to see."
Mr Watts whispers to George, "Michael sent us?"
"Yeah. Michael from the Sunrise planetarium in Charleston."
"Hum," Mr Watts mutters.
They all sat down on the floor of the ark. Noah's wife, their sons Shem, Ham, Japheth and their wives came into the ark bearing food for a meal.
Noah invites the travelers, "Help yourself."
"Thank you."
The pastor takes two fingers and dips them into a paste of some kind and puts it in his mouth. Then the others follow his lead. You might have described it as a really good tasting wallpaper paste.

But no one said that. Figs, dates and some other foods were on hand and they ate well.

"So," Noah's wife asked, "when is this flood coming? All the work has gone into this and there's not even a ------- in the sky."

"Wife! It will be in His time. The ark needs loaded with ------ for the animals to come."

"And who will gather these animals?"

"He will send them. We just need to help them on board."

They continued eating. Then Noah and all his family got up.

"Come my --------- and let me continue showing you around."

As they went up a ramp to the upper levels, Mr Watts whispered to George, "Is this translator working? It's missing a few words. They seemed garbled."

"The translator got hit with a new word and couldn't understand it. Might happen again. We have to use our heads and figure it out."

"My ------ come look here. This is a -------- pool I built in the ark. It makes for a more ---------- ride. It also changes the air inside. With all the animals on board the smell would be horrible."

"Yes," George said. "Very much."

"It is very seaworthy, Noah. Well done, good and faithful servant," said Pastor Bess.

"Forgive me, but I didn't catch all you said. It is a very sea what?"

"It will stay afloat very well." The pastor used some other words to get his point across. "You been working a long time on it. Keep the faith, Noah."

"The animals shall be coming soon, Noah," George spoke. "We'll be back soon. Just before the rains."

The four of them come out of the ark and start walking away. Many of the villagers saw them come out and started heckling them.

"Hey strangers, decided not to go sailing?"

"Maybe they're land lovers."

"They could be seasick."

George and the others just ignored them as they kept walking towards the XT1. When they were clear from the crowd Susan asked, "Why did we leave so soon? I would have loved to see more of the ark."

"Because the translator had been overwhelmed by the words it had to translate. It needs more memory space and faster processors. None of which has been invented yet, even in our time."

"Maybe you can build them, George."

"Maybe, Dad."

They approached the XT1 and George opened the door. It was like an oven inside. The heat just knocked you over. It was like a blast furnace.

"Oh gosh, what heat! No wonder the translator is not working right. The heat was just too much."

"Can we still take off, George?"

"I'd rather let it cool down, Dad, before even trying it. How about we camp out for the night and leave in the morning?"

"Sounds good to me," the pastor agreed.

" As long as no camels come poking into camp, I'll be fine," added Susan.

"Yes, my ears will be too," George teased her.

"Sorry about that, George."

Nightfall came and the temperature dropped quickly, but the campfire they were cooking on chased the cold away. George set up the telescope and stargazed till the late hours.

"George?" Susan broke the stillness. "Look at that star. It's moving very fast. Is it a falling star?"

"I'm not sure. I can't find it on the chart. Wonder what it is?"

"George, the pastor and I are turning in. It must be late."

"Okay, Dad. I think I will too. Susan, you going to sleep too?"

"I think I'll lay down and look up at the heavens. It looks so clear. It's amazing that it will be destroyed."

Day 3, 2427BC

The camp fire had gone out but some smoke was still escaping the hot embers. It had been a clear night. The previous night, dew had covered the ground but not this time. It seemed very dry.

"George!" Mr Watts shouted. "You getting up or going to sleep till the twentieth century?"

Mr Watts and the pastor had stoked up the fire and got it going again. Mr Watts was now frying up eggs and bacon and making toast. Then here came the pastor with a bottle of milk. No one asked where he got it. It did taste strange for milk. Hmm, wonder what he milked to get it. A camel or a goat, they thought. Anyway, breakfast was much appreciated. The XT1's door had been open all night so it had cooled down quite a bit. George went to service the rotor. He opened the service hatch in the floor to find sand had gotten in.

"Oh, man!"

"What's wrong, George?" Mr Watts asked, coming to look.

"Sand got in the rotor chamber."

"We okay for lift off ?"

"I think so, Dad. Just need to take the lower housing off, dump the sand out then put it back on. About half hour work."

"Okay George, let's get started. I'll hand you the wrench for this side and then I'll get the other. Susan can help pass the tools around. The pastor can help us get the shroud off."

Twenty minutes later the shroud was off and about a gallon of sand was dumped out. George got back up in the XT1 and took a deep breath and blew on the rotors. More sand came dropping out. As he came out of the XT1 everyone started laughing.

"What's up?"

"Look at your face, George! All covered in sand."

George sees his face in the window. White as a ghost. It was very funny looking. He just runs his fingers over his face and through his hair. Looked like his own private sandstorm.

"Come on, George," Mr Watts said, laughing. "Let's get the shroud back on."

Each person took a corner and lifted the shroud in place, taking turns with the wrench to put the nuts on the bolts. They used safety wire to secure the nuts the best they could.

Susan asked, "George, what would happen if the wire doesn't hold?"

"That's a good question; the nuts will vibrate loose and the shroud will fall off."

"Then what?"

"I would have to either retrieve it or make a new one. It's just a cover for the rotor. Obviously sand seems to still get in. Gotta work on that. We're ready. Climb aboard."
Pushing down on the forward pedal, the rotors start up. Some more sand blows to the outside. Then they go up about twenty feet or so. George hovers there a few minutes.
"George, everything okay?"
"Yes, Susan. Just clearing more sand out."
Then George pulls lever 2 slightly and eases off. The ark was still there. But it was just starting to cloud up in the east. Over to the north the shooting star was huge. Rumbles of distant thunder shook the XT1. The wind was picking up too. George turned into the wind. It was quite a bumpy ride. Lightning flashed before them. Rain came down hard.
"George!" Mr Watts shouted over the noise. "Maybe invest in better windshield wipers next time."
"I agree."
The rain, wind, lightning and thunder got worse. George had to give it more power to hold his altitude.
"DAD, I THINK IT'S TIME WE LEAVE!"
"YES!"
George does an instrument turn to start trying to head out of the storm. He kept going and going. No sign of it letting up.
"DAD!"
Lightning strikes the XT1 which sends it hurtling into time. A burning smell comes from the rotor and ….

Date unknown
….they were down, back into normal time on some sunny day. George slowed the XT1 down fast. It bounced twice on landing.
"Everybody alright? Anybody see whereabouts we came down to?"
"We're okay, George. Just shook up a bit. I saw a large city."
"They look friendly, Dad?"
"Didn't see."
"I saw it, George," the pastor added. "But I didn't recognize it. It had shipping and a port. Maybe repairs can be made."

"I hope so," Susan said in a trembling voice.

No one in the city seemed to have been looking up when they passed over. Looked like a million people down there. George had set the ship down in a valley near the city.

"Well, Dad, let's see what the damage is."

Climbing out, they could see where lightning had raked across the ship, ripping into one of the computers that regulates the rotor. And ALL navigation lights had blown.

"Well, George," the pastor remarked, "it could have been worse. We could have died in that flood."

"Yes, but we could be stuck here for a while. Wonder what the culture is like here. Maybe we should sneak around and see."

"I'll do that," Pastor Bess volunteered.

Pastor Bess heads off in the direction of the city. It was a crowded city. He still wore the translator but no sound was coming through. Maybe it would take a while to work. He continued walking around. Some people were staring at him as he wasn't dressed quite right for this culture. As he continued walking through the market place he was taking note of what was available. Listening to some people talking, it sounded as if they spoke about three different languages. One sounded like Greek. He could identify it, but not speak it. Then Latin. Oh good, he thought, I know it fairly well. As for the last language, he hadn't a clue what it was. Pastor Bess walked up to one vendor and asked in Latin if he knew of a blacksmith or any metal worker.

"Yes, stranger," the vendor replied. "If you go all the way down this road until you get to the harbor, turn right and you'll see many workers of iron and other metals."

"I might be back later. What is the common currency here? What do people pay with?"

"We take many. Talents, rubles, shekels in gold and silver."

"I have some silver coins from a far away land. Would you take them?" Pastor Bess hands him an American silver dollar.

The vendor looks at it. Rakes it across a small stone. Bites into it. "Yes. I would exchange it here. Strange writing on it. Is this from some far off land?"

"I got some during my travels. On my way back I might like to make some purchases. If I get lost how might I find you?"
"Just look for the sign above my stand."
Pastor Bess read the sign. 'Atlantis Fine Meats and Fish'
"Mine is the only one that says that."
"Thank you, sir. You're very kind. I'll look for it."
Pastor Bess walked and walked. It was a long way. Eventually he did get down to the docks, turned right as the vendor had told him, and saw the metal workers.
"Greetings," the pastor said. "I was looking for metal workers."
"You found many here. What you want? I'm busy."
"Just seeing what you can do. Got a friend that might need parts for a ship worked on."
"I can do anything with any metal. So can everybody here." The metal worker takes a metal piece and stretches it out long and thin.
"Can you do that with copper?"
"Over there on the bench."
On the bench was a huge roll of copper wire. It looked like thousands of feet. The pastor tried to look around and note where he was then headed back the way he had come and found the vendor again. For the weight of two silver dollars he bought four servings of some kind of steamed fish, fruits and figs. Thanking him kindly, he hurried back to the others.
Upon reaching them, he heard Susan shouting, "HE'S BACK!"
"Yes, I'm back. You miss me? Anyway, got you all some fresh food; fruits, figs and fish."
"We were beginning to worry about you, Pastor. What did you find out about this place? Whereabouts did we land?"
"Mike, you're never going to believe this. But we're on the island of Atlantis."
"Your joshin'! I always thought it was a myth."
"No, I read about it in seminary. It was said to be out the straits of Gibraltar past the pillars of Hercules."
"So you know about where we're at?"
George stops working on the XT1, opens a world map and the pastor looks at it. "Right there is where we are, George." He points

it out on the map.

"But Pastor, that island isn't shaped like this one."

"I know, George. The legend says part either sank or was blown away from a volcano, or maybe even something fell out of the sky."

"Well, I just want to get us home before anything else happens. Could use some insulated copper wire and at least two new batteries."

"A blacksmith in the city has copper wire. I doubt it's insulated. Could we insulate it with something?"

"How about beeswax, George? Mrs Watts use to run thread through it."

"That might work, Dad. I was going to use duct tape to patch up the coils. But that might be easier. We got anything we can trade for this stuff?"

"I paid for all this food with two silver dollars. They take talents, rubles, gold and silver. All the vendor seemed to care about was that it was real silver."

"Pastor, we got to be careful about leaving stuff from the future here. It might corrupt the time line."

"I thought so too but felt it was an emergency. We were out of food."

"Alright, Pastor. Could you get about a hundred feet of that wire, and beeswax? Might need some batteries."

"Yes, if your dad comes to help me carry it."

"Could I come too? I'd like to see the city."

"Go ahead, Susan, I got things okay here. Don't forget your translator."

"George, it doesn't seem to be working now. I had to translate Latin myself," said the pastor.

"Hum. I'll look into it while you're away."

George gets into the repairs. About half the main rotor coils were either beyond repair or damaged. The counter rotor seemed scorched but was useable. So George did the best thing he knew to do; started taking the main rotor coils off. Wire that was totally fried came off. That was easy because the wire just fell apart. Then

George went back into the XT1 and started pulling out the coils
mounted inside. One was burned to a crisp. Totally shot.
Unsaveable.
Just then our shoppers came back with supplies and food.
"George, we're back!"
"Great, Dad. I see you got everything needed to patch us up."
"Yep! I see you've been busy too. You do know how to put it back
together, don't you?"
"More or less. She might wobble a bit. Some the coils on the rotors
were shot. Just totally fried."
"But you can get us going again? We're not stuck here?"
"YES! I can do it."
"Good. Here, have something to eat."
Mr Watts hands George something that looked good. George
breaks it open and starts eating, as the others were doing.
"Hmm, taste like a haggis."
"Taste like a what?" Susan asks.
"Haggis. The national dish of Scotland. Stephen, in class, brought
it to school one day. But this taste better."
"What's in it?"
"Might not want to ask that, Susan."
She stared at him with a curious expression but ate anyway.
After they had finished their meal George showed the others what
to do to help him fix the XT1. All that afternoon they worked,
winding the copper wire on for the coils, insulating them with
beeswax. Then George would mount them back in one at a time.
By nightfall all was complete except for one thing.
"Batteries! Where on earth are we going to get batteries?" Mr Watts
exclaimed.
"Couldn't we make batteries, Dad?"
Mr Watts thought for a moment or two. "I guess we could. The
XT1 runs on twelve volts, doesn't it? I think we could."
"Yes it does, but it could run on less."
"How much less, George?"
"Could still get by at half that, Dad. Just shut down a bunch of the
electronic extras."

Well into the night they worked on making two six volt batteries to power the XT1. As George finally hooked up the batteries he said, "Dad can you hold this in place while I bolt it down?"

"ZZZZZZZZZZzzzzzzzz" Mr Watts and the pastor were both snoozing away. Susan was not far behind.

"Susan, I know you're tired but I'm almost done. Hold this in place while I bolt it down." Sleepy eyed, Susan did as she was asked even while nodding off. "That should do it, Susan."

"Zzzzzzz"

"Nite nite, Susan," said George softly, smiling, and just kept working at rechecking everything. "Finished! I hope." George was talking to himself. "Gee, the sky is so clear. Can see all kinds of stars."

Just then a shooting star goes by and he makes a wish upon it then glances at Susan. Stargazing was great but sleep caught up even with George.

Day 2 on Atlantis

Except George, everybody was up. Everyone left George alone to get some sleep that morning. He had worked about twelve or more hours straight.

"Hey George, honey. You going to sleep the afternoon too? Time to get up, sleepy head." Susan scratches his chin a little. Then he starts smiling. "George! Wake up. Out of bed, lazy head."

George opens his groggy eyes to the prettiest girl. "Good morning, Susan. What time is it?"

"Morning nothing, it's afternoon time," she says, smiling. "How late were you up? Anyway, got some food in town. Got some for you too." She hands him something to eat.

"I'd like to look around town myself. Might never get a chance to see it again."

"Well, you eat up. Then we'll all go. Can you secure the ship?"

"Yep. Sure can. I'll do that before we leave. Hope we don't need a translator. Although it seems to be working fine, it's just not communicating with us. Maybe the transceiver is burned up. Anyway, need parts to fix it when we get back."

George eats up, hoping he has fixed everything right. Then he gets up, secures the XT1 and heads off with the rest of the crew.

So many people there. Wonder where they all come from, George thought. The streets were lined with vendors with all kinds of goods. Out near to the inlet from the sea was a group of ships guarding the harbor. Just outside the city, in the higher elevation, there seemed to be dwellings. This is a major sea power. Whatever happened, nobody knows.

"Ready to go home, George?" his dad asks.

"I think so, Dad. This is an interesting place. Looks like could be a middle east port in our time."

"Yep!"

They all set off, back to the ship. As they board, they take one last look around. Down the way was the city.

"Wonder whatever happened to the people here," says Susan.

"Well everyone," the pastor says, "one theory is something from space hit it. Another theory says it was sitting over a magma when it built up pressure and just BLEW. And the last theory is it just sank."

"Yes," George exclaimed. "I think that I'm for leaving before we sink. Cross your fingers."

George pressed down hard on the forward start pedal. The rotors slowly started turning, the volt meter started coming up as the whole ship wobbled a little. The ship rose, though not like before, but it did well considering what it had been through. The rpm counter showed full speed.

"Pastor, any idea which way Great Britain is?"

"Go back east until we hit the coast then turn north, I'd guess."

"Okay then, here we go."

George took off, leaving the tiny island behind. Up ahead was the coast. Turning left, he headed north, over land until he saw what must be England. Reaching down for the time control lever, George gently pulled. As before, they had a great light show, timing how much and how long would be needed to bring them back to their own time. The XT1 wobbled a little more, then more. He dropped the time lever back down. The smell of something burning leaked a little bit into the cabin.

Sometime in the 12th Century (maybe)
"Are we there yet?" Susan said, like a little kid in a car.
"I doubt it, Susan. But we might be close. I was smelling something burning and thought we better put it down. I hope we can just land safely. Wish Stephen was here. He could point out landmarks or tell us about what time period it is, or was."
"We just want to get fixed and get out of here this time you all," Mr Watts ordered.
"We agree," everyone said.
George sat it down outside a small village that looked like it had a blacksmith shop, conveniently for them as one might be needed. They all got out to stretch their legs and look around.
"Well Dad, any idea when we might have landed?"
"No. But I'm for getting fixed and getting out of here."
"I'd love to have a look around myself."
"GEORGE!" everyone shouts.
"Okay, okay. Just let me look and see what I smelled."
George gets back into the XT1, takes the seats out then opens the hatch to look around the rotors. "I see nothing wrong. Yet."
Susan remarks, "Well, I smelled it too. So can we help you in any way?"
"Well, if you and Dad can take the outside panel off that got hit by lightning, see if everything looks okay, I'll get a closer look at the rotors and see if they're okay. Pastor Bess, can you scout around, see where we're at; that might help for plans to get back to our century." Pastor Bess scurries off in the direction of a village he saw while landing. Mr Watts and Susan start taking out the screws then the panel fell off with a clang.
"You all alright out there?"
"Yes George, Susan and I got that panel off like you said. Looks the same."
"I guess that's good. Just leave the panel ....." A buzzzzzzz sound came out from where George was working.
"What was that, George?"

"Susan, I found a short. Looks like the patch job in Atlantis wasn't good enough. All these coils needs to come out and be redone. What I was saying, just leave the panel off and go on to the next one." Buzzzzzzz "That was the same short. I'm working on it." CLANG, went another panel.

"George, as you heard, the next panel is off. It looks like, I don't know."

George comes out to look. "Uh oh, I see the problem with the transceiver; a diode blew. A half a cent item, two minutes of work, and the radio, universal translator and homing beacon would all be working again."

"Is that all, George? A half a cent item? You'll have that working in no time."

"Yes Dad, in the twentieth century. The diode has not been made till maybe mid 1900s."

"You'll think of something, George. You always do."

"Maybe I can take the part from a less priority unit."

"I have faith in you, George. I always did."

"Thanks, Dad."

"I do too, George." She kisses George on the cheek and he blushes. George starts getting busy on mending the rotors and the wiring going up to the brushes. A few of those had come loose and could have arced, causing the burning smell. So, to best be safe, George re-secured those wires and gave everything a good dose of beeswax. Next task at hand was to see if the transceiver could be fixed. He could take parts from something else. But maybe just leave it, fix it when they get home.

"Dad, I'm going to start up, see how goes it."

"Fire her up."

George starts up the XT1 at low speed. Buzz, buzz, buzz, buzz, buzz. Then he shuts it down. "I could use something to insulate these wire runners better."

"Like what?"

"Look here, Dad. The beeswax insulation is not thick enough. Sparks keep going through it. Could use rubber to coat the wires."

"Rubber might not be discovered for a few more centuries."

"George?" Susan suggests, "How about a fabric with a beeswax coating? I saw it in that old shantytown house we had in Chapman Grove."

"Hmm, maybe. That might make it thick enough to insulate better. But the only fabric we have is the clothes we're wearing."

"George, how about cut our t-shirts in long strips. Our other twentieth century clothes also."

"And go back looking like monks? That's an idea but I'm not overly keen on it."

"Well, we could go limping back to the twentieth century. Or live here," Mr Watts says.

"Think I'll go with Susan's idea. So whereabouts do I get more beeswax? Rob a beehive?"

Mr Watts says, "Yep. Find a beekeeper. Homes were probably lighted with candles."

"Find a person who plays bagpipes," says Susan.

"Huh?" George remarks.

"Yes, people use to coat the seals in bagpipes with beeswax."

"I think be easier to find candles. But we'll keep that in mind."

Just then the pastor gets back.

"Pastor Bess, so what did you learn on your walk?" asks Mr Watts.

"It's the second day of August 1100. The crowning of a new king, to be Henry the First of England, takes place on the 5th. He's to marry Princess Edith of Scotland, daughter of Malcolm the Third. We're just six miles from Reading."

"Can we get some fabric and beeswax anywhere?"

"At the village nearby, I think, George."

"Well, I gone about as far as I can without it. Let's see what we can get."

"Put your robes back on and we can look like monks traveling."

"Yes Pastor, we'll be very holy," Susan jokes.

George packs up his tools inside the XT1 and closes her up securely. Walking along the road for about half an hour they come to a sign at a fork in the road, ←6 Reading London 30→

"I take it London is a little far to walk, Dad."

"Good thing we're going the other way then."

"Dad, I think I'll go back to the XT1. Make some more preparations for when you get the supplies we need."

"That sounds good, George. Can you find it again? The XT1 was behind some trees. It might be hard to find."

"I can find it alright, Dad."

George went back to work for the better part of the day, doing what he could until the others returned. There wasn't much traffic on the road. A rider on a horse came by once, but it was mostly people walking. Near sunset, the others got back. In their hands they carried fabric and more beeswax. George had patched up some of the rotors until he ran out of supplies. The extra supplies Mr Watts, Pastor Bess and Susan got were a blessing.

All through the night they worked, finding shorts and patching them up. The men took off each coil that George had marked. When George finished the repair of each coil, they put them back on. Susan was the assistant, getting a lot of miles at the landing area as she ran back and forth between them. Then finally, all the coils on the rotors had been made worthy to get them home. It had been a bitterly cold night to do the winding. But morning was starting to peek out with clouds drifting overhead.

Pastor Bess had some leftover food from Atlantis. Passing it around, he told everyone to thank the Lord for this meal.

"George, do you think we can get home to the twentieth century now?"

"I think so, Dad. Let's get out of here before something else happens."

They clean up their campground, trying not to leave any trash in the past, climb aboard and start up the rotors.

"I'd like to still look around," suggested George.

"GEORGE, take us home," his dad firmly shouted.

George takes the XT1 up above the tree tops then sends them hurtling forward in time. Glimpses of history flashed past them. Just as they got to their time, radio traffic started coming back on again until they heard, "XT1 to Stansted control."

"Stansted, go ahead XT1."

"We're ready to depart. Waiting on instructions."

"XT1, make a U turn. Head to taxi way 16 behind TWA."

"Roger, Stansted."

"Stansted control, we're ready for take off. Also if we disappear off the radar screen, that's normal. No need for search rescue unless you see us crash."

"XT1, we know how to handle air space. You're cleared for take off."

It was strange hearing himself talking from back then. "Remember what you said last,Pastor?"

"Yes I do, George," the pastor shouts excitedly.

"Me too, George. He said punch it," Mr Watts comments.

"Let's land first." George puts them back into normal time and they hear traffic control talking to TWA.

"Stansted control, this is the XT1. We're home."

246

Chapter 18
Don't Let Me Find You Sleeping

Sunday, May29th 1966

"Keep a sharp lookout," Jesus said. *"For you will not know when I will come back- at evening, at midnight, early dawn or late daybreak. Don't let me find you sleeping."* (Taken from the gospel of Mark, chapter 13:35-36)

After service was over, Pastor Bess made a shocking announcement that he would be retiring soon and they would need to find a new pastor. He recommended Andy Brown as he is ordained and had filled in at many other churches when needed.

Monday, May 30th 1966

Morning came with George's alarm clock buzzing away. Since there was no school he just stayed in bed a few minutes more, thinking about church yesterday. The service was always good but yesterday's was kind of scary. But he dragged himself out of bed to the smell of bacon frying in the kitchen. George opens his bedroom door which goes into a short hall leading to the kitchen. Smoke from the cooking hits him right then. George hurries into the kitchen to find the bacon on low but unattended.

"DAD! The bacon's burnt to a crisp! I hope you like it burnt 'cause I sure don't. DAD, you here somewhere?"

Mr Watts didn't reply. Maybe he went outside to get the paper then started chatting with someone. That's how he is, so friendly. George turned off the stove and set the burnt pan of bacon on the back burner. He stepped outside to look for Mr Watts. He was not to be seen. Another funny thing, no newspaper. Looking down the road, George saw the paper boy's bicycle. It was just kind of lying there on the sidewalk. George walked down to the bicycle.

"Henry! Whereabouts you at?"

No reply. A fire engine races by followed by the garage's ambulance.

"Henry! I'm going to get Dad's paper!"

Hearing nothing, George gets the paper and looks at it while walking back to the house. Then he hears the phone ringing. So he races to the house, taking all the steps up to the porch in a single bound, into the house and grabs the phone just in time. "Hello?"

"Hello George, this is Bonnie. Is Jacob and the baby down there?"

"No, not seen Jacob since school let out."

"Well, neither one is here. I haven't seen them all morning. Let me talk to Dad."

"He's not here. Must have gone down to the school to close out the books before summer school begins."

"Well, if you see Jacob tell him to call me."

"I will, Bonnie. Take care sis."

George begins to wonder. He heads outside and walks down to the school. A few students were there, cleaning out their lockers. But not many. Most of them did that Friday. Dad's science classroom was empty and still locked. George heads into the office to find Mrs Harless typing away.

"Hello, Mrs Harless. Where is everybody today?"

"I'm really not sure, George. Maybe a bunch slept in today. Mr Sidebottom is not here yet, if you wanted to see him."

"No, I was looking for Dad."

"Isn't he home? Maybe he stepped out somewhere."

George heads back out the office and down the hall. As he passes Dad's classroom he tries the door one more time. Still locked.

George goes back to the house. It seems so empty without Dad. He scrapes out the frying pan and then makes himself some breakfast. Maybe Mrs Harless was right. Dad just took a walk. Maybe went to a store for something, like bacon, eggs, sausage, or juice. Just then Bonnie came in.

"George, have you seen Dad yet?"

"No, Bonnie. I went down to the school. He wasn't there. Maybe he took a walk."

"I tried phoning some of the others and most wasn't home either. I'm at my wits end for those two kids. Hate to tell their mom they're missing with her recovering in the hospital."

"Bonnie, relax. Jacob can take care of his sister. They might have gone for a walk. You know it calms the baby."

"But he ALWAYS leaves a note. This morning he was gone."
"He take anything with them?"
"No."
"There ya go. Just out for a walk."
"I hope so, George."
"Have some breakfast. I'll call Bob and have him watch for them."
George phones the sheriff's office. "Hello, Kyra. Is my brother Bob there? It's kind of important."
"No George, he's not here. He hasn't reported in to work today. Look George, if you see him tell him to get in here fast. Something's going on and I need help in here. What did you need the sheriff for?"
"Looking for Jacob and his sister from the foster home. Thought he might spot them and bring them home."
"Really? George, many people are missing. I've been getting calls for the past two hours. People missing, auto wrecks. I'll just add them to the list of missing."
"Alright, Kyra. Take care." George hangs up and heads back to the kitchen.
"So what did Kyra say?"
"She hadn't seen Bob this morning, Bonnie. But she'll tell him when she does."
"I hope so. Those kids are great."
"Maybe I should check with Mr McKee. Dad is always helping him."
"Best just go down there. You know they don't move well."
"And they're just across the street. Wait here and I'll go see."
George races across the road which seems very deserted. Down over the knoll to the McKee's house, the door to the garage was wide open. The car was just sitting there, engine running. Nobody around. The smell of exhaust was awful even with the door open. George reaches in the car and shuts the engine off.
"MR McKEE!" George shouted. "Mrs McKEE! I turned your car off. It was really stinking up the place. HELLO."
The door from the garage into the house was slightly open. George opens the door and shouts again.

"HELLO."
No reply. George goes into the house. The first room is the kitchen. Breakfast was on the stove. Whatever it was, it was burnt beyond recognition. It was about to spill out into the fire. Good thing he got there in time. The whole place would have gone up in flames. George continued on throughout the house, calling the McKees. But that was just met with silence. George went towards the back rooms; bedrooms, bathroom. In the bathroom, the washer had been running and was beeping to indicate it was done. George hit the button to acknowledge the load was done.
"HELLO. Anybody home?" George searches the whole house. "This is weird," he said to himself. "Somebody is always home here." George leaves, closing the door behind him. Exiting through the garage, he shut that door too then headed back up to the house. Bonnie was still there, using the phone.
"Who you calling, Bonnie?"
"Everybody. Most people in Dad's Rolodex are not answering. Here's a list of who I called and those who answered."
"Not many people answering, are they? It's a workday. Many will be at work, Bonnie."
"Were the McKees home?"
"No and it looked like they just up and left, leaving the car running in the garage, food cooking on the stove, laundry in the washer. It was weird."
"I'm tired of dialing this phone. Let's take a break. Turn on the radio or something. It's too quiet here."
"Okay, Bonnie. I'm going to grab something else in the kitchen then see if a few friends are on the shortwave radio."
Bonnie turns on the old radio in the living room. It's always preset to the gospel station in Wheeling. All she heard was static. She turns the dial until a news report comes in.
"Reports keep coming in. Some forty minutes ago, thousands if not millions of people that were here yesterday are not here today. To say the world is in shock would be an understatement. Planes crashing out of the skies over Chicago, New York, California and many parts of the globe. On busy highways cars and trucks went

out of control due to drivers disappearing from behind the wheel. Some fear that some alien force has declared war on our planet. Others feel it's the rapture as mentioned in the Christian Bible. If you're in your homes, stay there. Please stay off the telephones to your local emergency service personnel unless it's absolutely an emergency.

President Johnson is due to make a statement later today. Stay tuned in to your local network station."

George comes out of his room and seems in shock, his eyes glazed over in disbelief.

"George? Whats the matter?"

"I think Dad is gone!"

"Gone? Gone where?"

"Caught up. Went to heaven. The rapture."

"Oh George, don't be silly. It can't be. We're still here, aren't we?"

"Yes I know Bonnie, but what else could it be? On the shortwave they're saying thousands are missing. Jesus came and we have been left behind!"

"President Johnson will be making a statement today. They'll have the answers. If you ask me, I'll bet it's radiation with all that nuclear bomb testing."

"Let's see what the morning news has to say, Bonnie."

"Well, it's better than sitting around here."

The telephone rings.

"Let me get it, George, I need to talk to someone. Hello? Hi, Aunt Mary. No, Dad's not here. No, don't know where he's at. It's just George and I here. I was looking for the kids. They're missing. Aunt Mary, don't scare me like that, it's not the rapture. On the radio they think it's some alien force. You know what I think it is? Radiation. Yeah, from all that nuclear bomb testing. Oh, you say the president will be coming on soon? We'll warm up the TV and watch. Bye. I love you."

George had already jumped up and turned the TV on. The picture finally came on with a bulletin across the screen. Then the president appeared on the screen.

"My fellow Americans, this morning at approximately 7:51 eastern time, without warning, thousands of citizens of this country just vanished off the face of the earth. We have our top people here in Washington researching this phenomenon. Please remain calm and we will get though this crisis as we always do. I too have missing family and friends. You are not alone. Please restrict your travels to the bare essentials. If you do go out, please be back in your homes before sunset. I have mobilized all national guard troops to help law enforcement to maintain order. Thank you."

"Is that it?" Bonnie shouts. "We have thousands gone and he declared marshal law. What kind of action is that?"

"Bonnie, maybe we should go on a low level flight over Chapman Grove. In case the kids are in the area."

"George, you always were smart. Thanks. You're a honey."

They go out to the landing pad of the XT1. They open up the back door, board and get underway. George picks up the radio and calls in.

"Control tower, this is the XT1."

"XT1, go ahead."

"Control, XT1 requesting permission for some low flights over the Chapman Grove area."

"Purpose of this flight?"

"Searching for missing children for the foster home."

A moment of silence follows his request. "XT1, you have clearance for low flights over Chapman Grove."

"Roger, control. Well Bonnie, you ready?"

"No, I hate flying but let's do it."

George gives her the throttle and the XT1 gains in altitude.

"Bonnie, you watch the ground from your far left to right. I'll watch far right to left."

George started going down the main road almost to Moundsville area then turned around and headed back going north to Wheeling. Back and forth they went most of the day, going up and down each street, flying high enough to see all around.

"George, I've not seen any sign of them. Little Molly would be hungry now. Jacob hasn't got any of her food with him."

"We'll keep looking. Let's search the wooded area next."

"XT1, this is the control tower. All flights, by order of the FAA, have been canceled."

"Roger, control. Heading back to the landing pad."

"And you didn't even get to fly over the wooded area, George."

"Keep watching the woods, Bonnie, we can still make one pass as we go home."

They land with no luck in finding the children.

"Thanks for trying, George."

"You're welcome, sis."

"I think I'll go home. You need anything, George? You can come home with me if you're lonely."

"I'll be okay."

Monday, June 13th 1966

It was two weeks since the vanishings. There was not much happening in town. Summer school was canceled that year. Too many teachers were missing to run the school. The library was shut down due to a lack of funding.

George had the radio on, listening to music and reading some books off the shelf. Just then the evening news report came on.

"We interrupt today's music for an announcement from the Capitol in Charleston, Governor Moore speaking. We now take you there live."

"Good day, my fellow West Virginians. Two weeks ago the world was struck by forces unknown to us. Three days later looting, ransacking and other acts of violence started sweeping across America. As Governor of West Virginia, I have ordered that any further acts of this nature are not to be tolerated. All law enforcement personnel are, as of this date, to arrest people looting, by whatever force is deemed necessary. All citizens are to report to their local city hall or county courthouse to register their presence. This is to ensure law and order for a safe community. Please do so as soon as possible. Thank you."

George turns the radio off and thinks about what was said then heads outside to the XT1 which sat there idle. It looked sad, sitting there doing nothing. It wanted to FLY! George pulls off a few twigs that had blown down from a tree. Then he thought, hmm get the water hose out and give it a good washing. He got a ladder out and started on the top, worked his way down the sides then took a chamois cloth and wiped the whole thing down. After that George did the windows with glass cleaner, inside and out. Hmm, now what? George was just beside himself with not much to do without school. And most of the church membership was gone. George was going crazy.

Monday, July 4th 1966
A small group had been planning for the Fourth of July. EVERYBODY from Chapman Grove and surrounding area was there for the celebration. It had been such a boring summer, all the residents needed a break from just working. With so many people gone, others had to pick up the slack.
Also added this year was the new federal office of the census. It was their job to record the population. After a person was counted, a mark was placed on their hand or forehead. Most people were glad to stand up and be counted. Others would procrastinate, saying they'll do it later. They were too busy. George came by the census booth and watched a bit, but then one of his classmates hollered, "HEY GEORGE!"
"Hi Jake, what's up?"
"Isn't this great!"
"Yes, I been racking my brains trying to think of something to do."
"No, not the events happening here. This on my hand."
On the back of Jake's hand was a mark. It looked like a bunch of lines with a big long number under it.
"What is it, Jake?"
"It's my citizenship mark. I can now vote in any elections, buy what I need. Isn't that far out?"
"Yes," George said, somewhat unenthusiastic.
"Don't forget to do yours, George. No telling, they might run out of ink."
"Hmm."
George looks at the line for the federal census and thinks how hot it

is to be standing out in the sun. The sun felt like it could rip the skin right off you. He just wandered around the grounds, chatted with a few friends, got a drink or two, became bored and headed back home.

Monday, July 18th 1966

For the past few weeks, since the Fourth of July, George had devoted his time to the XT1. He took the whole rotors assembly apart then rebuilt the contact points as they seemed to be wearing out too fast. George cleaned his hands of grease then headed down to the hardware store to get new contacts. It was an old fashioned store, run by a nice old husband and wife.

George goes in. "Mr Tobin! You here?"

The floors were wooden. A counter top was made to match. Lots of things were on display for customers to pick up and look at. Everything else had to be asked for.

"George, is that you lad? Ah, it's so good to see ya boy. What can I get for you today?"

"Yes, Mr Tobin, it's me. I need some strips of brass, half inch wide."

"I got it. It's in the back. I'll go get it for ya."

Mr Tobin walks into the back, passing Mrs Tobin. She whispers something to him but George pays no mind. A hardware store was a kids' playground. Mr Tobin comes back out to the cash register, pushes the buttons for the cost of the brass then turns a crank on the side.

"Anything else, George?"

"No, sir. I think that's all for now."

"That will be twenty four dollars and fifty two cents."

George hands him a twenty and a five.

"George, I need to see your mark."

"My mark, sir?"

"Yes. I don't have a bar code reader yet but it's getting to be the law now, George. I can't sell you anything without it."

"Oh." George sadly walks out.

As he walks by the few other stores, he sees in the windows 'Bar code required.' His money will be no good without the bar code on his hand. So he just walks home. George goes in and makes himself a burger. No use cooking a big meal for just one. While that was frying up, George checked the mail. Bills, bills, more bills. George tried to call C&P Telephone Company. His phone was dead for non payment. So George just ate up and went to bed, listening to the radio. It was horrible. Mostly some kind of propaganda about the new world order. He shut it off.

Tuesday, July 19th 1966
George awoke to someone beating on the door.
"I'm coming. You don't need to break down the door."
George opens the door and some army guys come forcing their way in.
"Hey, you can't just come busting in like that."
"By order of the president, yes we can. You're George, Son of Mike Watts."
"I know that."
"We just want to be sure. Notice is hereby given you must register as a citizen or face dire consequences. You have one week to comply."
He then shoved a paper at George who had no choice but to take it. Another soldier came back from looking over the other rooms and said, "Nobody else here. Boy, if you love the world you'll comply." Then they stormed out, slamming the door.
This was just short of communism or when Germany was murdering the Jews. George had read the book by Ann Frank, about hiding in an attic. He decided to move into the basement and make the door going down there look like a shelf for food. He got busy immediately. But he'd have to use what he had. Nobody was going to sell it to him. George got the generator out of the garage and took it downstairs, hooked up some lights as it would be pitch black down there without it. Then he took a radio, his shortwave set. He moved all he could into the basement.

Thursday, July 28th 1966

George had been hiding out in the underground basement for almost a week. Then through the camouflaged basement door he heard people upstairs and the sound of wood breaking, dishes smashing, glass shattering and general destruction. Maybe they were searching for him. Bet they'll never find me, he vowed.

"He's gone, Sergeant. We've searched the whole house."

"Take what you can. Torch the house. If anyone runs out, shoot them."

Oh no, George thought. Torch the house! Hope the extra metal door will hold off the fire. Smoke was trying to come through the door. George stuffed rags in the cracks then went down and stayed low.

"God, help me."

The fire swept throughout the whole house like a wildfire.

Friday, July 29th 1966

George woke about mid-day. He climbed up the steps then tried pushing on the hot metal door. Taking some of the rags out he then used them to push on the door. Some of the unburnt timbers had fallen on the door. George propped the door open a bit more each time he pushed. He looked around. Nobody there. The back tool shed and the garage, all gone. The garden bulldozed. The old apple tree in the front yard that he loved so well, burnt to a crisp. His time machine wrecked.

Tuesday, August 2nd 1966

This would have been the beginning of George's senior year in high school. He walked down to the school and peeked in. Only one classroom seemed to be used, from what he saw through the window. All the students were dressed in orange jumpsuits. On a screen was a slide show. It looked like more propaganda. Become a citizen of the human world. God doesn't exist. Your old Christian ways are outdated. It went on and on like that.

George walked on down the street, hiding whenever a vehicle came by. Down at the old drive-in movie theater, there were more people. This time it was adults. Chained to each speaker, forced to listen to the same propaganda, they were also dressed in the same orange jumpsuits. But this time it looked as if they had been prisoners out in the weather for weeks. George just turned around and ran for it.

Saturday, August 13th 1966
It was cold that morning as George came up from his underground hideout, so he put on a warm sweater and thin gloves. The gloves could help hide the fact he had no citizenship mark. Maybe walk up the road towards Wheeling, see what's happening that way. George got far as the Ohio river bridge when he heard, "Psst! Hey, George, is that you?"
"Who's there? What do you want? I'm not George. George is dead."
"No, you're George alright. I'm Grace. Remember me from junior high? George, I need help. I'm hungry."
Coming out from under the bridge was a small spindly looking girl wearing the same orange clothes. She was very dirty and smelly.
"George, I can't make it alone. I heard of sanctuary up in Canada. Will you help me get there? We can both go. Any place is better than here."
George was always soft hearted for a girl in distress. "Okay, follow me. Best way to get to Canada is crossing the river then heading north."
She smiled. George gave his hand to her to pull her up. She had been under the entrance ramp to the bridge. The two of them started walking across the bridge. Off on the other side, some people started gathering.
"I think we might need to turn back. Too many people there to slip by."
They turn around midway across the bridge. Some army trucks had pulled in, blocking their exit back the way they'd just come.
"Maybe we should risk the Ohio side."
But that group also started moving towards them.
"Sorry, but I think we're trapped. Maybe jump in the water and swim for it down the river."
"Not me, George."
"What do you mean? They're after us."

"They're not after me, George. Just you."
She takes her lightweight glove off and shows the mark.
"You see, George, I'm a good citizen. You're just one of those
Christians who hate us. And I never met you before in my life."
"Stay away from me!"
George climbs over the rail. Others run for him and grab him by
the sweater.
"Let go of me!"
"Okay," they said with evil grins. They let go and George falls out
of control and splashes into the Ohio river.
"HELP!"

Monday, May 30th 1966
George wakes up, soaking wet. Mr Watts stood in the room with an
empty water bucket.
"I thought you were on fire again, George. Hope that put the fire
out for good."
George leaps out of bed and grabs his dad, saying, "I love you,
Dad!"
Puzzled, he replies, "I love you too, George."
"DAD! I love Jesus too. I want him in my heart."
"Just tell him, George. He will."

Chapter 19
Apollo 1[7]

The story so far is about to wind down but there are a few things still to tell.

Friday, January 20th 1967
Chapman Grove High students had turned the school around, now having top students in the state with many listed on the honor roll. The principal, Mr Sidebottom, couldn't have been prouder of them. Mr Sidebottom had arranged a special guest, Pilot Lieutenant Commander Roger Chaffee for the Apollo One Flight. All the students, who had gathered in the main auditorium, cheered. He presented a great slide program about the upcoming flight then a short talk followed by many, many questions from the students. Almost all questions were very intelligent. Some questions he couldn't answer but they were nonetheless interesting. Then they were dismissed for lunch. George thought, I can eat anytime. Many students stayed to talk more and shake the astronaut's hand. George was no exception. It took George twenty minutes to get to Lieutenant Chaffee.

"Lieutenant Chaffee, I'm George, a senior here. I have a question about the navigation system." George puts out his hand to shake with Chaffee.

"George, I heard a lot about you and want to talk more with you tonight at your home. Your dad invited me to spend the night." George takes his hand. A COLD damp chill goes all over George. Then he blacks out. Next thing George knows, he's in a room with the school nurse. He started hearing muttering voices as he came to.

"Is your son going to be alright?"

"Must have been the shock of getting to meet you, Lieutenant."

"Hmm, didn't know I was that famous."

"George," the nurse asks, "you doing better now? You been out like a light for a while. Why don't you get your dad to take you home."

"Yes, ma'am. I feel so embarrassed. I never fainted before in my life."

"To everything there is a first time," Chaffee joked.

Later that evening, Lieutenant Chaffee was sitting on the front porch swing with Mr Watts and George. It was such a clear night.

"This would be a great time for a launch. George, if you think about getting into NASA you look me up."

"Yes, sir. I will. Or maybe I'll get into designing your rockets. It seems I have dozens of colleges and universities scrambling to get me to enroll with them."

"That would be good, George. Maybe I'll fly a rocket you design."

"Lieutenant, cup of coffee?"

"No, think I'll turn in for the night. Been a long day."

"We have lots of rooms here, sir, but would you like to bunk with George tonight?"

"You think I'll get some sleep tonight if we bunk together?"

"Not a bit."

"Then George's room it will be."

The two of them go off to George's room.

" Lieutenant Chaffee?"

"Call me Roger, George."

"Roger, I keep having this bad dream."

"You want to talk about it?"

"I've not said much about it to anyone. I don't think I fully understand it myself."

"I'm listening."

"I'm in a rocket ready to blast off for the moon."

"Hmm hmm."

"We just got sealed in and the cabin was pressurized."

"Oh?" Roger's attention is riveted on George as cabin pressure is not public knowledge.

"Yes. We check all the electrical systems then a fire sweeps through the cabin. It's then I wake up. Is your flight going to happen on January the 27th? If it is, something bad is going to happen."

"No, we go in February. The engineers at NASA are the best. We've been training for this and all things that could happen. We'll be fine."

"I hope so, sir. I think you all are awesome."

The two of them turn in for the night.

Saturday, January 21st 1967

Lieutenant Chaffee was up with the sun.

"Lieutenant, you get any sleep last night?"

"Oh yes, George is a great bunk mate. We had a great chat. I'd love to go to the moon with him. He's a smart young man."

"He's been places you wouldn't believe. But I'll bet he'd go with you if you asked him. Would you like a cup of coffee?"

"Yes, please. Well, maybe some future flight George will go. I hear he's got universities coming after him."

Just then sleepy eyed George comes into the room and says, "Go? Go where? I'd need a drink first, Dad."

"Go to the moon with Lieutenant Chaffee."

"Okay, just need a drink first like I said."

The two men smiled, knowing George wasn't quite awake enough to catch what he said.

"HUH?" George remarked. It then clicked in.

"Lieutenant, how do you like your coffee?"

"You wouldn't have any honey, would you?"

"Here you are. Nice local honey."

"It looks like it's gone bad, Mr Watts. It's turned dark."

"No, that's the way the honeybees make it. It's dark like that because they worked on wildflowers. It will taste like them too."

He gets a drop of honey on his finger and tastes it. "Wow, that's great flavor. I've been getting honey from the local store, Publix®, in Florida and it don't taste this good. Where can I buy some?"

Mr Watts takes an unopened jar out of the cupboard.

"Here, you can have this jar. The beekeeper's contact information is on the jar. You see, Lieutenant, properly bottled honey never goes bad. Its color and flavor is from what the bees are working."

Later, about mid morning, Lieutenant Chaffee had finished packing to leave.

"Mr Watts, George, I guess I'm ready to head out. This was my last stop before heading back to Florida. Got to catch a flight out of Columbus."

"Would you like a ride?" George offers.

"No, I was going to just take a cab."

"Uh, no cabs in Chapman Grove," Mr Watts comments. "George can get you to Columbus or to Florida FAST."

"Really? Let's go then."

The two of them went out to the XT1 sitting on the landing pad. Lieutenant Chaffee stared at the strange looking craft. He couldn't see any propellers or jet engines. But to humor the boy he climbed aboard. George pressed on the starter. Lieutenant Chaffee looked worried when the XT1 made a sound as the rotors came to life. George got on the radio.

"XT1 to Wheeling tower."

"Wheeling tower to XT1."

"Wanting to make an unscheduled flight to Florida. Take Lieutenant Commander Roger Chaffee to NASA."

"Chaffee? The astronaut? Very well. Climb to 3000 feet and head due south. PLEASE hold your speed to 500 mph. We'll notify NASA of your coming."

"Thanks, Wheeling tower."

"George, this is an incredible machine. What makes it go?"

"In a nutshell? The rotors make it work by displacing magnetic waves of the earth away from the XT1 causing it to float. When you move the stick, like in a plane, it adjusts the rotor to turn it."

"If MIT wants you, that would be a good university to go to. The XT1? What's the T stand for?"

"Time. This ship will time travel."

"Hmm." Chaffee's not really believing it.

"Someday I'll show you, sir."

"You been anywhere special?"

"Well, first trip was a total accident. Ended up at Fort Randolph, Point Pleasant in the mid 1700s. Another trip, went to see the Wright brothers. Got my pilot license from them. Also been to see Noah's ark. On that trip, nearly got drowned in a rain storm, struck by lightning, had to sit down hard on the island of Atlantis, the one

that they think either blew up or sank in the sea, then made a short pit stop in twelfth century England. But we did have a good time."
The Lieutenant sat there, giving George the kind of look that says, you expect me to believe that?
"You get some leave and I'll show you."
"When we land at NASA let me show you around."
"NASA control to approaching aircraft, you're entering restricted airspace."
"NASA, this is XT1. I have Lieutenant Commander Chaffee on board, returning him to you."
"Really, XT1."
"Yep, just giving him a ride."
"George, let me tell him."
George hands him the mike.
"NASA! This is Lieutenant Commander Roger Chaffee aboard the XT1 out of West Virginia. Those folks have been kind enough to give me a direct flight home. But if you want, we can turn around and go right back and take a slow airline flight home."
Chaffee hangs up. Nothing else is heard for a moment. Then a jet comes alongside them. Chaffee turns and looks.
"Roger? You rookie, what are you doing in that funny looking thing?" The jet pilot's voice comes over the radio.
"Gus, you chasing me?"
"Just wanted to be sure it was you. I had orders to shoot you down too."
"You wouldn't shoot me down. Besides, you're a bad shot."
"Ha ha, Roger. Have your pilot follow me in."
"Follow that jet, George."
"Aye, sir."
They landed on the air force base next to NASA. Four MP jeeps came up with machine guns pulled.
"Hold on, men, it's me. We're cool."
The MPs didn't move and kept their machine guns pointed at them. Then a captain came up. "Lieutenant? This isn't protocol."
"George, if you don't mind, could you go ahead and leave. I'm sorry, I wanted to show you the base and Apollo 1. MOST officers

aren't jerks like this one."
George gets aboard the XT1 and takes off. Lieutenant Chaffee
starts heading to mission control.
"HALT, LIEUTENANT, OR WE"LL FIRE!"
"Go ahead, Captain. That will be a great way to scrub Apollo 1.
Shoot the pilot."
They didn't shoot.

*On January 27th 1967 at 6:31 pm during a pre-flight test, fire swept
though the Apollo 1 capsule of Gus Grissom, Ed White and Roger
Chaffee. All hands were lost and set back the American
race for the moon. This chapter is dedicated to their memory.*

Conclusion
Class of '67

Friday, May 19ᵗʰ 1967
It was the final day for George at Chapman High. He had done many things since his first year in high school. He sent bully Eddy Gulch running for the hills, got the town to start reviving with people moving back, built a time machine by accident, had lots of fun travels too, purchased lots of houses, fixed them up then sold or rented them out at a nice price. Most had been purchased. The land that used to have the lumber mill? It never sold. George decided to just keep it for himself, might start a business. Chapman Grove could use help to prosper. Absher's Grocery Store was sold to a chain store of modest priced foods.
George finally went to Georgia Institute with a really FULL scholarship. He had plans to open an engineering and research company in Chapman Grove. By the time he graduated from high school, he had made it to Eagle Scout and was elected into The Order of the Arrow. Some people to whom I told the story of George, asked, "Is he still rich?"
At this time his stocks, bonds, some real estate, a little bit of gold and other precious metals and bank balance, are valued at $3,692,487.49. But he was even more rich in family and friends.

His dad, Mike Watts, still teaches high school science, is still head deacon of the Chapman Grove Baptist Church, helps mentor kids and will still foster kids in need of a home.
Judge Mary Hanson was re-elected time and time again to the family court system, volunteers at the Chapman Grove foster home and thinks she'd like to travel the world; go to Great Britain, France or someplace.
Judy MacQueen went back to college to get her masters degree.
Sheriff Bob Shamblin was killed in the line of duty, assisting G-men in a shootout with the Dalton brothers, saving the lives of three G-men and two children.
Tom McKee still putters around the house with Mrs McKee, and

plans fairs, festivals and other gatherings for the town.

Stephen and his father moved back to England where he was educated at an independent school for boys in a small market town then went to Oxford, where he was awarded a Bachelor of Science. Stephen was a member of the Royal Air Force. Upon leaving the air force he went to work for border security.

Susan Hill moved with her parents a few more times while her father was employed in detecting corruption in government. She went to the University of New York State and graduated with honors then she started work at the Library of Congress.

Mathew Dunlap took over his father's apiary when his back was unable to cope with it.

Timmy went to work at the Virginia shipyards where they build for the Navy. But they didn't ever want to try any of his ideas.

Andy Brown became the new minister of Chapman Grove Baptist Church, but still loves to teach Sunday School to the little ones.

Jacob and Molly Hacker were reunited with their mother. The state welfare department assisted her to find work.

Richard Sidebottom is the name of a real former principal at Hayes Junior High School. He died in 1972. Even though events included in this book, from his life, might have been sensationalized, most people remember him as a 'man for the students.' In the story he continues as principal of Chapman Grove High School.

David Masters, George Warner, Helen Goldman, Erma Gulch, Ronald Biggarstaff and Jack Hall are still serving time at the state penitentiary for the November 3rd 1964 election rigging at Chapman Grove.

Pastor Bess retired to travel West Virginia and other states with his wife.

I really hope you enjoyed reading Time Voyagers: The Adventure Begins.

I'm planning some more adventures for George and his family and friends. Watch on Amazon Kindle for these books:

Time Voyagers: A Christmas Journey

The Solar Express

Time Voyagers Book 2

Time Voyagers Book 3

Have your name added to my email list at
thetimevoyagers@aol.com

[1] For Chapman Grove, WV I used a map of a WV town just to start off, then modified it for the story. Chapman Grove itself is a totally fictional town in WV.

[2] Acording to David Turnipseed of WV Forestry, it is highly unlikly that apple trees would grow as old as the ones in this book, but it could happen.

[3] Fort Randolph was an American Revolutionary War fort which stood at the confluence of the Ohio and Kanawha Rivers, where the town of Point Pleasant, West Virginia, is now located.
Built in 1776 on the site of an earlier fort from Lord Dunmore's War, the fort is best remembered as the place where the famous Shawnee Chief Cornstalk was murdered in 1777. The fort withstood attack by American Indians in 1778 but was abandoned the next year. It was rebuilt in the 1780s after the renewal of hostilities between the United States and American Indians, but saw little action and was eventually abandoned once again. A replica of the fort was built in 1973–74 and dedicated on October 10, 1974, the 200th anniversary of the Battle of Point Pleasant. The town of Point Pleasant had spread over where the fort had stood, and so the rebuilt fort was located at Krodel Park, about one mile from the original location. Visit their website at; www.fortrandolph.org/ *

[4] At one time West Virginia was a part of Virginia until the American civil war broke out and split it. "Into the Wilderness the Jesse Hughes Story" by Edward Clevenger (copyright 2008) was about settlers in the northwestern Virginia area which is present day West Virginia. From 1760 to 1829 is the time period in which Jesse Hughes and many others lived. "Into the Wilderness the Jesse Hughes Story" by Edward Clevenger is available only on Amazon Kindle.

[5] Currently, paddling is not practiced in 31 states in the United States, be it for corporal punishment or special occations. Some states however have banned the use of paddling. It was banned in West Virginia schools in 1994.

[6] The town of Kaymoor was named for James Kay, a Low Moor Iron Company employee who was in charge of building the town. Fifty houses were built in 1901, followed by 45 in 1902 and 17 in 1905. A suburb, called New Camp, was built in 1918-1919 with another 19-24 houses,

and represents the only extant town site remaining on the New River. Kaymoor town's public facilities were spartan, with no churches, saloons, banks or town hall, only pairs of segregated schools at top and bottom, company stores, a pool hall and a ball field. By 1952 Kaymoor Bottom had been abandoned, and in 1960 most of its structures were destroyed by fire. *

[7] Based on true events in history, sometimes with changes to work with the story. For example, the magnetic motor at this day and age, doesn't work.

[8] On the radio, originally told on Paul Harvey News.

[9] Prickett's Fort was built to defend early European settlers of what today is West Virginia from raids by hostile Native Americans (1768). Indians tended to avoid such strong points, preferring to ambush small work parties. In 1774, there were at least a hundred such palisades, blockhouses, and "stations" in the Monongahela Valley, many within a thirty-mile radius of Prickett's Fort. Perhaps as many as eighty families, several hundred people, gathered at Prickett's Fort during crisis periods, where they stayed for days or even weeks. Prickett's Fort was never attacked, although militiamen from the confluence area were killed by Indians elsewhere. *

[10] A U.S. Navy aircraft carrier.

[11] A Visit From Saint Nicholas aka The Night Before Christmas and 'Twas The Night Before Christmas, was written by Clement Clerk Moore in 1823. *

[12] 10-36, one code of many. Was called the ten code. 10-36 was a question asking what time is it? The ten code became most popular with two way radios called citizen's band.

[13] John Fitzgerald "Jack" Kennedy (May 29, 1917 – November 22, 1963), often referred to by his initials JFK, was the 35th President of the United States, serving from 1961 until killed by Lee Harvey Oswald in 1963. *

[14] Professor Stephen William Hawking, born 8th of January 1942 is an

English theoretical physicist, cosmologist, author and Director of Research at the Centre for Theoretical Cosmology within the University of Cambridge. He is a vocal supporter of quantum mechanics. *

[15] The underground railroad was a network of secret routes and safe houses used by 19th century black slaves in the United States to escape to free states and Canada with the aid of abolitionists and allies who were sympathetic to their cause. *

[16] "God is Good All the Time" was a song by Don Moen used in a Disney cartoon about Johnny Appleseed and is sung many times by the 4H All Stars before sitting down to a meal.

[17] Webelos. Stands for we be loyal scouts. This position was created for boys about the age of 10. They were getting kind of old for Cub Scouts but not old enough for The Boy Scouts of America.

[18] I have some fine family in Great Britain. One of them is a smart funny little lad named Alisdair. When he was real little, he used to create some small 'accident' then when someone would see it he would say, "Oh dearie me! Oh no!" as if he had just discovered this disaster.

* www.wikipedia.com. Lots of the information contaned in this book is based on researching the wikipedia, a free online service. However it's written to fit in the story line of Time Voyagers.